How Far Is Heaven?

By Laurie Hanan

Hoaka Moon Publishing
Honolulu, Hawai'i

Laurie Hanan

Published in the USA by Hoaka Moon Publishing

Printed in the U.S.A.

Copyright 2012 Laurie Hanan. All rights reserved. No part of this work may be reproduced without written permission of the author.

Cover by Laurie Hanan

ISBN-10: 0615588859
ISBN-13: 978-0615588858

This is a work of fiction. All names, characters, and places are fictitious or used fictitiously. Any resemblance to actual persons, living or dead, and any events is purely coincidental.

Also by Laurie Hanan: *Almost Paradise*

Laurie Hanan

This book is dedicated to my husband David
and my children Elan, Eliana and Yaron.

ACKNOWLEDGEMENTS

There are many people I must thank for the successful completion of *How Far Is Heaven?* My humble gratitude goes out to author William Bernhardt for his advice, counsel, and unwavering encouragement. His tough love approach has made me the writer I am today.

Mahalo nui loa to Gregory Field for working with me on the manuscript over a two-year period. His thoughtful and insightful advice added dimension to the characters and storyline.

All my love to my husband, David. Since the first day I set pen to paper, he's been my biggest fan and supporter. And to my three children, Elan, Eliana and Yaron, who cheer me on from the sidelines.

Mahalo to my old schoolmate Steve Protasio for the Chamorro translations; and to Diane Miller, Brenda Hovan, Linda Humes, Rick Ludwick, Pierre Guéret and Ross Mishima, who proofed early copies and offered support.

Laurie Hanan

Author's Forward

This book contains Hawaiian words and place names. If you are a mainlander, don't let that intimidate you. The Hawaiian language is simple, beautiful and melodious. Written words may appear impossible to pronounce, but by breaking them down into syllables, you'll probably come close. A syllable never contains more than two letters, and always end with a vowel.

There are five vowels and seven consonants in the Hawaiian alphabet, for a total of twelve letters. Several vowels may be used in a row, but consonants never appear together. Some words have no consonants at all and Hawaiian words always end with a vowel.

Consonants are pronounced as they are in English, with the exception of W. The letter W is sometimes pronounced the same as V, as in the traditional pronunciation of Hawai'i which is phonetically pronounced huhvi-ee rather than huh-why-ee.

Vowel Pronunciation: **a** *ah* **e** *eh* **i** *ee* **o** *oh* **u** *oo*

A symbol directly over a vowel, called a kahakō, indicates that the vowel sound is to be elongated. An apostrophe-like symbol, called an 'okina, indicates a quick break in the word, like in English when we say *oh-oh*. So, for the Hawaiian word ka'a, which is the word for car, it would be pronounced: *kah-ah*.

The meaning of most words should be clear from the context. If you aren't sure, you can refer to the glossary at the back of the book. The Hawaiian people are accepting of outsiders. If you show an interest in learning the language and culture, you will be embraced. Speak a Hawaiian word with a smile and aloha, and you can't go wrong.

Laurie Hanan

Without stirring abroad, one can know the whole world.
Without looking out of the window
one can see the way of heaven.
The further one goes, the less one knows.
Lao Tzu

How Far Is Heaven

CHAPTER 1

All that stood between me and sudden death was a faded yellow line. Westbound commuters, hepped up on coffee, whizzed past me. God bless caffeine.

My portable radio blared *Jingle Bell Rock.* I considered flinging it out the window, but I was waiting for the six o'clock evening news. After the news, I'd fling the radio.

My name is Louise Golden, better known this time of year as Louise McScrooge. I work for the U.S. Postal Service. Neither snow, nor rain, nor heat, nor gloom of night ... and all that good stuff. In Hawai'i we don't have to worry about snow, but the rain in winter can be real humbug.

My headlights reflected off the wet road. I leaned forward, hoping the change in position would ease the pain in my back. I'd spent the last twelve hours delivering Christmas cards and packages in this miserable weather. I was cold, I was wet, I was beyond exhausted. Santa Louise. Ho ho ho, merry Christmas!

Through the downpour, a figure appeared in the road. She was young, maybe twenty. Her long, dark hair and oversized white tee-shirt clung to her thin, pale frame. Her feet were bare. If she'd just continued across the road, she would've been fine. But she didn't. She stopped in front of me, frozen. I hit my brakes and swerved hard. At the same moment, the woman doubled back the way she had come. Right into the path of my truck. My tires skidded on the wet asphalt, and there was nothing I could do to avoid hitting her.

A sickening thud shook the truck. She flew several feet and landed on the muddy roadside.

I had my cell phone out and was dialing 9-1-1 before my truck came to a full stop. I switched on the emergency flashers and remembered to lock my door. I pocketed the keys, stepped into the rain, and ran to where she lay.

I stood over the crumpled body. I hadn't been going very fast when I hit her. I didn't see any injuries, but she sure wasn't moving. The phone rang on the other end.

"Nine-one-one. Police, fire or ambulance?" said the disembodied voice of the operator.

My Red Cross emergency first aid class taught me to ask for the police first. They would determine if an ambulance was needed. "Police."

"Is this an emergency?"

"Yes."

I held the phone to my ear, knelt beside the woman—more of a girl, really—and touched her neck. Rain spattered her face. Her skin was cold to the touch. I didn't think I felt a pulse, but my own heart was pounding so hard I wasn't sure.

"Police. What is your emergency?"

"I hit a pedestrian. She's not moving."

"You say you hit a pedestrian?"

"Yes! With my truck. I'm a mail carrier."

"Is the victim breathing?"

"I don't know…I can't tell…"

"Where are you located?"

I looked around. Where exactly was I? I couldn't remember the last mile marker I'd passed.

"Kāne'ohe. On the eastbound side of Kam Highway. About a mile east of the Hygienic Store."

My tears mixed with the rain on my face. My body shook from cold, exhaustion, and fear. The operator was still talking, but I'd stopped listening. I collapsed onto the mud and rocks and sobbed.

In the distance, sirens wailed. As they grew nearer, flashing blue lights pierced the darkness.

Chapter 2

I have no memory of the drive home. It was after midnight when I parked my Z-3 and trudged up my front steps.

I didn't bother to check the mailbox. There'd be plenty of time to do that tomorrow. I'd been suspended. Standard procedure, but it still stung. I'm a good driver, not a single accident in the five years I'd been working for the post office. Until today.

Without turning on the light, I dropped my purse on the floor, locked the door, and reset the alarm.

Sage barked and raced through the living room in excited circles. I couldn't help smiling. Moondance hissed and spit. Only a cat could derive no vicarious pleasure from a Westie's exuberance. I picked her up and draped her over my shoulder, and she vibrated with a deep, throaty purr.

I left my wet clothes in a heap on the floor, pulled on my red flannel pajama pants and an old sweatshirt, and crawled into bed without brushing my teeth. With one furry companion on either side of me, I closed my eyes.

As soon as my head hit the pillow, my mind went into overdrive. I stared through the semi-darkness at the striped shadows made by the partially open blinds. The accident played through my mind again and again—the dark, wet road, cars whizzing past me in the blinding rainstorm, my headlights illuminating the woman who appeared out of nowhere, the look of terror frozen on her face, the thud …

Someone was knocking on my front door. I opened my eyes and squinted at the clock on the nightstand. Eight o'clock.

"Just a minute," I said under my breath.

I dragged myself to my feet, rubbed my eyes, and padded to the living room.

Emmeline saw me through the window and waved. I punched in the alarm code and opened the door.

"Hi, Louise. Why are you in your pajamas? Were you sleeping?"

I held the door open for my thirteen-year-old neighbor and her brown and black dog, Dazy.

"I had a late night."

"You look tired."

"I didn't sleep well."

Emmeline spread her arms. "Hug."

I held my hands up. "I haven't brushed my teeth."

Emmeline plopped onto the couch. She sat cross-legged, and clicked on Cartoon Network.

I headed for the bathroom. "I'll be right there."

Dazy paused to look through the bedroom doorway where Sage and Moondance slept on the bed, then followed me. *Scooby Doo* came on in the living room. I ran the water in the sink and studied myself in the mirror.

"What a mess."

Dazy let out a whimper.

"You agree, huh?"

I washed my face, brushed my teeth, and fluffed my curly blond hair. "That's the best I can do."

Dazy followed me to the kitchen. She watched me grab my favorite sailboat mug, fill it with water, add a teabag, and zap it in the microwave.

I heard a low yowl. Moondance was crouched in the kitchen doorway, ears back, tail twitching. I lifted her onto the countertop. Dazy didn't take her eyes off me as I took a can of vegan cat food from the fridge and dished some onto a saucer.

I formed a blob of the food into a ball. "Here, Dazy. Catch."

She caught it in mid-air and swallowed it in one motion.

Sage's toenails tapped on the hardwood floor and her face appeared around the doorpost. She yawned, sniffed the air, and stared vacantly into the room. The vet says she's been blind from birth, but even without her eyes she sees more than most people.

I tossed some cat food to Sage and joined Emmeline on the couch.

Emmeline bears no resemblance to the bubbly eight-year-old

who befriended me when I moved into the neighborhood five years ago. She'd recently cut off her waist-length honey-colored hair and donated it to an organization that makes wigs for children with hair loss. What's left of her hair is dyed henna-red and trimmed in a short shag. Gone are the chubby cheeks that made her resemble a chipmunk, replaced by the strong jaw and prominent cheekbones of a high fashion model. Only her eerie amber eyes remain the same.

Every few minutes, Emmeline's phone whistled. Her thumbs flew over the keys as she texted with her eyes glued to the TV. Dazy and Sage tumbled and chased each other through the house. Moondance crept into the living room and, without taking her eyes off the dogs, slinked across the Persian rug and jumped onto the piano. She glared at the dogs before curling up and closing her eyes.

When *Scooby Doo* ended, Emmeline turned off the TV

"Okay if I practice on your piano?"

"Of course."

The piano is in my living room by default, rather than by design. My friend Marta, the garage sale junkie, found it at an estate sale. She'd already paid for it before she realized it wouldn't fit in her overcrowded house. She insisted on moving it into mine. I did not want a piano, and all the memories it would evoke. My mother had been a piano teacher. She died when I was fifteen, and I haven't touched a piano since.

Marta convinced me I needed something to fill the empty space in my living room. Now the piano takes up one wall of the sparsely furnished room and, for the most part, gathers dust. I have to admit, though, it's an exquisite piece of furniture. It gives the room a lived-in feel, as if people might gather here for a festive evening. It also makes itself useful as a display shelf for my collection of glass fishing floats, and a dog-free zone for Moondance.

Most important, the piano gives Emmeline an excuse to be here, where she can practice away from her eight-year-old brother, Jackie.

Emmeline shoved the phone into her back pocket. She sat at the piano, lifted the fallboard, and played Bach's *Toccata and Fugue in D minor*. I closed my eyes. I still knew it by heart. As a child, it was my favorite recital piece. Emmeline played expertly, but I knew her heart wasn't in it. Her real love is the electric guitar.

When she finished, she stood and curtsied. I applauded.

"I'm playing a Christmas song for my recital. Wanna hear it?"

"Of course."

I never told Emmeline how much I dislike Christmas music. I was just happy to have her in my home.

Her phone whistled. She pulled it out, sent a text, and put it back in her pocket.

She played several verses of *O Holy Night*, making it sound like a slow dirge. I fought the temptation to sing along.

"That was beautiful."

"That was horrible. You really need to get this thing tuned," she told me, for the hundredth time.

"I have to go now. I have a riding lesson at eleven."

I see a lot less of Emmeline since her dad bought her a horse for her thirteenth birthday. Emmeline and Journey Bleu were taking dressage lessons in preparation for competitions next summer. She was growing up.

She gave me a hug. Her phone whistled as she ran down my front steps. She pulled it out and texted, with Dazy trotting beside her.

I needed to do something to fill the empty space they'd left behind. "Come on, Sage. Let's go see if Dan and Doug are home."

Sage shot through the house, and waited for me at the back door.

I opened the door. "Watch the steps, girl." It took her a while to learn that steps not only go up, they also go down. After a few tumbles, she now takes them with care.

Dan and Doug's cars were in the driveway and their front door was open. Sage and I crossed the lawn and climbed the front steps.

At a time when everyone else was coming out of the closet, Dan and Doug moved here from San Francisco to go *into* the closet. At least, that's my theory. It's my good fortune that they have no use for the mother-in-law cottage on their property. They've been renting it to me for five years now. They still try to pass themselves off as a pair of swinging bachelors. But hey, that's fine by me.

I peered through the screen door. "Knock, knock!"

"Come on in, Louise," Dan said.

Dan and Doug were at the dining table, enjoying their morning coffee and sharing the newspaper.

"Join us for coffee?" Dan asked. He's ten years older than me, which puts him at fifty. At six feet tall, with curly dark hair and a neatly trimmed mustache, he could pass for an older, stockier

Marlboro Man.

"Sure. Thanks."

"It's in the kitchen. Help yourself."

"Morning, Louise," Doug said.

"Hi, Doug." I closed the screen door behind me and went to the kitchen.

"Would you like a cinnamon roll?" Doug called. "I just made them. They're still warm."

Originally from Wales, Doug is softer and paler than Dan. He works as a chef in an upscale restaurant in Waikīkī and practices his culinary skills at home. Every now and then I get to try one of his creations.

My stomach growled when I saw the cinnamon rolls cooling on a cookie sheet. I couldn't remember the last time I'd eaten. With a mug of coffee in one hand and an oversized cinnamon roll in the other, I joined Dan and Doug. Sage sat at my feet, her nose twitching.

"I see you made the newspaper again," Dan said.

"I did what?"

Dan turned to the *Hawai'i* section of the *Honolulu Advertiser* and pushed it in front of me. I put a hand over my mouth when I saw the headline.

> **Mail Truck Hits Pedestrian**
> **Friday Rush Hour Traffic Snarled**
> (Kāne'ohe December 11) Traffic backed up in both directions yesterday when a pedestrian was struck by a mail truck on Kamehameha Highway. The accident happened just before 6 p.m., when an unidentified woman attempted to cross the road. She was not in a crosswalk. The woman, who appears to be in her twenties, was taken to Castle Hospital where she remains in a coma, in serious but stable condition.
>
> The 40-year-old driver of the truck, mail carrier Louise Golden, has been suspended pending further investigation of the accident.

A tear rolled down my cheek and over my fingers. "Oh God."

Doug laid a hand on my arm. "Are you okay?"

I couldn't answer.

Dan stood behind me and put his hands on my shoulders. "Drink some coffee."

I took a couple of deep breaths and obediently sipped my coffee.

"Have you had breakfast?" Doug asked.

"No." It came out like a croak.

"You might feel better if you eat," he said.

"Douglas, why don't you make her some eggs," Dan said.

"No. Really. This is fine." I took a bite of the cinnamon roll.

Dan massaged my shoulders. "How did it happen?"

"I was driving back to the station at the end of the day. It was dark and raining. I don't know where she came from. She was just there, in the middle of the road. It was a moment I've always dreaded. I'll never forget the sound …"

No one spoke. Dan kneaded my neck with strong thumbs.

After a minute, Doug said, "The paper says she's in a coma."

I nodded. "She was taken to Castle. They were going to assess her condition, then move her to Queen's Trauma Center, if necessary. After I filled out the accident report at work, I went to Castle to see if I could find out how she was doing. She was still there but they wouldn't give me any information on her condition.

"I hung around, hoping to learn something. At ten o'clock, the shift changed. One of the nurses who came on duty was in a talkative mood. When I told him I was the one who hit her, he said the CT scan was negative and they didn't think her injuries were serious."

"That's good," Doug said.

"She's unconscious, and that's never good. They have her down as a Jane Doe."

"They don't know who she is?" Dan asked.

"She wasn't carrying any ID. I'll go back today and see if I can find out more."

"How old do you think she is?"

"Young. I thought at first she was around twenty. Now I'm thinking she could be as young as fourteen or fifteen. She was barefoot, dressed in nothing but panties and a long tee-shirt, soaked to the skin. She'd been outside for a while."

"Her family must have reported her missing." He went back to his chair.

He worked as a skip tracer for a local loan company, and knew all about people who went missing. He went back to his chair.

I lifted Sage to my lap and hugged her. She strained toward the cinnamon roll.

"Did they really suspend you?" Dan asked.

I nodded.

"But why? It wasn't your fault."

"Standard procedure."

"You can probably use a little time off," Doug said.

I nodded again.

Dan said, "I bet she was on drugs. The way she ran into the road, in the dark and the rain, without looking where she was going. Did they do toxicology tests on her?"

It hadn't occurred to me. "They must have."

"You'd better try and find out," Dan said. "If she was high, it would remove any doubt about negligence on your part. Ask the investigating officer."

"I will." I brushed away more tears.

"It wasn't your fault. There was nothing you could have done."

I knew what he said was true. I hadn't been negligent. Even so, I couldn't forgive myself. If I hadn't been there at that precise moment, the young woman would have made it across the road. I pulled Sage to my chest, buried my face in her coarse fur and sobbed.

Laurie Hanan

CHAPTER 3

"Do you want to skip the party tonight?" Dan asked.

He was referring to his office Christmas party. I'd accompanied him to the party the past four Christmases, and had agreed to be his date again tonight. It may be part of his attempt to make his coworkers think he's straight, but I like him and don't mind helping out.

A couple days ago, I went to Ross and bought a dress and shoes for the party, and even picked up some makeup and nail polish. Dan would be disappointed if I didn't go, and I'd have to fight the crowds again to return the dress and shoes. There was nothing to be gained by spending the evening home alone, worrying about Jane Doe.

"No. I'll go. I want to visit the girl in the hospital again this afternoon, but I'll be home in time for the party."

Dan smiled. "That's my girl. We'll have a good time."

Rain had washed mud and rocks across Pali Highway. Police were directing traffic through the one lane that had been cleared. The drive to Castle Hospital, which should have taken fifteen minutes, took nearly an hour.

I picked up a vase of pink baby roses in the hospital gift shop before stopping at the Information desk. The woman behind the desk had to be ninety years old. She peered at me through thick glasses. "Good morning. Can I help you?"

"I'm here to visit a young woman who was admitted last night."

"Her name?"

"Jane Doe," I tried.

"How do you spell the last name?"

"D-O-E."

She ran a crooked finger down her roster. "Here she is. Room three-eleven." She smiled. "Have a good day."

The door to 311 stood open. I hesitated, then stepped into the room. The girl in the bed looked like Sleeping Beauty. The only signs that she wasn't just resting peacefully were the IV drip in her arm, the bleeping heart monitor, and the dark purple scrapes on her almost translucent skin.

I set the flowers on the window ledge and took a seat in the upholstered visitor's chair. There was no reason to move so quietly, but I did just the same. I watched Jane Doe, unsure what to do.

"Newspaper?"

I looked up to see a woman in a red flowered smock. The tag on her chest read, VOLUNTEER.

Before I could answer, she handed me a copy of the *Honolulu Advertiser*.

"Thanks."

I left the newspaper on my lap, unopened. I closed my eyes and tried to ignore the story I knew was buried in its pages.

Footsteps startled me out of a light sleep. A man in a white coat stood at the foot of the bed. A stethoscope hung from his neck, the end tucked in his pocket. He was so young, I thought he must be a student.

He was looking at me. "I'm Doctor Pan. I'm the ward doctor today."

I stood and shook his hand, unsure how much of an introduction was required on my part. "How's she doing?"

Dr. Pan studied the chart in his hands. "Last night when she came into the ER, we did a CT scan and took X-rays. Nothing looked abnormal. We aren't sure why she's still unconscious."

I couldn't think of anything to say.

He looked at the chart, then back at me. "Are you a friend, or a relative?"

"No. Actually..." It was difficult to say the words. "I'm the one who... hit her."

Dr. Pan's stare made me feel the need to explain. "She ran in front of my truck. There was no way I could stop."

"Do you know her name?"

I shook my head. "I'd never seen her before."

"According to her chart, she wasn't carrying any ID. So far, no one has reported her missing."

Her family must be frantic with worry. Why hadn't they reported her missing? "Is she...will she be okay?"

"The longer she remains unconscious, the greater the chance of lingering cognitive problems. She has some bruises and contusions consistent with the accident. She also has a broken rib and a ruptured eardrum. Those didn't happen last night. When she wakes up, we'll assign a social worker to talk with her about how she got the other injuries. For now, all we can do is watch her and hope she comes out of it soon."

Dr. Pan left and I went back to watching the girl in the bed. Had someone beaten her up? Is that what drove her to dash across the road on a cold, rainy night, barefoot, wearing next to nothing?

I wear a dress exactly once a year, for Dan's office party. I buy a new one each time, so now I own five. I opened my closet and took the new dress out. It was a simple style, sleeveless with a v-neck. The material was raw silk in a deep cranberry red.

I put on new red lace panties and bra, then slid the dress over them. The shoes were shiny patent leather in the same red as the dress. I added a string of tri-color pearls and matchig earrings and stood in front of the full-length mirror. The dress fit well, and the color looked good on me.

I've been blessed with my mother's curly blond hair and have worn it the same way for twenty years. I keep it short, so all I have to do is wash it, brush it out, and fluff it with my fingers. In the bathroom I tore open the new packages of makeup, the first makeup I've owned since I was a teenager. I applied shiny earth-tone gloss to my lips and dusted a bit of blusher on my freckled nose and cheeks. Good enough.

Hefting mail bags is hard on my nails. They were a mess. I sat at my desk, dug a nail file out of the drawer, and filed the ragged ends the best I could. I shook a bottle of cranberry nail polish, opened it, and applied it to a thumb nail. The polish just emphasized how stubby my nails were. I finished painting them, and blew on them to dry the polish. Tonight I was really stepping out of my comfort zone.

There was a knock at the back door. Sage woofed and scurried to the kitchen.

"Dan?"

"It's me."

"The door's unlocked."

He came in and stood beside me. "Ready to go? *Woo hoo.* I've never seen you do your nails before."

I touched a thumb nail. The polish was still tacky. "This is the first time. I think it'll take another five minutes for my nails to dry."

I blew on the polish again, then closed my eyes.

"You okay?"

"All this blowing is making me lightheaded."

"Better ease up. I don't want you passing out before we even leave the house."

I gave him a warning look. Three years ago, I was invited to the wrap party for a Trent Nellis movie that was filmed here. I didn't have a date, so I asked Dan to go with me. At the party, someone slipped me a Mickey, and I passed out, face down in the middle of the lawn. Dan and the bartender were the only two people who had handled my drink. I've always suspected Dan was the culprit, though I can't imagine why he would've done such a thing. It wasn't something I liked to be reminded of.

"I'll just sit on your couch and wait, if that's okay." He switched the TV on to *CNN* and made himself comfortable.

I blew on my nails for a few more minutes and tested them again. "Okay, they're dry."

I took the car keys from the desk and tossed them to Dan. We have an understanding when we go out. We take my Z-3, he drives on the way there, and I'm the designated driver for the trip home.

We left the top up for the short drive to Yacht Harbor Towers, next to Ala Moana Shopping Center. Dan's boss lives in the oceanfront condominium complex and reserves the restaurant for the Christmas party every year.

Dan pulled into the parking garage and came around to open the car door for me. As we walked to the restaurant, he draped his arm loosely over my shoulders.

Ten tables had been set for four people each. White tablecloths created an elegant atmosphere. Each table was decorated with a centerpiece of Hawaiian greens and white flameless candles.

"Look at the beautiful cake," I said.

We walked over to admire the square three-tier cake. It had white fondant icing and was decorated with green holly leaves, red sugar roses, and white pearls.

Dan led me to a couple who were sitting at one of the tables.

"Louise, you remember our secretary, Donna?"

"Good to see you again, Donna."

Donna was chubby girl in her twenties. She wore a large red mu'umu'u, and fresh flowers in her hair. "Louise, Dan, this is my fiancé, Jason."

The tall, thin man with her had longish hair and a wispy mustache. He stood and shook our hands.

Dan kissed Donna's cheek. "You're engaged? That's wonderful. Congratulations."

We sat with them. The other tables filled up while a quartet played jazzy Christmas music. Bow-tied waiters opened wine bottles and poured the wine. Dan chose red, I had a glass of white. It would be my only drink for the evening.

Dan's boss, a tall, rugged man of about sixty, stood. The room fell silent. He made a toast to the company and its employees. Glasses were raised all around.

Salads and baskets of hot bread were brought to the tables. The choice of entrée was beef or chicken. Dan had beef, accompanied by mashed potatoes and mixed vegetables. Donna and Jason both opted for the chicken. My vegetarian plate, ordered ahead, held a passable rigatoni with pesto and a side of asparagus.

Once the dinner plates were cleared, the cake was cut and distributed and coffee served. I took a cup of coffee. Dan had already polished off one bottle of wine. He raised the empty bottle and asked the waiter to bring another.

The band switched from Christmas songs to swing. Donna and Jason finished their cake, then joined several couples on the dance floor. I glanced at Dan. He used to teach ballroom dancing at Arthur Murray, but usually prefers drinking over dancing.

His eyes caught mine as he took a swig of wine. "Wanna dance?"

I nodded.

In spite of the large amount of alcohol he'd consumed, Dan was light on his feet. After a few fast numbers, the band played *Unchained Melody*. More couples filled the dance floor. Dan put an arm around my waist and pulled me closer, so I was pressed against him. It made me uncomfortable, but I didn't pull away.

"Are you doing okay?" he said into my ear. I smelled the wine on his breath.

"Yes."

"You seem a little quiet."

"I'm fine. It's a very nice party." I leaned my head back so I could look into his eyes. "Thank you for bringing me."

He pulled me close again and put his cheek against mine.

His skin was smooth, his cologne sensual. "Did you go to the hospital today?"

"Yes." I relaxed against him. Anyone who saw us would've thought we were lovers. "She's still unconscious. I talked with her doctor. He said the CT scan didn't show any damage."

"So why is she unconscious?"

"They don't know. But he told me something even more disturbing. She has injuries that didn't come from the accident. A broken rib and a ruptured eardrum."

"Sounds like someone beat her up."

"The police are being notified, and a social worker will talk with her when she wakes up."

The song ended and we sat down. Donna and Jason joined us. Dan, Donna, and Jason all refilled their wine glasses. I asked the waiter for more coffee.

"How long have you two been together?" Donna asked.

Dan looked at me. "How long has it been?"

I shrugged. We weren't *together* at all. "We met five years ago."

"That's a long time," Jason said.

"So, are you two thinking of making it permanent? Sealing the deal?" Donna asked.

This was awkward.

Dan laughed and shook his head. "I've been married twice. That's enough for me."

Chapter 4

"Auntie Louise!" Jackie's voice was unmistakable.

I pushed myself up out of my desk chair. "What is it, Jackie?" I asked through the screen door.

Sage hid behind my legs.

"Wachu doin?"

"I'm checking my e-mail."

"Can I come in?"

I tried hard to think of a reason to say no. Aside from Emmeline, I'm not fond of kids in general. I don't think anyone is fond of Jackie.

"I'm kind of busy. Don't you have Sunday school this morning?"

"It's Christmas break."

"Sunday school takes a break for Christmas?"

"Of course." He rolled his eyes. "Everybody takes a break for Christmas."

"Everybody but Santa Claus and the post office," I said under my breath.

"What?" Jackie's eyes pressed against the screen.

"Nothing"

"Can I watch your TV?" He reached for the door handle.

"Okay. Come on in. Just keep the volume down, okay?"

He opened the screen door, kicked off his rubber slippers, and came inside. Sage and Moondance retreated together to the bedroom as Jackie headed for the couch.

"Shut the door, please."

"Sheesh," Jackie mumbled, and did an about-face.

"Nicely, please. Don't slam it."

"Sheesh," he repeated.

He closed the door, then stood in the middle of my living room and looked around. "Where's your Christmas tree?"

Sheesh. "I don't have one."

"Well, when are you getting one? Can I help you decorate it? My dad says I'm big enough this year. I helped decorate my tree. I did one side and Emmie did the other. My side is better."

How could I explain to an eight-year-old that some people don't identify with the whole Christmas holiday experience?

"I'm not getting one."

Jackie frowned. "How come?"

"I'm Jewish."

It was a half-truth. My father was Jewish, my mother Irish Catholic. Which doesn't technically make me Jewish, but sometimes it's the easiest way to explain my lack of participation in the Christian traditions.

"What does *Jewish* mean?"

"It means I don't celebrate Christmas."

"Doncha know Santa won't bring you any presents if you don't got a tree?"

"Doncha know it's my job to help Santa deliver the presents?"

Jackie's eyes grew wide. *"Really?* Is he bringin me a phone? That's *all* I want."

"If I knew, I wouldn't tell you. But I do know one thing."

"What?"

"He won't bring you anything if you aren't very, *very* nice. To everyone. That includes your sister."

Jackie rolled his eyes, settled on the couch, and clicked the remote.

That afternoon, I went back to the hospital. This time, my knock was answered by a quiet, "Come in."

I opened the door a crack. "Hello?"

"Come in," she said again.

Thank God, she was awake! She'd been watching TV with the volume turned low. Her dark waist-length hair had been washed and brushed out. It was still drying. The abrasions on her face were less raw than yesterday. Her breakfast tray was pushed aside, her meal barely touched.

"Not hungry?" I asked. It seemed as good a way as any to start a conversation.

Her mouth opened, but she didn't speak. She turned the TV off. Her stare was disturbing.

"I'm Louise."
She didn't respond.
"What's your name?" I asked.
She looked away and shrugged one of her delicate shoulders.
What now? I looked around the room and saw the dry erase board on the wall by the sink. It read:

Date: Sunday, December 13
Jane Doe
Weight: 96
Nurse: Nadine
Fall precautions: up with help

They still didn't know who she was.
"How are you feeling?" I asked.
She stared into the center of the room, blinked a couple of times as though assessing how she felt, then looked directly at me. "I have a headache. And I'm a little dizzy."
"Is it okay if I sit?"
She nodded. I pulled the chair closer to the bed.
"What day is it?" she asked.
"It's Sunday."
"Sunday. That's right. The nurse told me that."
"Do you know your name?"
She turned her hands over and examined the scrapes on her palms.
"You don't know your name?" I asked, as gently as I could.
She bit her lip. A tear rolled down her cheek. I wanted to reach out and touch her, but wasn't sure it was the right thing to do. I couldn't begin to imagine what it would be like to wake up in a hospital and remember nothing, not even who you are.
"Do you know why you're here?"
"They told me there was … an accident."
"You don't remember the accident?"
"No." Her gaze moved to the window and landed on the vase of roses. "Did you bring me the flowers?"
"Yesterday."
"They're pretty. Thank you."
"I'm glad you like them.

Her eyes met mine again. "Do I know you?"

"Not really."

"Then why are you here? Why did you bring me flowers?"

This wasn't going to be easy. "I was driving the truck that hit you."

She looked away.

"I'm so sorry," I whispered.

She stared out the window. Her room was on the back side of the hospital, and the view was of a rusted trailer and a stack of plywood. Had the bump on her head caused the amnesia—or had she been mentally ill before the accident? I'd heard stories of mentally ill people who were abused by family members. Was that the case here? Had she been running from someone? An abusive parent? A boyfriend? A husband? Why hadn't anyone filed a missing person report?

I could think of nothing to say to keep the conversation going. "I have to leave now. Is there anything you need before I go?"

She seemed not to have heard me. I stood and turned to leave.

"Louise?"

"Yes?"

"Will you come back?"

I hesitated.

"Please. Please come back. Tomorrow."

She was so young. So fragile. Almost like a porcelain doll you never took off the shelf for fear she might break.

I nodded. "I'll come back tomorrow."

She almost smiled. "Thank you."

I stepped into the hallway. A Filipino nurse hurried by with a box of adult diapers in her arms.

"Excuse me," I said.

She stopped and turned. "Can I help you?"

"I'm looking for Nadine."

"I'm Nadine."

She was shorter than me, with shoulder length hair. Her scrubs had a print of the Grinch. A woman after my own heart.

I lowered my voice. "I wanted to ask you about the patient in three-eleven."

"The Jane Doe. Are you a relative? Do you know who she is?"

"No. I'm ... I'm the one who hit her. With my truck. I'm worried about her."

"She's much better today."

"I'm happy she's awake, but she doesn't remember anything. She doesn't know who she is. The doctor says she has injuries that ... are not consistent with the accident. Someone will eventually be looking for her, and I want to be sure she's safe. That she has protection."

"At this time, we are not sure how she got the other injures. The doctor has scheduled a psychiatrist and a social worker to speak with her today."

I was relieved to know that Jane, as I'd begun to think of her, would get the help she needed.

"I'll be back tomorrow to look in on her."

"Thank you." She hurried away to deliver the diapers.

Laurie Hanan

CHAPTER 5

I belong to a fast-growing subculture in Honolulu that few people are aware of. Folk dancing. There are a variety of dance groups here that include Greek, Scottish, Israeli, contra dance, and square dance, to name the most popular. One could folk dance every night of the week here, and many people do.

I needed to get out of the house and clear my head. I dressed in a tan tank top and a batik skirt, put on a jacket, and headed for the Ala Wai Golf Course, where the international folk dance group meets every Sunday night.

Music reached me from the second floor of the clubhouse as I turned into the parking lot. I locked my car and climbed the concrete staircase.

Frankie sat on a bench on the lanai, smoking a cigarette. It's illegal in Hawai'i to smoke within twenty feet of the entrance to a public building, but I wasn't going to be the one to say something.

Frankie's frequent bouts of paranoia keep her away from crowds, but she likes to watch the dancers through the floor-to-ceiling windows. Three years ago, a motorcycle accident nearly killed her. Except, it wasn't an accident at all. A man named José Luis Diaz ran her down with his truck. José Luis had been stalking me, and Frankie was trying to protect me from him. She almost died because of me.

Most of her bones had been broken and she needed extensive skin grafts. She spent weeks in the hospital and months in rehab. After the accident, Frankie seemed to age thirty years in a month's time. Her black hair turned white. The fat melted from her body until skin draped against bone.

I sat on the bench beside her and resisted the urge to fan away the smoke. "How's it going?"

"Pretty good, pretty good." She took a drag on her cigarette and flicked the ashes onto the walkway. "I gotta go to work in an hour."

"You got a job?"

She nodded and released a trail of smoke. "With a janitorial service. We clean office buildings after hours. It pays pretty good, cash, so I can still collect my Disability. I can't complain."

It worried me that she was riding a motorcycle again. With her cataracts, she doesn't see well in the dark. But no one could tell her what to do.

"It's good to see you. You have my number if you ever need anything …"

Frankie waved her hand, partly to disperse the cloud of smoke in front of us, partly to dismiss my words.

"I'm fine. I'm doing good. You go in and dance."

I pushed the glass door open and went into the ballroom. A Hungarian tune played on a portable CD player plugged into overhead speakers. I sat against the wall on a folding metal chair, took off my jacket and sandals, and watched couples spin around the room. In a group where women outnumber men ten-to-one, some of the couples were made up of two women.

It didn't take long for Janet to spot me. Since the day we met, she's had an odd fascination with me. Hard as I try to avoid her, she always manages to corner me sooner or later.

The music ended and Janet hurried over, grinning. Some of her bright red lipstick was smeared on her teeth—but hey, it wasn't my job to point it out to her.

She sat in the chair next to me, leaned into my personal space, sniffed, and wrinkled her nose. "Have you started smoking?"

"I was talking to Frankie…"

"Oh."

I glanced around for an excuse to get up.

Janet said, "I saw you in the newspaper. It said you hit a pedestrian with your mail truck."

Sheesh. I'd better set the record straight, or she'd invent a half-truth to spread around town. "She ran into the road in front of me. there was nothing I could do."

"And she's in a coma?"

"No. She's not in a coma. She's doing fine."

Janet's smile dropped. "Oh." She seemed disappointed by this piece of news. "Are you still suspended?"

The DJ put on a *hasapiko*. Dancers formed lines of three or four and grasped shoulders.

"I'm going to dance," I said, and walked away before she could say any more.

I squeezed between Dick and Roger and put my arms across their shoulders. Both were members of the international dance troupe and dressed in full costume. I did my best to follow their expert dips and steps to the lively Greek tune.

Brian came through the door. His eyes caught mine and he winked at me, then joined the end of our line. Brian is a tropical Keith Urban, complete with guitar and great voice. He always looks like he just came from the beach. I wouldn't say he's my boyfriend, at least not to his face, but he's the closest thing I have. For six years we've been dance partners and on-and-off lovers.

Brian had been looking rougher around the edges lately. Not so most people would notice, but I did. His hair had grown longer than mine so it nearly touched his shoulders. He hadn't shaved in two or three days. His aloha shirt needed ironing, and his jeans looked like they could use a wash.

The *hasapiko* ended and the DJ put on an easy Israeli circle dance. Brian took my hand and we joined the circle.

The song ended and Patty, the club president, rang a dinner bell. "Announcement time!"

The crowd hushed and gathered around her.

"We'll be dancing every Sunday at the usual time, through the holidays. Don't forget caroling on Christmas Eve. We'll meet at six o'clock at Anita's house in Nu'uanu and carol in her neighborhood for a couple hours. When we're done, we'll meet back at her house for our Christmas party. Everyone bring a pot luck dish."

The music started to play and the dancing resumed.

At nine-thirty, the caretaker of the city-run facility came to lock the doors. After helping to put away the folding chairs, Brian walked me to my car.

I unlocked the car with my remote and opened the door.

"Louise."

"Yes?"

He hesitated. "Do you mind if I crash at your place tonight?"

What was up with that? In the five years we'd known each other, it was the first time he'd ever *asked* to spend the night. That's not to say he never slept over, he just wasn't comfortable being locked into a plan.

"Not at all," I said.

"Meet you there."

The red light on my answering machine blinked rapidly, which meant the four-minute memory chip was full. I hadn't checked my messages since my name had been splashed across the news yesterday.

"Coffee?" I asked Brian.

"I have something better." He opened his duffle bag and pulled out two bottles of beer. He stuck them in the freezer and said, "They'll be cold in no time. I really could use a shower. Do you mind?"

"Go right ahead."

He took his duffle bag to the bedroom. A minute later, the shower came on. The scent of Irish Spring drifted from the bathroom. Brian had brought his own soap.

I sat at my desk, rummaged in the top drawer for a pen, flipped over an unopened bill to take notes on, and pressed the PLAY button on the answering machine. The first few messages were from friends who wanted to know if I was okay. I'd have to send out a group e-mail explaining what had happened. A couple of the messages were from reporters who wanted to interview me.

The next message was from my brother.

"Louise, this is Mike. Dad …" His voice broke, and he continued in a whisper. "He's had a stroke."

Chapter 6

We sat on the couch and drank our chilled Coronas. Brian's hair was wet and he smelled of Irish Spring. Moondance slept curled on his lap, Sage on mine.

"I haven't thought of him as *Dad* in nearly thirty years," I said.

"Sounds like he wasn't much of a dad to you."

"Not after my mom died."

Brian didn't reply. He isn't much of a talker, but he's a good listener.

"Mike has never called me before," I said.

"Never?"

"He leaves it up to his wife, Victoria. She calls twice a year, on my birthday and Christmas. She says a brief hello, then hands the phone to Brittney. My thirteen-year-old niece is expected to make conversation with an aunt she's never met."

"How old is your father?"

"He was thirty-five when I was born. That would make him seventy-five now." After a few minutes I said, "I don't know why I was so unprepared for this. In all these years, I don't think I ever imagined him aging like the rest of us."

"When was the last time you saw your brother?"

"Twenty-three years ago. He was fifteen when I left home. Just a kid."

"And you were seventeen?"

I nodded. "I left, and never went back. Just kept heading west."

"Are you going to call him back?"

"It's five in the morning in New York. I'll wait till I get up tomorrow."

Brian took a long sip of his beer, leaned his head back, and closed his eyes.

"What's going on with you?" I asked.

"Things are rough."

"Work?"

He nodded without opening his eyes. "Everyone's holding onto their money, waiting to see which way the economy will go."

He was a contractor, did everything from carpentry, to plumbing, to drywall, to electrical wiring. Since the housing market exploded in the eighties, he'd had more work than he could handle. He renovated multi-million dollar homes, and lived in them while he did the work.

"Where are you living now?"

"In my van. It's not so bad. I surf all day, then hit the showers at the beach." He took another sip of his beer. "You know Dave?"

"The tile guy?"

"Yeah. He was out of work too, so he opened a used car lot. Calls it Ishimoto's."

I burst out laughing, gagged on a mouthful of beer, and spewed it down the front of my shirt.

"What's so funny?"

I was still laughing. "Isn't he Israeli?"

"Yeah. So what?"

"Do you know what *Ishimoto* means in Hebrew?"

"Hebrew? I thought it was a Japanese name."

"It is. But I think Dave is playing on words. In Hebrew, *ish* means *man*. *Im* means *with*. *Oto* means *car*. So, *Ishimoto* means *a man with a car*."

"Ah. Okay. That's pretty funny. Dave's doing good with the cars. That's the business to be in now, while the economy's slow. He needs someone to do body work and detailing. I'm going to start helping him tomorrow."

I woke before seven. Brian was asleep on his side, his back to me. I eased myself out of the bed. Sage groaned, then let out a light snore. I made a cup of tea, took it to my desk, and stared at the phone. I really did not want to call Mike back. But I'd better get it over with.

I made a cup of tea, took it to my desk, and stared at the phone. I really did not want to call Mike back, but I'd better get it over with. Where was his number? I dug around, found it, and dialed. Hopefully they'd be at work now and the answering machine would pick up.

"Hello?"

"Mike?"

"Louise?"

"I got your message. What happened?"

"Dad is in a coma. He went out to walk his dog yesterday and didn't come home. Lillian"—he referred to my father's current wife—"went out to look for him. She saw an ambulance down the street and ran to see what was going on. A mail carrier had found Dad lying in the snow, unconscious, and called for the ambulance."

I didn't know what to say. Mike and my father were close. I wasn't happy my father had a stroke, but I couldn't bring myself to say I was sorry.

"We need to make a decision," Mike said. "I want you to be in agreement before we do anything."

"What do you mean, *make a decision*?"

"Dad is being treated with antibiotics to prevent pneumonia. They're hydrating him and feeding him through a tube. A physical therapist exercises his muscles. There's a possibility he won't come out of the coma. He doesn't have a living will or an advanced health care directive. We have to decide how long we're going to continue this kind of care. If it's his time to go, we don't want to prolong his suffering."

"Is he aware of what's happening?"

"We don't know. He's in what they call a light coma. He has some brain function. When he's awake, his eyes move. He responds to pain, but doesn't respond when spoken to. Lillian has been with him since he arrived at the hospital. Victoria, Brittney, and I relieved her this morning so she could eat and rest. We took turns reading to Dad from the Bible."

Lillian married my father fifteen years ago. I knew little about her, but sorely resented the fact that she lived in the Manhattan apartment where I grew up.

"Shouldn't Lillian be the one to make the decision about withdrawing treatment?"

"She wants us all to be in agreement. Including you. She won't make a decision the rest of us aren't comfortable with."

This was too much for me to take in. My father might be approaching the end of his life.

When I didn't respond, Mike said, "Louise, you need to be here. Do this one last thing for Dad."

"There's no way I can leave work right now," I fibbed. "It's a week and a half to Christmas. The post office doesn't give time off for anything."

I wasn't about to tell him I'd been suspended. There was just no way I could sit in a hospital room and watch my father die, while my brother and his wife took turns reading to him from the Bible. And then there was Lillian. I couldn't intrude on their grief.

"I'm sure in a case like this…"

"I'm allowed three days off to attend the funeral of an immediate family member. But just to visit someone in the hospital, regardless of their condition, there's no way I can get time off."

"I'm sorry to hear that. I feel it's important the family be together now."

As opposed to when our mother died, and Dad shipped us off to camp so we wouldn't be there when it happened. There was little point in holding onto the bitterness I felt toward my father for not telling us our mother was dying. For not allowing me the chance to say good-bye. But it rose in me now, tightening my chest, making it hard to breathe.

"I can't." I struggled to keep the anger out of my voice. Anger that was not in any way directed at Mike.

"Okay." I knew he was disappointed. "The CT scan shows Dad had a series of small strokes before this last big one. His body and brain are shutting down. When the time comes, we feel he should be allowed to slip away with as much dignity as possible."

For all the hatred I'd felt for my father, I took no pleasure in his suffering. I had only pity for him now. "Please, do whatever you feel is right."

"Do you agree to withholding all treatment except feeding and hydration?"

It's what I'd want for myself in the same situation. Maybe this was one last gesture I could make toward my father, giving my permission for him to pass from his body in peace. "Yes."

We said a few final words, then hung up.

I remembered my father as a dark, towering, bookish man with prematurely thinning hair and one of those faces that screams *Jewish*. During my mother's lifetime he observed, but preferred to stay in the background of, the day to day activities my mother orchestrated with precision.

After she was gone, my father's darkest side emerged. My last memory is of him screaming at me in a blind rage, "You killed her! If you'd behaved like a *normal* daughter ... if you'd shown your mother one ounce of respect ... she would not be *dead*!" I stood frozen, even as he picked up a chair and swung at me. I ducked out of the way a moment before the chair smashed against the wall.

Now I tried to get my mind around the image of my father as an old man, lying in a hospital bed, waiting to die. I pictured him with tubes going into and out of his shriveled body, only a few wisps of white hair on his liver-spotted head, his dentures removed so he wouldn't swallow them, his mouth caved in where his teeth used to be.

Even if I wanted to, I could conjure no hatred for him.

Laurie Hanan

Chapter 7

Brian hadn't told me what time he'd be starting his new job today. Instead of zapping a cup of tea, I brewed a pot of coffee. He'd need something to eat before he went to work, wouldn't he? I opened the fridge. There wasn't much in there. I didn't normally eat breakfast.

I turned on the TV and checked my e-mail while I listened to the morning news. There was no mention of my accident.

The shower turned on. A few minutes later, Brian came into the kitchen wearing yesterday's jeans and a tee-shirt that needed a wash. Maybe I'd offer to do a load of laundry for him after work. He poured himself a mug of coffee and opened the fridge.

"There's bread, if you want toast," I said. "You can have cereal with soy milk. And I have some bananas."

"Do you want anything?" he asked.

"If you're making toast, I'll have some."

Brian set a plate with two pieces of toast on my desk. He went back to the kitchen and came out balancing a bowl of cereal, a mug of coffee, and a plate of toast, and settled on the couch to eat. I followed him to the living room and sat cross-legged on the Persian rug. Sage came out of the bedroom and sat in front of me. Her nose twitched at my food.

"What time do you start work?" I asked.

Brian shoveled cereal into his mouth, took a bite of toast, and washed it down with coffee. "Dave keeps pretty loose hours. He said to call him around eleven. I don't know when I'll get in tonight, either. What time will you be home from work?"

"Did you see Saturday's paper?"

"I don't usually get the paper. Why?"

I sighed and rubbed my eyes with both hands. "I had an accident."

"An accident?"

"With my mail truck."

"Why didn't you tell me? Are you okay?"

"I hit a pedestrian. I've been suspended from work while they investigate."

"Was it your fault?"

"She ran into the road, right in front of me. I swerved, but at the same time she doubled back. There was no way to avoid hitting her."

"How badly was she hurt?"

"She was unconscious for two days. I went to the hospital Friday night after I hit her, then took her some flowers Saturday. I sat in her room and just looked at her. I felt so helpless."

"I'm sorry. I can't imagine."

"Yesterday, I went back again. She's awake now."

"That's good."

"But she has amnesia. She doesn't remember the accident, or anything else. She's just a young girl, maybe a teenager. They have no idea who she is. She seemed so frightened and confused. She made me promise I'd come back again today."

"I didn't hear anything about it on the TV news."

"I think they hushed it up. Her doctors suspect someone beat her up before I ran her down, and they're bringing in the police. It wouldn't do to have someone show up at the hospital to finish her off."

Jane Doe smiled when I walked into the room. "Louise!"

I was encouraged she remembered my name.

She turned the TV off and raised her bed to a sitting position. "Thank you for coming. Do you want to sit down?"

I pulled the chair closer to the bed. "You're looking good. Are you feeling better today?"

"Yes, I am."

How was I going to keep a conversation going, when her memory went back only three days? It didn't leave a whole lot to talk about.

I needn't have worried.

As soon as I was seated she said, "Louise, I want to talk to you. But you have to promise me something."

I looked into her eyes. I had no way of judging her mental state, but she appeared as sane as you and me.

She reached out and laid a hand on my arm. "Louise, promise me you won't tell anyone what I'm about to tell you."

I immediately had second thoughts about her sanity. How could I promise not to repeat what she said? If she was insane, maybe intent on harming herself, somebody had to be alerted. "That depends ..."

She gave me a pleading look. "Please. Promise me."

I was curious. "Okay. I promise to keep your secret."

She studied my face. "Can I trust you?"

"You can trust me."

She glanced at the door. I'd closed it when I came in. "I'm scared. I need help."

Was her paranoia a result of the head injury, or was she just plain nuts? I stared into her dark eyes as they studied me. She was dead serious. And she was terrified.

"I remember everything," she finally said.

This was a surprise. "Your memory is coming back?"

"I never lost my memory."

"*What?*"

She glanced again at the closed door and lowered her voice, even though there was no one who might overhear. "I was afraid to give them my name. I think someone's trying to find me."

I thought of the injuries Dr. Pan had told me about—the broken rib, the ruptured eardrum.

"Who's trying to find you? Who is it you're afraid of?"

"His name is Raymond."

I waited for her to continue. When she didn't, I leaned forward and whispered, "Who is Raymond?"

She didn't answer.

I glanced at her hands. She wasn't wearing a ring. "Is he your boyfriend? Your husband?"

A tear escaped her eye. She brushed it away. "It's complicated."

Of course it was. Relationships are always complicated. "Let's start with your name."

"Enid." She looked into my eyes, as though seeking my approval.

"Enid." The name suited her. "Tell me about Raymond."

She didn't speak. I waited.

"I met him at Fullerton College," she finally said. "I was

studying biology. I wanted to be a nurse. I noticed him in one of my classes. He was soft-spoken and serious, and seemed more mature than the other students. I was attracted to him. Not just his looks. It was everything—the way he smiled, the way he looked into my eyes when I talked. He had a way of making me feel as if I were the most important person in the world."

She stared at her clasped hands.

When she didn't continue, I said, "Go on."

"We started dating. I mean the old fashioned kind of dating, where he'd pick me up in his car and take me out to dinner, or a movie.

"He told me he grew up on Guam. After high school, he spent four years in the army. When he got out, he came to Hawai'i. Some of his brothers and sisters joined him here. They saved their money and when they had enough, they opened a restaurant. A year later, Raymond left his siblings here to run the restaurant, and went to Fullerton to study Business Management.

"One night, he told me the story of how his heart had been broken. Right out of high school, he married his sweetheart. He went to boot camp in Missouri. While he was there, he received a letter from Marie. She was expecting their baby. Raymond was thrilled. After boot camp, he returned to Guam. Marie was eight months pregnant. Shortly after their daughter was born, the army moved Raymond and his family to Hawai'i.

"At this point in his story, he opened his wallet, took out a photo, and put it in my hand. It was a little girl, about a year old, with curly hair and a smile like an angel. She was dressed all in pink, with ribbons in her hair. 'Her name's Celeste', he said.

"Raymond was deployed to Iraq. While he was there, he got the news. His baby girl was dead and his wife had been arrested for her murder.

"Raymond took the photo back from me. He looked at it, and started to cry. At that moment, I knew I was in love with him."

Enid stared at nothing. Her face showed no emotion, but her breathing had accelerated. "Raymond was allowed to return to Hawai'i for the funeral. Celeste was buried in a little white casket, thousands of miles from Raymond's home.

"In court, Marie said she hadn't meant to do it. She'd been at her wit's end, so far from her home and family, never knowing from one day to the next if her husband would come back alive. Celeste threw tantrums that went on for hours. She cried through the night. Marie was exhausted. All she wanted was a little quiet. She held a pillow over Celeste's face. Just to stop the noise.

"A jury found her guilty of second degree murder. She's still serving her twenty-year sentence.

"Raymond and I moved in together. We worked hard, studied hard, and spent what little free time we had in each other's arms. I knew I could give him enough love to heal his broken heart.

"It wasn't long, though, before he dropped out of college. He said his brothers were mismanaging the family business and he had to go back to Hawai'i to straighten things out. He asked me to go with him, said I could continue my studies on O'ahu. He was sure there was a demand for nurses on the island, and I'd have no problem finding work after I graduated. By then, I couldn't imagine life without him. Living in Hawai'i with the man I loved sounded like an exotic dream."

She took a couple of deep breaths, then spoke in an even voice. "The dream turned into a nightmare."

"What happened?"

She studied her hands again. "He brought me to a muddy, filthy pig farm and a dilapidated house that he shared with three brothers and two sisters. I was never allowed to return to school. They took my money, took everything I had, and kept me locked in an upstairs room with only the clothes on my back. Raymond's sisters, Tatum and Lourdes, divided my belongings between them. They liked to dress me as if I were a doll." She paused. Her face crumbled, but her voice didn't falter. "All six of them used me as a… as a…plaything."

She stopped.

I touched her arm. "Did they hurt you?"

She nodded. "When I cooperated, I was rewarded with food. When I didn't cooperate, Raymond beat me."

She turned away and brushed tears from her cheeks. "I did what I had to do to survive," she whispered.

"Anyone would."

"The house and farm are surrounded by a high fence. They must have a dozen pit bulls that bark like mad when anyone goes in or out the gate. I'm terrified of those dogs. The window of my room opened onto the roof and there were always two or three dogs outside my window. Sometimes they slept. When they weren't asleep, they stared at me through the glass and salivated."

"How did you get away?"

"The first time I escaped was a few months ago. Every evening, Raymond goes to the restaurant. Usually, his brothers and sisters go with him. They'd bring my dinner, then leave me alone, locked in my room.

"One night, I hid some chicken. When they'd all gone for the evening, I slipped the chicken out the window. The dogs gulped it down and begged for more. I opened the window and climbed onto the roof. The dogs danced around me, but didn't bark. I jumped off. The dogs shot into the house through another window and ran down the stairs. By the time they got outside, I was over the fence.

"I hitched a ride with some surfers. They let me out a few miles down the road, and I started walking. Headlights approached. I stuck my thumb out again. The car pulled over. By the time I realized the driver was one of Raymond's brothers, it was too late.

"I told Raymond I was sorry for trying to run away. I told him I loved him, and promised it would never happen again. I cried. I begged. It didn't help. He beat me. He starved me. He sealed my window shut with big screws. When I was given food, it was drugged. I ate it any way. The drugs were my only escape. I pretended to enjoy …" She let out a sob, and clamped a hand over her mouth.

"It's okay."

She took time to compose herself. "I pretended to enjoy the … attentions … of Raymond and his brothers and sisters.

"After months of good behavior, Raymond said he was rewarding me. He started taking me with him to the restaurant in the evenings. But he made sure there was no opportunity for me to run. When Tatum and Lourdes dressed me to go out, they made me wear shoes with five-inch heels. I could barely walk in them. If I needed to go to the restroom, Tatum accompanied me. She linked her arm through mine like we were best friends, and stood outside the stall while I used the toilet."

Enid sighed. "Poor Tatum. She doesn't have a mean bone in her body. And she's madly in love with me. The only person she loves more is Raymond. She's his most devoted watchdog.

"I never stopped looking for another chance to escape. I knew the next time my plan had to be perfect. Failure would mean death—or worse.

"Every day, while the dogs stared, I worked at the screws that sealed the bedroom window. Finally, I could pull them out with my fingers. I left them in place, and waited.

"Friday evening, I saw my chance. The noise of the rain pounding against the tin roof would cover any sound I might make. Nobody would be outside. When we were about to leave for the restaurant, I told Raymond I felt sick. I ran into the bathroom, shut the door, and stuck my finger down my throat. I vomited up my drugged dinner, all over the outfit Tatum had just dressed me in.

"Raymond was disgusted. He ordered Tatum to clean me up, and left with Lourdes and two of his brothers. Tatum and the oldest brother, Joseph, were left to guard me.

"Tatum removed the soiled dress. She washed me, slipped an extra large tee-shirt over my head, and put me to bed. I heard her lock the door from the outside.

"I was about to pull the loosened screws out of the window frame, when a car drove through the gate. Tires crunched on the gravel, and the dogs barked madly. The three dogs outside my window dove into the next room and raced down the stairs.

"The car stopped in front of the house. Car doors slammed. Joseph's ungodly laugh rose above male voices speaking in loud Chamorro. Footsteps pounded up the front steps, into the living room. Joseph yelled at the dogs to shut up, but they kept barking.

"As far as I could tell, everyone was in the living room. I had to hurry. The dogs would grow bored with the visitors soon enough. I pulled out the screws and slid the window up. I crawled onto the slippery roof and peered over the edge. The ground below was invisible in the dark. Before I could change my mind, I swung my legs over the edge of the roof. I lost my grip, fell maybe ten feet, and landed hard. Without stopping to check for injuries, I ran, barefoot, over rocks and mud. I collided with the chain link fence, took a fast look around, and climbed over.

"I felt my way along the fence, through the property next door. I found a driveway and walked to the road. This time I didn't hitchhike. I stayed behind trees and bushes. Under the cover of rain and darkness, I made my way toward Kāne'ohe.

"There were no sidewalks. Without shoes, the going was difficult on my side of the road. I thought it might be easier to cross the highway and follow the beach. The rain came down harder. My body trembled so hard I could barely move. I was cold and terrified I'd be caught. An opening between the ironwood trees looked like access to the beach. I waited for a break in the traffic. When I was sure there was no one who might see me, I dashed across the road."

Her eyes locked with mine and she shook her head. "That's all I remember."

I sat in shocked silence, trying to process the horror story I'd just heard. "You're safe now," I finally said. "There are people who can protect you."

Enid's eyes filled with fear. "No."

"You have to tell the police."

"*No*. If I tell anyone who I am, Raymond will find me."

"There are shelters where he can't find you. Where you'll be safe until you can go home."

"Raymond took my money, my clothes, my ID. I have absolutely nothing."

"The shelter will give you clothes. They'll help you get in contact with your family."

"I can't."

"I'll tell your nurse you want to speak to a social worker. They deal with situations like yours all the time."

"There is no other situation like this. There is no other person like Raymond."

Chapter 8

I sat cross-legged on the floor, a mug of coffee in my hands. Brian had picked up some groceries yesterday after work and he made breakfast this morning. A plate of French toast with maple syrup sat on the floor beside me. Sage lay with her nose pointed in the direction of my breakfast. I was either going to have to start going to a gym, or watching my diet.

I'd done Brian's laundry. He was dressed in clean clothes, faded jeans and a tee-shirt, ready for his second day at work. This was getting downright domestic.

I'd just finished telling him Enid's story, as she told it to me.

He shoveled a big piece of French toast into his mouth and washed it down with coffee. "If she's that scared, I don't understand why she doesn't ask the police for help."

"She's terrified. She doesn't trust anyone, won't even talk to a social worker. She thinks if anyone knows who she is, Raymond will track her down."

"She seems to trust you."

"She does. But she swore me to secrecy."

"She's held it in for so long, I guess she needed to tell someone. To unburden herself. But you can't protect her from Raymond. You have to convince her to talk to the authorities. It's the only way she'll be safe."

Sunlight glinted off the highway as I headed toward the mountains, making it difficult to see. On the other side of the Pali tunnel I drove into thick, fog-like clouds. I moved to the right lane, reduced my speed, and concentrated on the curves in the road.

In the hospital parking lot, a cold wind nearly knocked me off my feet. A dark sky threatened rain.

The door to Enid's room stood open. I lifted my hand to knock, then heard voices in the room. Did she have visitors?

I gave a quick knock. "Enid?"

The voices stopped. I peeked through the doorway. Two men stood in the center of the room, and a woman sat on the bed with her back to me. Enid was on the visitor's chair, fully dressed in too-short shorts, a green tee-shirt, and pink rubber slippers.

The four people in the room stared at me as I stepped in. I said, "Hi," in a cheery voice.

One of the men walked over to me. He was five-foot eight or nine, with dark skin and neatly trimmed black hair. He wore expensive looking shoes, gray slacks, and a long-sleeved black dress shirt that almost obscured the thin, gold watch on his left wrist.

He held out his hand and I shook it.

"I'm Raymond." His grip was firm, his hand strong.

So, this was Raymond. To look at him, I never would have imagined him capable of the things Enid described.

I glanced at Enid. Her eyes were wide, her face paler than ever. She shook her head almost imperceptibly. Warning me away from … what?

I took my eyes off her and met Raymond's gaze. "Nice to meet you, Raymond. I'm Louise."

Raymond looked to Enid. "Louise …?"

Enid hadn't told him about me. Had she hoped to be gone before I returned? Was she running away from me this time?

"I'm a friend of Enid's," I said.

"A friend? Of Enid's?"

Enid looked at the floor as she spoke. "Louise visited me every day while I was here. When I lost my memory and didn't know who I was, she kept me company."

Raymond crossed his arms in what would normally be a defensive gesture, but his smile seemed genuine. "Well, Louise. I certainly thank you for all you've done for Enid. I can't tell you how much I appreciate it."

Before I could think of an answer, he nodded toward the other man. "This is my brother, Joseph."

I smiled at Joseph, but I didn't offer to shake his hand. His legs were shriveled and deformed, and he supported himself on two forearm crutches. He was a good twenty years older than Raymond, but seemed to defer to him. His curly salt and pepper hair was long and unkempt. His jeans and white tee-shirt had seen better days. He stared directly at me with his right eye, which was dark brown, while his cloudy left eye strayed to the side. He grinned, showing several missing teeth, but didn't speak.

"And this is my sister, Tatum," Raymond said, indicating the woman sitting on the bed.

Tatum stood and took my hand. She said, "Hi," then sat again.

Tatum was half Joseph's age, twenty-five or so. A classic apple shape with wide shoulders, her belly was so rounded I thought at first she was pregnant. Her upper body was padded with fat that hung over her bra strap, but she had no breasts to speak of. Her legs appeared too thin to comfortably support her weight. Her frizzy brown hair was so sparse I could see her scalp. She'd be bald before she reached forty.

"We're just glad we found Enid," Raymond said. I pulled my eyes from Tatum and looked back to him. "And that she's okay. We were frantic with worry about her."

I bet you were.

"You've done so much for me, Louise," Enid said. "I was so confused. It helped to have someone to talk to."

I stared hard at her, trying to read her expression. Was there a hidden plea for help in her words?

"Okay, are we ready to go?" Raymond asked, his eyes on Enid.

She stood, keeping her eyes averted. Tatum got up and put an arm around Enid's waist, as though to help her walk.

I stepped back and let them pass, watching as the strange entourage escorted Enid out the door.

I gave them time to move down the hallway before I looked out. Raymond walked ahead of the rest. He was the only one of the bunch who appeared normal. Joseph propelled himself forward on his crutches with difficulty, dragging his misshapen legs along the floor with a scraping sound. Tatum and Enid took up the rear. Tatum waddled, duck-like, on the sides of her flat feet, halfway on, halfway off a worn-down pair of rubber slippers. Enid held herself rigid, as though resigned to the fate that awaited her.

I took a last look around the room. The vase of pink roses still sat on the window ledge, forgotten. When the elevator door closed, I ran down two flights of stairs to the ground level.

I spotted them in the parking lot. The breeze lifted Enid's long, dark hair. She looked frail, almost swallowed by Tatum's bulk. They got into a black pickup truck. Raymond took the driver's seat and Joseph sat beside him. Tatum and Enid climbed into the truck bed. Enid's outfit was too skimpy for a ride in open air on such a cold day.

Raymond started the engine, and the truck pulled out of the lot. I walked casually toward my car, hoping to catch their license number. They were too far away.

I jumped into my car, started the engine, and pulled out of the lot a few cars behind Raymond's pickup. I followed at a distance. The pickup made a right on Kam Highway. A mile down the road, it turned into the lot of a small liquor store. There was no way I could pull into the same lot without being seen. I drove another half mile, pulled into a gas station, and positioned my car so I could see the pickup when it passed.

I filled my tank without taking my eyes off the road. The pickup hadn't gone by. I got in my car, waited fifteen minutes, then got back on the highway and headed toward the liquor store. The truck was gone. I turned around and followed Kam Highway through Kāneʻohe, to the area where I hit Enid, and several miles beyond.

Raymond's pickup was nowhere in sight. I'd lost Enid.

Chapter 9

I sat with Sage on my front steps, sipped a cup of tea, and watched the sun sink over Honolulu Harbor.

"Wassup, Louise?"

Sage lifted her head and sniffed as Emmeline and Dazy climbed the steps. Emmeline sat beside me, and Dazy made herself comfortable on the step below.

"Just thinking."

Her phone whistled, and she typed a text message with her thumbs. Messages flew back and forth for a few minutes before she put the phone in her pocket, apparently done with the exchange.

"What are you thinking about?" she asked.

"I don't know. Lots of things."

"Like what?"

"My father is very sick."

"What's wrong with him?"

"He had a stroke."

"A security guard at my school had a stroke. I made a big card for him out of poster board. Everyone at school signed it, even the teachers and the office staff. I took it to him at the hospital and he was so happy he cried."

"That was so nice of you. How's he doing now?"

"He's still paralyzed on one side and it's hard to understand him when he talks. But he's home now and he's learning to walk with a cane. I think he misses coming to work.

"I bet he does."

"Is your father in the hospital?"

"Yes, he is." I'd always done my best to shield Emmeline from life's harsher realities. But she's got a good head on her shoulders and at thirteen is probably better equipped to handle them than most people. "He's in a coma. They don't think he'll wake up. We're thinking of telling the hospital to stop his care, except for feeding."

Emmeline thought for a minute. "When it's someone's time to go, we need to let them. I think your father wants to be with God."

I nodded. "I think so too."

"Does it make you sad to let him go?"

"Not really. Maybe just a little bit sad to think of him trapped in a body that he doesn't want to be in any more."

"But will you miss him?"

"When I was your age, I was very close to my father. But as I got older, we ... drifted apart. I haven't seen him since I was seventeen."

"That's a long time."

"It is."

"Maybe you should go talk to him now. Before he leaves his body. You need to tell him you still love him. Tell him you're sorry the relationship wasn't better. And, most important, give him your permission to go. People in a coma hear everything. He'll hear you, if you just go and talk to him."

As much as I hate work during the Christmas season, I was frustrated and bored at home. The investigation into the accident was wrapping up and I'd be back at work soon. In the meantime, I was running out of ways to pass the time.

I'd let Enid slip back into Raymond's grasp, right in front of my eyes. I'd failed at something as simple as following them home. I didn't know her last name or Raymond's. I didn't know the name of Raymond's restaurant. I wanted to help her but had no clue where to start.

I know. It wasn't my problem. Just because I ran into her with my truck, it didn't mean I was responsible for her the rest of her life. Even so, she'd shared her story with me. The abuse was real, the injuries documented. She was genuinely terrified. And I was the only one who knew the conditions she was living in.

I had to help her. But how? Should I call the police? What could I tell them? The hospital had already reported her injuries as possible domestic violence. Enid had the opportunity to file charges against Raymond while she was in the hospital, but chose not to. She left the hospital with him willingly. Would the police investigate simply on my say so? I doubted it.

There was someone who might know how to find Enid, and what

to do to help her. It was a long shot. I only met him once, years ago. Did I still have his number?

I searched through my desk. His business card was tucked inside my address book. Freddy Friedman was one of a dozen reporters who attended the funeral of one of my customers, Mrs. Santos, after she was murdered. He interviewed me at the funeral and gave me his business card. I stuck it in my back pocket, and forgot I had it. A week later, I found it when I was doing laundry, put it in my address book, and never looked at it again. Until today.

I held the card up and examined it. Should I give it a try? Would he remember me? I had a feeling he would. Was the number on the card still good? There was one way to find out.

I dialed and got his voice mail. *Hey, this is Freddy. I'm glad I can't come to the phone, because it means I'm out enjoying Paradise. Leave your name and number, and I'll get back to you.*

"Hi Freddy. This is Louise Golden. Remember me? You interviewed me three years ago, at the funeral for Conchita Santos. I have a ... tricky situation I'd like to talk to you about. Maybe get your take on it. There might even be a story in it for you."

I hung up. Five minutes later, the phone rang. I looked at the caller ID. It wasn't Freddy, it was Gene.

Gene is my eighty-something-year-old friend and neighbor. He's more than a friend or a neighbor, really. Over the years, he's become like a mother and a father to me, all wrapped up in one. Gene and I get together about once a week. We talk, then he plays the piano and I sing. Gene loves the same songs my mother loved. Without knowing anything about her, he always picks her favorites to play for me. Funny enough, my mother's name was Jeanne.

"I left a message for you Sunday," Gene said. "I saw the article in the newspaper. I've been worried about you."

"Oh Gene, I'm sorry. I got so many calls after the story, I never got around to listening to all the messages. I should've called you. I should've realized you'd see the news and worry."

"Are you okay?"

"I was shaken up by the whole thing, but I'm fine now."

"And the young woman you hit? How is she doing?"

"Much better. I visited her in the hospital every day. Yesterday she was released."

"Wasn't she in a coma? It sounded like she was seriously

injured."

"She was unconscious for a couple days, but her injuries were minor. Once she regained consciousness, she recovered quickly."

"Thank God."

The phone beeped. Freddy was trying to call.

"Gene, I have an important call coming in. I'll call you back." I disconnected before he could reply.

"Hello? Yes?"

"Louise?"

"Yes, this is Louise."

"It's Freddy Friedman."

"Freddy. Thanks for calling back. Do you remember me?"

"Of course I remember you. I saw you made the paper again a few days ago. Is that what you're calling about?"

"Yes, and no. What I want to talk to you about is related to my accident Friday night, but only indirectly."

"I don't like talking on the phone. Can we meet?"

The first time I saw Freddy, I was momentarily attracted to him. He was nice to me, but I was sad and distracted. Now, I was surprised at the butterflies I felt at the thought of seeing him again.

"That sounds good. I'm not much of a phone person, either."

"I'm taking my sailboat out this afternoon. Can you join me? We'd have privacy, and plenty of time to talk."

Sailboat? I'm notorious for getting sick on boats. And in airplanes, in cars, even on carnival rides. But the *idea* of sailing has always appealed to me, even if the reality never sits well.

"I haven't been sailing in years," I said, neglecting to tell him the reason I refrain.

"That's no problem. I'll do all the work. Your only job will be to sit tight and hold on."

And not puke on your boat. "I think I can manage that."

"I saw a whale the other day. Maybe we'll see more today." A chance of seeing whales this early in the season made his offer that much more appealing. "Can you meet me at Ko Olina at three o'clock?" he asked.

"Ko Olina?"

"That's where my boat's docked. Is that too far for you to drive?"

The western shore of the island is uniquely beautiful. But other than the beaches, there's no reason to make the long drive out there. I hadn't been to the west side more than twice in the five years I'd been on the island.

"Not at all. It'll be fun."

"Fantastic. Try to be here no later than three. I want get back in before it's completely dark. Bring a jacket. It gets pretty cold on the ocean when the sun starts to set. Do you you know where Lagoon Four is?"

Brian and I went to Ko Olina just once. He wanted to check out the man-made lagoons. The beach was clean, quiet, and mostly vacant of tourists. I liked the added assurance of nets at the mouths of the lagoons to keep sharks out. Brian found the whole setup artificial and distasteful. After fifteen minutes, we left and headed down the coast to Ka'ena Point.

"I think I can find it."

"Turn at the sign for Lagoon Four. "Drive up to the marina gate on your left, then give me a call. I'll open the gate for you."

"See you then."

I called Gene back. "Sorry for cutting our call short."

"Oh no, not at all. I know you have a lot going on in your life."

Gene didn't know the half of what was going on in my life, but I wanted to tell him. "I do have a lot going on. I'd like to come over and talk to you about it. Soon."

"Of course. You know you're welcome any time. It doesn't have to be just once a week."

"Thank you. I'm going sailing in Ko Olina this afternoon. I might be home late. Can I come over tomorrow night?"

"Of course, Louise. Whatever is best for you. I'm always here. You know that. Have a great time sailing, and I'll look forward to seeing you tomorrow."

I went into the bedroom and searched through my dresser. I'd just agreed to go out on a sailboat, alone, with a man I'd met only once and hadn't spoken to in years. We'd be in the middle of the ocean. No one would hear me if I called for help.

But I had a good feeling about Freddy. He seemed like a decent guy, and someone I wouldn't mind getting to know a little better.

Laurie Hanan

CHAPTER 10

Freddy had said it would get cold. I dressed in a pair of jeans and a cropped sea green tee-shirt. My *Ski the Volcano* sweatshirt went into my backpack, along with my wallet, hairbrush, and Chapstick. What else did one take on a sailing trip? I had no idea.

I said good bye to Sage and was on my way.

Ginger is supposed to prevent sea sickness. I made a stop at the natural food store and picked up a bottle of ginger capsules. I wandered through the store and grabbed a cold six-pack of ginger beer as well.

Back in the car, I twisted open a bottle of ginger beer and washed down a handful of capsules with the soda. I set the radio to the oldies station and cranked up the volume. I put the top down and pulled onto the freeway with one hand on the wheel, a ginger beer in the other, my hair tousled by the wind. I sang with the radio, *Brandy, you're a fine girl, what a good wife you would be/but my life, my love and my lady is the sea ...*

It was a gorgeous December day in Hawai'i, and I was going sailing!

Twenty minutes later, flying down the H-1 and singing *Torn between two lovers, feelin' like a fool...* a red Mustang convertible pulled alongside me. I took a swig of my ginger beer and tried to ignore the other car as it matched my speed. I heard hollering, and glanced over. Four military guys with blond crew cuts, half my age, fist-pumped and grinned at me. I get that reaction sometimes from guys who like my car. But their car was newer than mine, with an engine twice the size.

The Mustang increased its speed and pulled in front of me. The two guys in the back seat turned around and hollered and hooted as they sped out of sight.

I took another sip of the ginger beer, then noticed the bottle. It looked exactly like a beer bottle. Good thing it hadn't been a cop that pulled alongside me.

The rush hour traffic hadn't started yet and I made good time. I slowed as I approached the guard shack at the entrance to the resort and shoved my empty bottle under the seat.

A young Hawaiian guy in an aloha shirt signaled me to stop. "Welcome to Ko Olina. Where you headed?"

"The marina."

"Have a great time." He smiled and waved me through.

To my left, ducks and black swans rested near a manmade waterfall. On the right, I passed Paradise Cove, the Ihilani Hotel, multi-million dollar condos called the Beach Villas, Marriott timeshares, and the beginnings of what would be a new Disney resort.

I made a right at Lagoon Four and checked the time. It was only two-thirty. I was half an hour early. I pulled to the side of the road and dialed Freddy's number. He picked up on the first ring.

"I'm a little early," I said.

"No problem at all. Where are you?"

"Outside the gate."

"I'll be right there to let you in."

I drove up to the electronic arm at the marina entrance. I didn't have a clear memory of what Freddy looked like, but when he approached the gate I knew it was him. He wore only a pair of loose khaki shorts and slippers. He wasn't tall—maybe five-eight, dark-skinned, hard-muscled, with dark hair on his arms, legs and chest. And his head was completely bald.

He grinned and waved. He swiped a key fob over the electronic box at the gate, the wooden arm went up, and I drove in.

I found a parking spot and stuffed the remaining bottles of ginger beer into my backpack. Freddy caught up with me as I was latching the convertible top. I hoisted the backpack to my shoulder.

"Can I carry that?" he asked, and took it from me. "Whoa. What have you got in here?"

"A few bottles of ginger beer."

He used his key fob again to open a metal gate. "You get sea sick?"

"Sometimes, if the water's rough," I under-exaggerated.

He led me down a flight of concrete steps. Sailboats, fishing boats, catamarans, and a few pricey looking yachts bobbed in the calm water.

"How many boats are docked here?" I asked.

"Around three-hundred, give or take."

"Is that the pirate ship from *Pirates of the Caribbean*?"

"Yes. The *Queen Anne's Revenge*. They're keeping it here, for now."

We stopped in front of a brick structure. "If you want to use the restroom before we sail, this is it."

I recalled operating a toilet on a sailboat at sea can be tricky, and took advantage of this last opportunity to use the on-land facility.

When I was done, we walked to a thirty-foot sailboat. The name *Makutu* was painted in blue script across the stern.

"This is it," he said.

"It's beautiful."

Freddy kicked off his slippers. "You can leave your slippers here on the dock. No one will take them."

I took my slippers off and left them next to Freddy's. If I didn't come back, at least I was leaving a trail of evidence.

He climbed onto the boat. "Watch your step." He held out a hand to help me.

"I'm fine. Thanks."

"You can sit on the bench here." He set my backpack on the floor. "Can you swim?"

Why was he asking me that? "I know *how* to swim. I don't particularly *want* to swim today."

He laughed. "Well then, hopefully you won't have to. But just in case, the cushions float and there are lifejackets below your seat."

With all the sharks in the water, what good would a life jacket do me? I nodded, realizing I had more to worry about than seasickness.

Freddy busied himself with getting the boat ready to sail.

"Can I do something to help?" I asked.

"If you're not an experienced sailor, I'd prefer you just sit tight until we're out at sea."

"I can do that."

A few minutes later, he untied the mooring line and started the engine. The boat eased away from the dock. We turned and moved slowly through the marina.

"That's the *Splendour*," he said, pointing to a small, unimpressive boat. "It's the boat Natalie Wood was on when she died."

He pointed out several large yachts and told me the names of their celebrity owners. We passed within a few feet of the *Queen Anne's Revenge*, with its skeleton masthead.

When we were through the channel, he turned the engine off. He raised the sails, and we headed up the Waianae coast, with Nanakuli on our right.

In no time, I started to feel queasy. I pulled a bottle of ginger beer from my backpack, twisted the cap off, and took a sip. It was lukewarm. I shifted so the wind hit my face, trained my eyes on the hills in the distance, and tried not to think about the rocking of the boat.

"Feeling okay?" Freddy asked.

"I think so."

"Want to steer for a while?"

Anything to take my mind off my stomach. "Sure."

"Come right here. Set your drink in the holder, stand in front of me, and take the wheel."

I gripped the big, stainless steel wheel.

He reached around me and put a hand beside each of mine. "See that hill over there? Just head straight for it."

It wasn't difficult. With my mind on steering, I didn't notice my stomach as much. After a few minutes Freddy took his hands off the wheel. "You're doing great. Take it just a bit to the right … that's it. Keep an eye out for whales. This is where I saw one just a couple days ago."

I kept the boat on a steady course, heading north toward Makaha.

"Now, what was it you wanted to talk to me about?" he asked.

"You already know about my accident last Friday."

"What happened?"

"She ran into the road, right front of me. I swerved, but she doubled back, into the path of my truck."

"That must have been horrible for you."

"It was. For her too, I'm sure. Except, she has no memory of the accident."

"Wasn't she in a coma?"

"She was unconscious for two days. When she woke up, she said she didn't know who she was."

"So she's still unidentified?"

"Officially. I visited her several times. Finally, she confided to me that she was faking the amnesia."

"Faking? Why?"

"That's what I wanted to talk to you about. The story she told me is almost too bizarre to believe. She made me promise not to tell anyone."

"So, why are you telling me?"

"I think she's in danger."

I repeated Enid's story about Raymond, his brothers and sisters, Enid's first failed attempt at escape, and the second attempt that landed her in the hospital. "She's a sweet girl who got caught up in a situation beyond her control," I finished.

"You believe she was telling the truth."

"While she was still unconscious, one of the doctors talked to me. Besides some minor injuries from the accident, she has broken ribs and a broken eardrum. The doctor said those injuries happened before the accident."

"Strange that a doctor would give you any medical information."

"He was just the ward doctor that morning, and wasn't clear about the situation or my relationship to the girl."

"The hospital should have reported her injuries to the police."

"They did. But Enid refused to speak to the police or a social worker."

"But she's in a safe place for now?"

"No. When I went back to visit her yesterday, Raymond was there with one brother and one sister. Enid was fully dressed and ready to check out. She left the hospital with them a few minutes after I got there."

"Was she upset? Scared?"

"She looked resigned."

"If she didn't want to go home with them, that would have been the time to speak up."

"I think she's so terrified of Raymond, she didn't dare. I followed them to the parking lot and watched them get into a pickup truck. I followed the truck to Kāne'ohe, but lost it."

"It sounds like you gave it a good try."

I nodded. "I can't get Enid out of my mind. The first time she tried to run away, Raymond beat her and starved her. I can't stop thinking about what he's doing to her now."

"What do you want to do?"

"I'd like to find her and get her out of that situation, once and for all. Maybe help her get back to the mainland, to her parents or some other relative."

"I make my living as an investigative reporter and, I have to say, I'm pretty good at it. Let's look at the information you do have, and see where we can go from here."

"I have almost nothing to go on."

"Not true. You have first names. Enid isn't a common name. You know she's from California. She's how old? Around twenty?"

"Old enough to be in college."

"And you have the family from Guam. One brother named Raymond, another named Joseph. Two sisters, Lourdes and Tatum. Raymond drives a big, black pickup truck. The family owns a restaurant, probably in the Windward area. They live on a small pig farm. Enid couldn't have gone too far on foot before you hit her. The farm must be in that area."

"There are miles of farms along that stretch of road. Most of them have pigs."

"It's a place to start. Then there's Raymond's wife. Normally, a mother on trial for killing her two-year-old would be big news. I don't recall hearing anything about it."

"Neither do I. Could the military have hushed it up?"

"If it happened on base, definitely. This is all pretty intriguing. Let me see what I can come up with. It might turn into a good story."

Now the boat was parallel to Makaha Beach. As the sun neared the horizon, the wind picked up and shook the sails. I shivered.

"Cold?" Freddy asked.

"A little."

"Did you bring a jacket?"

"In my backpack."

"Go ahead and sit down. I'll take the wheel. We'll be turning toward the land, into the wind, and heading back to Ko Olina."

I took my ginger beer from the holder and sat on the bench.

"There's a bit of a south swell," Freddy said.

"What does that mean?"

"It means the ride back might be rougher."

When the boat had circled around, the sunset was to my back. I faced forward with my legs crossed on the bench, and looked toward the horizon. The boat seemed smaller now as it pitched through the swells. Only one other sailboat was visible, near the horizon. It listed so severely that waves washed over its side.

I took a sip of my ginger beer. Please God, don't let me puke on Freddy's immaculately clean boat.

"Look over there!" Freddy pointed. "Dolphins!"

A pod of dolphins swam just below the surface, maybe a half mile away. Their dorsal fins showed black above the water, silhouetted by the setting sun. "Do you see them?"

"They're beautiful." I watched the dolphins until they were gone.

My stomach roiled. My head felt heavy, but I resisted the urge to lie down. I didn't want Freddy to worry. I finished my ginger beer, stuck the empty bottle in my backpack, and rested my head in my hands.

"Are you okay?" he asked.

At this point I was calculating the angle I'd need to puke over the side to avoid messing the boat. "I'm feeling a little queasy."

"Are you going to throw up?"

I nodded. I was mortified, but too sick to hold onto my dignity.

Freddy let go of the wheel, made his way to the stern, and opened a little gate. "This is my sick seat. You can sit here and be as sick as you want."

I gripped the sides of the pitching boat, eased through the two-foot opening, and sat on a small platform inches above the water.

"There's a hose here, if you need it." Freddy said.

I bent over and heaved into the water as Freddy said, unnecessarily, "Just hold on tight so you don't fall in!"

I kept my feet on the seat, lest any sharks should happen by and want a bite of me. I puked my guts out, holding on for dear life with one hand, running cold water from the hose over my face and head with the other.

At least Freddy's back was to me, giving me some small amount of privacy.

"How are you doing back there?" he called out.

"Okay." I tried to sound more chipper than I felt.

"We'll be back in a few minutes. Hang in there."

Did I have a choice?

Freddy brought the sails down and started the engine. We motored into the marina, past boats decorated with colorful strings of lights, Santas, and reindeer. Freddy's boat was one of the few without gaudy decorations.

He eased into the slip and jumped to the dock with the mooring line.

"Would you like to go to the restroom and freshen up?" he suggested.

I stood. My legs wobbled.

He held my elbow to steady me. "Easy. It'll take a minute to get your land legs back."

I smelled absolutely revolting and was beyond caring how I looked. I made my way down the concrete dock to the restroom, washed my face and hair with liquid hand soap, and wiped at the vomit on my shirt with paper towels.

When I got back to the boat the nausea had passed, but I still reeked.

"Do you need help up?" Freddy asked.

"I've got it." I climbed onto the boat and sat on the cushioned bench.

Freddy had unfolded a small table and set out a bowl of strawberries, slices of cheese, crackers, and dip. He held a bottle of Heineken.

"Beer?"

"I'd better stick with ginger beer." I pulled another out of my backpack.

"I'll get you some ice."

He climbed down a ladder, into the cabin below. A minute later he came back with a plastic cup of ice and a small electric menorah.

Freddy wasn't bothered by long silences, a skill that had to serve him well in his work as a reporter. Sailboats bobbed around us. The evening turned deep shades of apricot. Pink and purple cirrus clouds feathered the sky, mirrored by the still water. Three years ago, Freddy and I had shared another sunset. Was he remembering it, too?

I bit into a strawberry and chewed, testing my stomach. "I might have to go to the mainland for a few days."

"What for?"

"My father's in a coma. They don't think he'll come out of it. My stepmother and brother want to withhold treatment. They're asking me to come and say good bye to him first."

"I am so sorry."

I looked at the sky. "He hasn't been part of my life since I was seventeen. It isn't like I'm going to miss him."

"You sound as if you don't want to go."

"I see no reason to. My brother thinks my father hears what people say, and will know I'm there."

"And you don't think so."

"I'm not sure I care."

We were silent for a while.

"Why hasn't your father been part of your life?" Freddy asked.

"My mother died when I was fifteen."

"I'm sorry. How did she die?"

"I know now that she died of colon cancer. At the time, no one told me anything." I sipped my drink, and turned to look at Freddy. "When it became obvious my mother was ill, my father gave us strict instructions not to speak of her illness. We went about our lives pretending nothing was wrong. I picked fights with her, just to reassure myself everything was normal. I mean, when someone is dying, you don't fight with them, right? Maybe my mom had the same idea. We argued over clothes, hair, lipstick, boys, you name it. It was my childish way of denying anything was wrong.

"One day, I walked into her bedroom with my head shaved. It shocked her so bad, she didn't notice my newly pierced ears."

After another silence, Freddy looked up. "I can see four stars in the sky." He plugged in the menorah and turned the bulbs until seven were lit. "How's that?"

"It's ... simple and lovely."

"An electric menorah isn't kosher, but I don't want candles on the boat."

I'd never celebrated Hanukkah. It was the last thing I expected when I came to see Freddy this afternoon. The menorah's bulbs illuminated his face. He was smiling at me.

"What?"

"I'm still trying to imagine you bald." He rubbed his head.

I said, "It isn't such a bad look," unsure if I really meant it. I've never found bald men attractive, and didn't know if I could make an exception now.

We laughed a bit. Freddy finished his beer and took another from a cooler under the table.

I sipped my ginger beer. "That summer, when my mom was sick, my dad sent my brother and me to camp. She died while we were away. Some distant relatives came to pick us up, and brought us home for the funeral. I don't remember the funeral, but my brother tells me I was there."

"What happened between you and your father?"

"He wasn't the same after my mom died. He locked himself in his room for days—weeks—at a time. He wouldn't speak to anyone. This was the time I needed him most, and he wasn't there for me. Months passed. He started spending more time out of his room. He wouldn't let me forget how I fought with my mother while she was dying. Finally, he accused me of actually causing her death."

"You know you didn't make her die."

"Back then, part of me believed I did. After a while, his accusations turned to blows."

"He hit you?"

I nodded. It wasn't something I talked about. Not to anyone. "My father was enraged with me because I was still alive, and she was dead."

I took another strawberry and bit into it. A CD somewhere played Jimmy Buffet's *A Sailor's Christmas*.

"Did you know he was born on Christmas?" Freddy asked.

"Who?"

"Jimmy Buffet."

"No, I didn't."

"Did you look like her?" His question surprised me. I didn't answer right away. "I mean, before you shaved your head, of course."

I couldn't help smiling. "I looked very much like her."

"That must have made it harder on your father, seeing her every time he looked at you."

"I suppose so. She was a true Irish beauty. I was lucky to get her hair and her build. Unfortunately, I got my father's nose."

"What's wrong with your nose?"

"It's …" I shrugged. I didn't want him to think I was fishing for compliments.

He surprised me by reaching out and touching my chin. "Let me see your profile."

I complied.

"Nothing wrong with your nose. It's strong and … distinctive."

I laughed. "I guess I'm pretty well used to it by now."

"So, what happened when you were seventeen? Did you leave home?"

I nodded. "Before I even finished high school.

"Where did you go?"

"I ran away with a neighbor boy named Josh."

"Your boyfriend?"

"Not at all. He just conveniently wanted to run away at the same time. We went to Greenwich Village and lived in an apartment with about twenty other people. I changed my name to Willow.

Freddy chuckled. "Sorry. I can't picture you as a bald girl named Willow."

"Add thick glasses to the image."

"You wore glasses?"

"High voltage. A lot of the time I just took them off. It was my way of not having to deal with the world."

"And now?"

"I had laser surgery a few years ago."

"I'm sure it's an improvement."

"The downside is I can't retreat into the haze any more. I have to meet whatever comes, face to face. And things have a way of landing in front of me."

Laurie Hanan

Chapter 11

An oversize pair of neon-pink slippers lay on my front porch. There were voices in my living room. Did Brian have company?

I let myself in through the unlocked screen door. Marta was sitting beside Brian on the couch, her feet up on the chaise. She wore black slacks and a loose-fitting leopard print blouse. Today she was a blond, her hair freshly cut and styled. Her neon pink nail polish matched the slippers outside the door.

The Comedy Channel played on the TV.

"Hey, Louise," Marta said.

"I see you've met Brian."

When I spoke, Sage jumped from Marta's lap and ran to me. I picked her up. Marta's old black lab, Ele'ele, stirred in front of the couch. She opened one eye, then closed it again.

"I read about your accident in the paper," Marta said. "I left a message, but you didn't call back. I came over to see how you're doing, and Brian let me in."

"I tried to call you an hour ago," Brian said.

I dug my phone out of my backpack. There was a missed call.

"I was driving. I guess I didn't hear the phone."

He looked wounded, but I didn't think I needed to answer to him for where I went, or what time I came home.

Marta wrinkled her nose. "What's that smell?"

"It might be me." I sniffed my shirt. "Sorry. I threw up on myself."

"Are you sick?" Brian asked.

"I'm feeling better. I'll just take a quick shower and put on some clean clothes. Be right out."

I dropped my backpack on the bedroom floor, pulled plaid pajama bottoms, a sweatshirt, and clean underwear out of my dresser, and headed for the bathroom.

After my shower, I stood in the hallway, out of sight. Brian and Marta were speaking softly, their words too low for me to make out.

I stepped into the living room.

"Do you feel like eating?" Brian asked.

"After I threw up, I had some strawberries and ginger beer. I think I'll hold off eating anything more tonight. Go ahead and eat if you want."

"I made dinner earlier. When you didn't come home, Marta and I ate."

"He's a good cook," Marta said, her eyes on Brian.

Brian was definitely her type, which is to say male. But his taste runs toward smaller, younger women.

"Your brother called," Brian said. "He asked me to have you call him back."

Mike must be trying to put more pressure on me to visit my dad. "It's one in the morning in New York."

"It sounded urgent. I think you should call now."

"Let me make a cup of tea. Then I'll call him."

"I'll make the tea," Brian said. "You make the phone call."

"Mint tea, please."

I dug my address book out of the desk and found Mike's number. My hands shook as I punched the number into the phone. Why was I so nervous? Hopefully Mike and Victoria were asleep and their voicemail would pick up.

It rang once, twice.

A woman's voice said, "Hello?"

"Oh ... Victoria?"

"Louise. I'm glad you called."

I didn't reply.

"Louise." She hesitated. "I'm very sorry. Dad died tonight, just after midnight."

I didn't speak.

Half a minute went by before Victoria said, "The funeral is Friday afternoon. Please, come."

"Friday? Why so soon?"

"It's Jewish custom to bury the body within a day after death."

Growing up, I knew my father was Jewish only because I overheard the neighbors say it. In my mind, Jewish was an ethnicity, the same way my mother was Irish and some people were Italian or Polish. I never thought of him as different from anyone else. Hearing Victoria speak of Jewish burial customs threw me off.

She continued, "We wanted to give you time to get here, but of course the funeral can't take place on the Sabbath."

Of course not. My head reeled. They were waiting for me to get there? "I … I don't know if I can …"

"Sunday would be too late, so we decided to have the funeral Friday."

When I didn't reply, she repeated, "Please, come."

"I'll see what I can do." I pressed the phone's OFF button.

Brian set a mug of tea on the desk. "Your father?"

I nodded. "He died. An hour ago."

"I'm sorry." Brian touched my shoulder, then pulled his hand back.

I took my tea to the living room, sat on the Persian rug beside Ele'ele, and rubbed her head as she snored. Sage climbed into my lap.

Brian took his spot beside Marta again.

"Are you okay?" Marta asked.

"You heard?"

Marta nodded. "I'm sorry. Where …?"

"New York."

"Is that where you're from? New York?"

"Manhattan. But I haven't been to New York since I was seventeen. They put off the funeral until Friday, to give me time to get there."

"Are you going?" Brian asked.

"I don't know."

"I think you should go," Marta said. "It's your obligation as a daughter to bury your father."

"My brother is taking care of everything. It wouldn't matter if I'm there or not."

"It does matter," Marta said.

For a few minutes, no one spoke. Marta dug around in her large purse and pulled out a business card.

"Here. This is my travel agent. She should be able to get you a good deal on a ticket."

I took the card, but didn't look at it. "Thank you."

That night, I couldn't sleep. I stared at the slatted shadows on the ceiling and tried not to move. Brian lay on his side with his back to me, snoring softly.

I got out of bed, walked through the house in the semidarkness, and lay on the couch. Sage jumped off the bed and followed.

The sun showed gold through my closed eyelids. I smelled coffee, rubbed my eyes, and opened them. "Brian?"

"In here," he called from in the kitchen. He came into the living room with two mugs of coffee, handed me one, and sat beside me. "Why did you sleep out here?"

Brian didn't spend the night often. When he did, we always slept together.

"I couldn't fall asleep. I didn't want to disturb you."

"You okay?"

I rested the mug on my knee and rubbed one hand over my eyes. "No."

Brian waited for me to continue. When I didn't, he asked, "Have you decided to go?"

"The funeral is tomorrow. I'd have to leave today. I'll call Marta's travel agent and see if I can get a flight."

"It's going to be hard for you, isn't it—going home?"

"*This* is home. Everything I need is here. I see no reason to leave."

"A trip to New York, seeing your brother, might give you some … closure."

"I don't need closure. I need to be left alone, to live my life in peace. The thought of going back to New York is … the scariest thing I can think of."

"It'll be like pulling a rotten tooth. Painful, but once it's out, the agony will be a thing of the past. You'll be able to move on."

Chapter 12

I took my coffee to the desk and turned the computer on. It was a little after eight.

I called Marta's travel agent. Mike and Victoria live twenty minutes from Stewart Airport, in Newburgh. The agent said the next flight would leave Honolulu at two P.M. today, and arrive at noon Friday. There'd be enough time for Mike and Victoria to pick me up and still make it to the funeral.

I asked for a return flight Monday. The weekend would be more than enough time with Mike's family. I gave the agent my credit card number before I could talk myself out of it.

There was a lot to do before I checked in at noon. I didn't have any warm clothes. Didn't even own a suitcase. I'd have to make a quick shopping trip. There were phone calls to make, people who needed to be told I was leaving.

"What time are you going to work?" I asked Brian.

"Dave doesn't usually get in until noon. I thought I'd wait and take you to the airport, then head to work from there."

That meant no privacy for making phone calls. I waited until Brian went into the kitchen, then dialed Freddy's number. His voice mail picked up. Maybe he was still asleep.

"This is Louise. My father died last night. I'm flying to New York this afternoon, and coming back Monday. I was wondering if the e-mail address on your card is still good. It might be the easiest way to communicate while I'm gone."

Next, I typed an e-mail to Ilan Katz. I met the Israeli stuntman three years ago when he was working on the set of a movie being filmed on the North Shore. Besides being drop-dead gorgeous, Ilan is the nicest guy you could ever know. But our age difference—he was twenty-nine when we met, I was thirty-seven—put any thought of a relationship right out of my mind. Not to mention the fact that he was living with his long-time girlfriend, Echo.

When they were done filming here, Ilan headed back to L.A. with the rest of the film crew. He recently moved to New York to work on a new TV show being filmed there. Echo chose to stay in Los Angeles.

Over time, my e-mail exchanges with Ilan grew more flirtatious. With the safety of thousands of miles between us, it seemed a harmless game. Tomorrow, I'd be within sixty miles of him. Maybe there'd be a chance to see him.

> From: GoldenGirl
> To: MrKatz
> Subject: Coming to New York
> Date: December 17 08:28
> Shalom, Ilan. My father passed away last night in New York. I'm flying out this afternoon, the funeral is tomorrow. I'll be staying at my brother's house in Highland Mills. I doubt I'll get to the city, but maybe I can call you while I'm there.

Freddy returned my call. "So you've decided to go."

"I bought a ticket this morning. I can't back out."

"I know it won't be easy, but it's good you're going. Send me an e-mail now, to the address on my card. That way I'll have your address, in case I need it. Today I'll start work on locating Enid. I'll keep you updated."

"I appreciate your help. Thanks for yesterday. I had a good time."

I glanced toward the kitchen. Brian was standing in the doorway.

"I enjoyed it too," Freddy was saying.

"Bye." I closed the phone.

"Who was that?" Brian asked.

"An investigative reporter. He interviewed me three years ago about Mrs. Santos's death. I contacted him yesterday, thinking he might have an idea how to find Enid."

Brian didn't reply.

"The girl I hit?"

Brian nodded, then went back into the kitchen.

I e-mailed Freddy, then changed my Yahoo password, deleted my history, and disabled my cookies. Brian would be using my computer while I was away and I didn't want him snooping.

I called my boss, Darren. "My father died last night."

"I'm really sorry."

"Thank you. I'm leaving for New York today for the funeral."

"When will you be back?"

"Monday."

"Okay. Plan to be back at work Tuesday."

"They've finished the accident investigation?"

"Yes. You've been cleared of any fault."

Thank God.

I searched my closet and dresser and took out several pairs of jeans and a couple of sweatshirts. The rest of my wardrobe consisted of party dresses, shorts, tee-shirts, tank tops, and a few flimsy skirts for folk dancing. The only enclosed shoes I had were a pair of Reeboks.

There was a knock at my front door. Sage barked.

"Hi Sage" It was Emmeline. "Louise? Are you home?"

I opened the door.

"I saw your car," she said. "Is it your day off?"

"I'm taking a few days off."

"What for?"

"Remember I told you about my father?"

Emmeline's amber eyes stared into mine. She was as tall as me now. "Are you going to visit him?"

"He died. Last night."

"Oh. I'm so sorry."

"The funeral is tomorrow. I'm leaving today."

"Why is the funeral so soon?"

"My father was Jewish. According to Jewish law, he has to be buried as soon as possible. The Jewish Sabbath starts at sundown Friday. If we don't bury him by then, we'd have to wait until Sunday."

"Just like Jesus."

"Jesus?"

"The Easter story. Jesus died on a Friday. They couldn't bury him on the Sabbath. That's why they were in such a hurry to bury him before the sun set Friday."

A chill passed over me. I rubbed my arms.

I had to move fast if I was going to make it to the airport on time.

"I need to make a quick shopping trip to pick up a suitcase and some warm clothes."

"Can I go with you?"

Normally, I prefer to shop alone. Today, Emmeline's company might be just what I needed. "Go ask your mom. Hurry!"

We breezed down the freeway with the top down. Ironically, the last time Emmeline rode in my car, three years ago, we were on our way to a funeral.

I put in my *Abbey Road* CD. Emmeline held her phone in both hands and texted, while singing along with me and the Beatles. *Here comes the sun, here comes the sun, and I say it's all right…*

Children's minds today must develop so differently from my generation.

The song ended. She laid the phone on her lap and asked, "Why didn't you get along with your father?"

I turned down the volume as the next song came on. "I told you my mother died when I was fifteen, right?"

"I can't imagine losing my mom."

"It was a hard time for my father, too. He couldn't handle living without her. He took his grief out on me."

"Did he hit you?"

Should I tell her? Maybe she's old enough to hear it. "Yes, he did."

"What did you do?"

"When I was seventeen, I ran away from home."

"You *did?*"

"I did."

"Where did you go?"

"This crazy place in New York called Greenwich Village. I changed my name to Willow."

Emmeline laughed. "Really?"

"Yes, really."

"How long did you stay there?"

"Not long. After that, I went to a place called Woodstock."

"I know about Woodstock. My dad told me about the big concert there."

"The big concert was before my time."

"Was it a very cool place?"

"It was still a pretty weird place in the eighties."

I described life in Woodstock, but left out the part about the nudist who ran the boardinghouse where I rented a room. She cooked and cleaned stark naked, wearing only a sling to hold her baby. Maybe when Emmeline was older I'd tell her about that, too.

"How long will you be in New York?"

"Just over the weekend. I'll be back Monday."

"Do you want me to take care of Sage and Moondance and Bob?"

"My friend Brian will be staying in my house. But thanks."

"Can I still look in on them? And take Sage for walks?"

"Of course. I'll let Brian know you'll be coming around."

I got off the freeway at Kinau and made a right onto Ward. Two blocks down, I pulled into the Ross parking lot.

The suitcases were stacked three and four deep along the left wall. They'd certainly been improved upon since the last time I travelled. Most stood upright on wheels that swiveled in every direction.

Emmeline pulled a zebra-striped suitcase out of the pile. "Look at this one! I can't believe how cute it is!"

"I'm not sure it's my style."

"How about this one?" She picked up a green and purple paisley suitcase.

"Uh…"

"What *is* your style?"

"I'm not sure. Something that won't make people look at me."

"Why be like everyone else? I wish I was going to New York with you. In May I'm going to Washington DC for my class trip. I won the essay contest and got a scholarship for the trip. I'm gonna ask my mom to buy me this suitcase."

I lifted a red Eddie Bauer softside into my cart. "I need shoes."

"What size are you?"

"Seven."

"My feet are bigger than yours. I'm an eight. Let's try some on. I brought my babysitting money."

We spent fifteen minutes trying on shoes. Emmeline chose a pair of black suede slouch boots with straps and buckles. I settled on a pair of simple black leather boots. They'd match my Coach backpack, and I could wear them with jeans or a skirt.

I looked through the racks of clothes while Emmeline headed in another direction. I picked out a somber black wool skirt and blazer, and a full-length gray herringbone coat. Next, I looked at sweaters. I chose a turtleneck in black, and one in gray. Then, I couldn't resist a bright blue V-neck sweater that would bring out the color of my eyes.

"There you are!" Emmeline said. "Look what I found!"

She held up two pairs of skinny jeans.

"Cute," I said.

"And look at these! I love them!"

"Does your mom let you wear shorts that short?" I sure didn't want to get in trouble with her mom.

"Everyone wears them. I tried them on and they aren't as short as they look. And see this?" She held up a brief Roxy bikini. "Don't worry, I'll wear board shorts over it."

I noticed several bras in her cart. "Maybe I should get some new underwear too, as long as I'm here."

"Over here." She led me to the underwear rack. "What size bra are you?"

"32B."

"I'm a 32C. It's a hard size to find."

When did she grow up?

I selected some comfortable looking bras and panties, and we moved toward the checkout line.

Emmeline picked up a gray beret. "I think you should have a hat. So your head doesn't get cold." She put it on my head.

I looked in the mirror. "I don't care for this look."

She handed me a black fedora. "Try this."

I set it on my head. It did have a certain panache. "I never wear anything this…attention-getting."

"Well, I think you should. No one in New York knows what your style is. This is your chance to reinvent yourself."

I tried the coat on with the hat, and stood in front of the mirror.

Emmeline put a black scarf around my neck. "How's that?"

It looked and felt like cashmere. I checked the price tag. Definitely not cashmere, but who'd know?

"I like it. I need gloves, too." I picked up a pair of black gloves and looked at the tag. "Oh, look. They're vegetarian."

"Cool! You have to get them!"

My shopping trip set me back a week's pay, but there was no getting around the need for warm clothes.

I stuffed clothes and shoes haphazardly into my suitcase. That done, I hooked the leash to Sage's collar and headed to Gene's house. He deserved more than a phone call before I left.

Gene sat in his favorite chair, with Pipsqueak on his lap. Pipsqueak once belonged to Mrs. Santos, the elderly woman on my route who was murdered. I brought Pipsqueak to Gene's house for a music session, and they've been inseparable ever since.

I told him about Enid, and how Freddy offered to help find her.

"You've certainly been busy," he said.

"I'm leaving for New York today."

"You're *what?*"

"My father passed away last night."

Dan's car was in the driveway. I climbed his steps and peered through the screen.

"Dan?"

"I'm in the kitchen. Come on in."

I went in and closed the screen door behind me.

He came out of the kitchen with a Heineken. "Beer?"

"No, thanks. I can only stay for a minute. I didn't expect you to be home today."

Dan went to the living room and sat on the sofa. "I took off early to get a few things done. What's up?"

I sat across from him in a matching chair. "I'm going to the mainland for the weekend. New York."

"This weekend? What for?"

"I'm leaving today. I have to be at the airport in an hour. My father died last night and the funeral is tomorrow."

"I am so sorry. Don't worry about your house and your pets. We'll take care of everything."

Dan disliked Brian. I'd hoped Brian would be gone before Dan realized he was staying with me. "Actually…I asked Brian to stay in my house while I'm away."

Dan took a swig of his beer.

"I hope that's okay," I said.

"I've told you, that guy's no good for you."

Dan may be right. Brian wasn't the best relationship material. But Dan's dislike for Brian had nothing to do with protecting me.

"I know you feel that way. But I can handle my relationships."

"I'm not so sure," Dan said under his breath. "How long will you be gone?"

"I'll be back Monday."

"If Brian knows what's good for him, he'll stay out of my way until then."

Chapter 13

Brian pulled his van up to the walkway outside the departure area. We got out and he set my bright red suitcase on the sidewalk.

"Got everything?" he asked.

"Laptop, cell phone, wallet, itinerary, hairbrush, Chapstick ... I think I'm good."

Brian wrapped me in a big hug. I pressed my face into his chest and clung to him for an extra moment. He was the last familiar thing I'd touch before heading into the unknown.

He kissed the top of my head. "Okay?"

"I don't know if I'm ready for this," I said into his clean tee-shirt.

"You'll do fine. I know you will."

I pulled back and looked into his brown eyes. "I don't know what I'm walking into."

"Just stay detached from any family drama. Don't forget your brother was close to your dad. He has to be feeling a huge loss right now, even if you aren't."

I nodded. "Take care of Sage and Moondance."

"I will."

"And don't forget to feed Bob. He's kind of quiet, so it's easy to forget ..."

"Don't worry. They'll be fine. I promise."

"I better go."

Brian put his hands behind my neck. He kissed me on the lips once, then again. "Take care. Call me."

Halfway to the terminal, I looked back. Brian stood beside his van, watching me. Our eyes met. He gave me a nod, got into the van, and drove away.

I turned and walked away from everything I love.

A security guard instructed me to put my suitcase on a belt that would carry it through the agricultural inspection machine. It weighed forty pounds, at most, and I lifted it easily. At the other end of the machine, another guard stuck a strip of bright pink tape through the handle.

I wheeled the suitcase to the long check-in line. In front of me, two guys laughed and talked too loud in thick cockney accents. I didn't mind. It took my thoughts off of the reason I was there. A Filipino family got in line behind me, with a grandma in a wheelchair and five kids ranging in age from one to about ten. The kids whined and shoved each other.

Dear God, please don't let me sit near any kids!

I realized I was staring at the other passengers. They stared back. This flight was headed to San Francisco, where the weather was sure to be cold. But most of the passengers chose to dress in shorts and slippers. Their brightly colored aloha shirts clashed with painful looking sunburns that would start to peel in a day or two. I understood why they wanted to stay in island mode as long as possible. Once they got off the plane there would be no avoiding a hard reality that did not include warm sunshine and the scent of plumeria blossoms.

I stood out like a sore thumb in my black boots, jeans, and blue cable knit sweater. My fedora sat on my head, and my wool coat was draped over one arm. I did my best to ignore the stares as I inched my way to the front of the line.

The ticket agent was a pretty, dark-skinned woman, with heavy makeup and flowers in her hair. Her movements were quick and efficient. "Here. Just fill out this luggage tag."

I did so. She attached it to the suitcase and handed me my boarding passes. "Your bag is checked all the way to Stewart Airport. Have a great trip!"

The security line moved even slower than the check-in line. Passengers were removing their shoes and I immediately regretted wearing my boots, however stylish they may have been.

The British guys were ahead of me again.

"Take off your jacket!" a burly female TSA agent ordered the shorter one.

"My jacket?"

"Off!"

"Ja vol, mein commandant!" He saluted.

He took his jacket off, laid it in a bin, and held his arms out. "Would you like to check me trousers for hidden weapons?"

The agent's face grew red. A blood vessel stood out on her forehead. She breathed heavily, but didn't reply.

The guy shrugged and said, "And a bloody sad day it will be when a terrorist comes through here with a machete down his Y-fronts!"

His traveling companion burst out laughing, and several people snickered.

The female commandant shouted, "Next!"

She was looking at me. I lifted my carry-ons to the conveyor belt.

"Open the laptop and put it in a separate bin! Jacket and purse together, shoes in another!"

I rushed to do as she said. I leaned against the counter, struggled with my boots, then finally sat on the floor to pull them off. Next time, I'd wear the Reeboks.

I made it through without setting off the metal detector, thus avoiding a pat down.

The walk to the gate must have been two miles. Before I was halfway there, sweat beaded my forehead and trickled down my sides under my sweater. The strap of the laptop case cut into my shoulder, and my new boots rubbed blisters on my heels and toes.

Almost every chair in the waiting area was occupied. Aloha Airlines had recently gone bankrupt. Other airlines had cut flights to and from Hawai'i to ensure every flight was filled to capacity. I sat on a carpeted ledge in front of the window, where several small children played. The air conditioning was too cold, considering how most people were dressed. I put my coat on, pulled it tight, stretched my legs in front of me, and stared out the window.

Elderly and handicapped passengers and people with infants boarded first. The Filipino family I'd seen earlier gathered their children and wheeled their grandma down the Jetway. First class passengers boarded next. Finally, the rest of us were called up by row, and I was herded onto the plane with hundreds of other people.

I located my aisle seat in row thirty-three. An elderly man had the window seat, and a woman sat in the middle.

"My name's Polly," the woman said. She was sixty-something and wore a light blue pantsuit.

"Louise."

"This is my husband, Bob."

Bob turned from the window and I gave him a wave. He was a good ten years older than Polly and bore an uncanny resemblance to Bob the Goldfish.

"Where are you headed?" Polly asked.

"New York."

"Is that home?"

"Hawai'i is home. I'm visiting my brother."

"For Christmas?"

I nodded.

"We live in Nevada. I was attending a real estate convention in Waikīkī."

I supposed that's what real estate agents do when there isn't enough work to keep them busy.

Polly continued, "Bob is retired, and likes to come to my conventions with me. We had an ocean view room at the Hilton Hawaiian Village. He spent most of his time in the room. He enjoyed sitting on the lanai and looking at the view." She looked at Bob. "Didn't you, Honey?"

Bob nodded and gave me a brief smile before turning his gaze back to the window. The plane taxied to the runway. After a ten minute wait for clearance, we took off into the night sky. Within minutes, Bob was snoring shamelessly. Polly pulled a novel from her carry-on. I closed my eyes, leaned my seat back, and wished I'd remembered to pack a book.

Almost six hours later, we landed in San Francisco.

In a sundries store I picked up Listerine strips, deodorant, and gum. Next, I found a book store and browsed through the bestseller section. No discounted books here, they were all sold at the full cover price. Maybe someday I'd get a Kindle. But I do enjoy holding a book in my hands, turning the pages, then setting it on a shelf when I'm done reading it. I pulled out my credit card and left the store twenty-eight dollars poorer, with a six-hundred page thriller that promised to be distracting.

I got a latte at Starbucks, took out my laptop, and checked my e-mail. Nothing from Freddy. I turned my cell phone on and listened to the voicemail. There was a message from Ilan.

"Louise, I'm so sorry about your father. I'm forty-five minutes away from Highland Mills. Let me know where the funeral is, and I'll be there."

It was almost three in the morning in New York. I dialed Ilan's cell, hoping he turned it off while he slept. His voicemail picked up.

"This is Louise. The funeral is at three o'clock, at the Cemetery of the Highlands. It's in Highland Mills, on Brigadoon Drive. I'd love to see you."

In no time, I was on another plane, smaller than the last. I had two seats to myself for the five-hour flight to Philadelphia. I pulled my boots off, tucked my legs under me, draped my coat across my lap, and stared out the window. I took my book out, read a few pages, and drifted to sleep.

When we landed in Philadelphia, I was hungry. There was no time to grab lunch before boarding the flight to Newburgh. This time, there were only about twenty passengers on the small jet. I accepted a cup of coffee and a bag of pretzels from the flight attendant. I tried to read, but couldn't concentrate. Instead, I leaned my forehead against the window and watched the frozen landscape creep by below.

Stewart Airport has only one baggage carousel. As I waited for my suitcase, I realized I was the only person in Baggage Claim. Apparently, I was the only one on the flight who had checked in luggage. After ten minutes, my lone red suitcase rose up the chute and slid onto the carousel. I watched it make a full round, then picked it up and set it on the floor.

What now?

I followed the signs and headed toward the exit. My footsteps echoed in the empty terminal. There wasn't another person in sight. I passed the rental car counters, decorated with Christmas lights and tinsel garlands, but seemingly abandoned.

The automatic door hissed open. I stepped into dim sunlight and biting cold, pulling my bag behind me, and faced a half-empty parking lot. A car door opened and closed somewhere. A short, slight man stepped out from between the cars. His gray hair was thinning, his three-piece suit tailor made, his shoes expensive.

I recognized him, but only from photos Victoria had e-mailed me.

Laurie Hanan

Chapter 14

"Louise?"

I held out my hand and he shook it. "Hi, Mike."

He took my bag and I followed him to a blue Audi A4. He popped the trunk and put my suitcase in. I opened the passenger door, moved his coat aside, and slid into the front seat.

"I'll take you to the house first. You can freshen up and eat something before we head to the cemetery."

Mike did his best to make conversation, something he was clearly not good at. I wasn't much help. My brother and I were together for the first time since we were kids, and I couldn't think of a thing to say.

The two-lane highway was wet from recent rain. Large pine trees and old houses lined both sides of the road. Many of the houses had been converted into businesses: a real estate office, a photographer, a bakery, a funeral home. All were decorated with Christmas lights and wreaths on the doors.

Mike turned left onto a narrow road. It wound up a hill and two minutes later a subdivision of mini mansions came into view. The nearly identical homes sat on park-like lots. Now all the trees were bare, but it was easy to imagine the scene would be breathtaking in the spring and fall.

We took the third right, then a left, and entered a cul-de-sac where five large homes sat in a semi-circle. They were all painted the same shade of eggshell, with only slight differences in each model. I bet the residents had trouble finding their own house at night—especially after a few drinks.

Mike pulled into the driveway of the middle house. A nativity scene sat on the bare, frozen lawn. He pressed a remote. The garage door opened, and we parked beside a red Mercedes C63. He dragged my suitcase up a set of concrete steps. I followed him into an impressive kitchen that smelled of pot roast.

A grey miniature poodle came around the corner and trotted up to me, wagging his tail.

"Well, hello. Who are you?" I asked.

"That's Lillian's dog, Nigel," Mike said. I crouched to pet Nigel, and he licked my face.

A woman with wide hips and dark hair worked at the stove. She didn't turn around when I came in. Two more women and a teenage girl sat at a small table in a breakfast nook. I recognized Victoria and Brittney. The other woman must be my stepmother, Lillian.

Victoria stood. "I am so happy to meet you, Louise." She put her arms around me. She was several inches shorter than me and I had to bend to hug her. "I'm sorry it was such a tragedy that finally brought us together," she said, "but I'm glad you're here. Come, sit with us. This is Brittney, and Lillian."

"Hello, Aunt Louise," Brittney said.

I saw nothing of Mike in Brittney's features. She had Victoria's straight, blond hair, blue eyes, and flawless skin. At thirteen she looked so much like her mother, they could almost be twins. Victoria's hair was cut in the same precise bob she'd always worn, but Brittney's hair had grown to just past her shoulders.

Lillian patted the chair next to her. "Sit here, Louise."

Nigel jumped to the chair. Lillian pulled him onto her lap. As soon as I was seated, she reached out and took my hand in hers. "It's good to finally meet Howard's daughter."

She must have been implying that I should have showed up sooner. Like, while he was still alive. This was the woman who had taken my mother's place, had taken over my mother's home and husband. What sort of impression did she have of me, based on what my father told her?

Lillian was four years older than my father, which put her at seventy-nine. Her straight, white hair was cut in a short, fuss-free style. She was dressed in a stylish black pantsuit and boots. She looked haggard, but under better circumstances she'd be pretty.

"I'm sure Louise is hungry," Mike said.

"What can I get for you?" Victoria asked. "We're drinking coffee."

"Coffee would be great."

"Milk and Sugar?"

"Black. Thanks."

Victoria set a mug in front of me and refilled Lillian's. Brittney had a half-full glass of something that looked like Coke.

"Gabrielle is making pot roast and mashed potatoes for later. We'll have people over here after the funeral," Victoria said. "Can I have her make you a sandwich for now? Ham and cheese?"

"I'm a vegetarian."

"Oh … that's right. You did mention that. I'm sorry. I totally forgot. Would you like a tomato sandwich?"

I stood. "I can make it."

"No. Of course not. You sit and visit with us. Gabrielle will make it. Is mayo okay?"

"Sure."

"Cheese?"

"That's fine." I was trying to get away from eating dairy, but I'd eaten almost nothing in the past twenty-four hours. I wasn't going to be picky.

"Gabrielle, please make Louise a tomato and cheese sandwich."

Gabrielle turned. She was Hispanic, in her fifties. "*Jes*, Mrs. Golden."

"I'll take your suitcase to the guest room," Mike said.

He disappeared around a corner with my bag, and I heard him go down a flight of wooden stairs. Brittney excused herself and went upstairs. Victoria sat and we sipped our coffee, not speaking.

"I hear you work for the post office," Lillian finally said.

"I'm a mail carrier."

"Do you like it?"

"It's pretty routine, but it has its moments."

Lillian and Victoria both nodded.

I'm not good at small talk, even under the best of circumstances. I was exhausted, starving, and generally freaked out over finding myself in New York, face to face with relatives I barely knew, about to go to my father's funeral. My mind was a blank.

Lillian said, "Until a few years ago, I taught at the New York School of Interior Design."

She'd certainly one-upped me on career choices.

Gabrielle brought me a sandwich on a plate.

"Thank you."

"*Jou're* welcome, Miss."

Lillian and Victoria watched me take a big bite of the sandwich.

It was sliced tomato, American cheese, and Miracle whip on white bread. It stuck in my throat and I gulped my coffee.

Mike appeared in the entryway. "We need to leave in fifteen minutes," he said. "Louise, do you want to change?"

I was still in my jeans and blue sweater. "Yes. Thanks."

I quickly finished the sandwich and washed it down with coffee before following Mike through the living room.

"Your room is in the basement." He opened a door and flipped a switch. A light came on, revealing a steep, carpeted stairway. "Down here, first door on the right."

The stairs ended in a family room, complete with a fireplace, built-in book cases, and a wide screen TV. On the left, doors opened to a fitness room and a sewing room. I saw my suitcase just inside a doorway to my right.

"Baruch atah adonai eloheinu melech haolam, dayan ha'emet," the rabbi intoned. The Hebrew was archaic, very different from the modern language I learned during a year spent in Israel. But I understood the prayer: *Blessed are you, Lord our God, Sovereign of the Universe, the Judge of Truth.*

The rabbi handed torn strips of black cloth to the family members, and we pinned them to our coats. The strips are the modern day answer to rent clothing, the traditional Jewish sign of mourning.

Mike joined a group of bearded, black-hatted men beside the hearse, and together they lifted out the casket.

Snow clung to blades of grass around the bases of the headstones. In spite of my warm clothing, a cold wind found its way up my skirt to my bare thighs. I tucked my scarf around my neck, put my gloved hands in my coat pockets, and shivered.

More men arrived and joined the procession with the casket. They would walk a short distance, then set the casket down. Each time they stopped, the rabbi chanted. The casket was lifted again and moved closer to the grave.

Someone laid a hand on my shoulder.

I turned. "Ilan. Thank you for coming."

Three years had added maturity to his face. His brown eyes looked into mine and I was hit once again with the feelings of a teenage crush.

"I'm sorry about your father."

"Thank you."

He gave my shoulder a squeeze, then joined the men. Seven times, the procession stopped and started again. Finally, the casket was set beside a hole that had been neatly cut by a backhoe.

About twenty-five people huddled against the biting wind while the rabbi gave a short eulogy. The younger mourners were probably neighbors and co-workers of Mike and Victoria. The older ones must be friends of Lillian. The rest, men with black hats and beards, had come with the rabbi to ensure a *minyan* so *kaddish* could be said.

When the rabbi was done speaking, Mike said a few words. Lillian sobbed. Victoria put an arm around her. Brittney stood alone and it was impossible to tell what she felt.

The rabbi motioned for the family to gather beside the grave. The casket was lowered by straps attached to a portable winch.

Mike turned to the mourners. His voice broke as he said, "Please, help me bury my father."

He picked up a small spade that sat on a mound of dirt. He scooped up some dirt and spilled it into the grave. He set the spade down and Victoria picked it up. She dropped dirt into the grave and set the spade down again. Lillian's hands shook and she dropped the spade. Victoria helped her scoop up some dirt and drop it onto her husband's casket. Brittney picked up the spade, dropped dirt into the grave, and set it down. It was never passed from hand to hand.

Everyone looked at me.

I took my gloves off and put them in my pocket. I approached the grave and knelt at the edge of the hole. Stones cut into my bare knees. The pain felt good. I filled my bare hands with clods of icy-cold dirt and stared into the hole. The simple pine box, adorned only with a Star of David on the lid, held all that remained of my father.

I let the dirt slip through my fingers. It landed with a series of thunks on the coffin.

The rest of the mourners took their turns. I watched Ilan pick up the spade and drop dirt into the grave. He put it down, then caught my eye.

The rabbi moved to one side, and the Jewish men gathered around him. I kept my eyes on Ilan as he joined them. The men swayed and bobbed as if in a choreographed dance. Their collective voice rose above the small gathering of mourners.

"Yitbarach v'yishtabach v'yitpa'ar v'yitromam v'yitnasei v'yithadar v'yitaleh v'yit-halal..."

The incantation was a repetition of sounds, elemental, like a heartbeat. The prayer shifted back and forth from Hebrew to long-dead Aramaic, the words secondary to the hypnotic rhythm. The consonants were strong. The vowels that connected them moved and flexed and altered. Then, the consonants changed too, and the vowels began their dance again.

The words drifted across the cold, empty cemetery and were dispersed by the wind.

The long prayer ended with the Hebrew words, *"Oseh shalom bim'romav, hu ya'aseh shalom aleynu v'al kol Yisrael. V'imru amein"* *He who makes peace in high places will make peace for us, and for all Israel. And let us say, amen.*

The mourners formed parallel lines leading away from the grave. As our family walked between the lines, the Jewish men called out to us, *"Hamakom y'nachem etchem b'toch sha'ar avelei tziyon virushalayim."* *May God comfort you among all the mourners of Zion and Jerusalem.*

CHAPTER 15

The rabbi and his entourage disappeared after the funeral. They had to get home before the sun set, and *Shabbos* officially began.

Mike stood by the door to take coats and scarves. Gabrielle had set chafing dishes on the long kitchen countertop, along with a salad, and store-bought dinner rolls. She accepted casserole dishes of lasagna, scalloped potatoes, and kugel from arriving guests. One couple brought a whole salmon. Several brought cakes or pies.

Victoria took Ilan's hand. "So good of you to come." She searched his face, but was too harried to ask who he was.

"This is my friend, Ilan," I said.

Ilan piled his plate high with pot roast, salmon, mashed potatoes, and carrots. I recalled that he had a healthy appetite. I took some salad, mashed potatoes, and kugel. I skipped the carrots, because they'd been cooked with the pot roast.

"Wine?" Mike asked us.

"Red. Thank you," Ilan said.

"Ilan, this is my brother, Mike."

They shook hands.

I took a glass of red wine and led Ilan to the living room. A fire burning in the big fireplace made the room too warm. Lillian sat on a couch with Nigel on her lap, surrounded by elderly friends. The other couch and several chairs were taken. Ilan and I sat in the only spot available, a small loveseat. We set our wine glasses on the floor and balanced our plates on our laps. Our shoulders touched as we ate. When I was done, I settled back into the seat. My leg rested against Ilan's. He didn't pull away.

A few minutes later he said, "That's a nice tree."

The sixteen-foot pine, covered with twinkling white lights, took up one corner of the room. Oversized pale blue glass ornaments hung on the branches between blue silk poinsettias. The silver star at the top of the tree touched the ceiling. Even the gifts under the tree were color-coordinated, wrapped in pale blue paper and tied with wide silver ribbon.

I didn't see the gifts I mailed a week ago. I'd wrapped them in bright green paper with the words *Mele Kalikimaka* emblazoned in red. Either my gifts hadn't arrived, or Victoria had hidden them away so they wouldn't clash with her perfect ensemble.

"Growing up, I always wished we could have a real Christmas tree in our apartment," I said. "I love the way they smell. But my mother put up the same artificial tree every year."

"You had a Christmas tree?"

"My mother was Catholic. We never talked about religion in our house, but I don't think my father minded about the tree. My mother had this big box of ornaments, each one different. Every year, she'd take the box down from the closet shelf, and Mike and I would watch her unwrap the ornaments. As she unwrapped each one, she'd tell us the story of how she got it. Some were passed down from her mother and grandmother in Ireland. Some were souvenirs of her travels. Others were gifts from friends or relatives. She told us the same stories year after year, but we never got tired of hearing them. Last, she'd unwrap the ornaments Mike and I had made in school. She always said those were her favorites. After all the ornaments were unwrapped and the stories told, Mike and I hung them on the tree by metal hooks. Then, we'd drape silver tinsel on the tree that would give an electric shock to anyone who passed too close. We always thought that was hilarious. There were never any presents under the tree before Christmas. They appeared Christmas morning, magically, while we slept."

"You have some nice memories," Ilan said.

"I wonder if Mike ever thinks about those days."

Ilan finished his food and drank the last of his wine, then looked at his watch. "I have an hour's drive back to the city. I'd better get going."

"I'll walk you out."

We took our dishes to the kitchen and got our coats from the closet. Outside, the temperature had dropped with nightfall. Strings of lights around the roofline and windows cast a soft blue light. On the lawn, the plastic Mary, Joseph, and baby glowed from within, ghostlike.

I shoved my hands into my pockets. "Thanks for being here."

Ilan's cologne mingled with the sharp winter air. "I'm glad you contacted me. I'm sorry about your father. If there's anything I can do, please let me know."

Our breath came out in white clouds.

"Thank you. It helped to have a friend here, among all the strangers."

"What about your family?"

"When my brother picked me up at the airport today, it was the first time I'd seen him in twenty-three years. I met his wife and daughter for the first time, just before the funeral."

Ilan raised an eyebrow. "And your father? Were you close to him?"

"I had no contact with him since I was seventeen. I met his wife, my stepmother, today for the first time, too."

The porch light picked up flecks of gold in his eyes as he looked into mine. "I can't imagine how difficult it was for you to come here."

"It's definitely been awkward."

"I'm sure there's a good story behind all this. One of these days, you'll have to tell me."

"I will. We'll keep in touch."

"It's been good seeing you again."

He kissed my cheek. I watched his tall, lean figure go down the steps, cross the driveway, and walk down the road. I wished he was older. I wished he didn't live so far from me. And even as I wished it, I knew how foolish it was. He was young and elegant, and rubbed shoulders with the most beautiful people in the world. His life was a blaze of excitement and achievement, untouched by mediocrity. I was a middle-aged postal worker.

He got into a car. The door slammed. The headlights came on and I saw it had started to snow.

I sat on the bed and opened my laptop. There was an e-mail from Brian, and one from Freddy. I opened Freddy's first.

>From: FFriedman
>To: GoldenGirl
>Subject: Raymond & Enid
>Date: December 18 16:43
>Did you get thru the funeral OK? How's it going with

your brother & family? I looked into business licenses, found a restaurant in Kaneohe called Lago Bar & Grill. Heard of it? The owner is listed as Raymond Lago. Going to check it out tonight. Thinking of you. Freddy

I tapped out my reply:

From: GoldenGirl
To: FriedmanF
Subject: re: Raymond & Enid
Date: December 19 00:01
It's been too much in one day. The long flight, seeing my brother for the first time in 23 years, meeting his wife and daughter. The funeral was unreal. Like being in a movie about someone else's life. I met my father's wife Lillian. Tomorrow they're driving her home. She lives in the apartment where I grew up. They expect me to come along. I'm trying to think of a way out.
    Never heard of Lago. Good detective work. I'll be waiting to hear more. L

From: GuitarMan
To: GoldenGirl
Subject: Missing you
Date: December 18 09:10
HEY HOWS IT GOING? HOW WAS THE FLIGHT? YOUR BROTHER/HIS FAMILY? THE FUNERAL? MOONDANCE LONELY, SAGE LOOKING FOR YOU. BOB DOESN'T KNOW YOUR GONE. CAN'T WAIT TO SEE YOU MONDAY. BRIAN

From: GoldenGirl
To: GuitarMan
Subject: re: Missing you
Date: December 18 23:15
The flight was long and uncomfortable. Not enough

to eat, no sleep. My head is spinning. How can I describe the funeral? Beautiful and bizarre at the same time. Not a single flower. A bunch of men with bushy beards and black hats showed up with the rabbi to say the prayers. I knew my father was Jewish, only because I overheard the neighbors say it when I was a kid. We never talked about it. I thought he was just like everybody else. Today, I watched them bury him in a plain pine box with a Star of David on the lid. It was like he was someone else, someone I never knew. And you know the weirdest thought I had at the funeral? Here is a whole society of people who've found a way to opt out of Christmas.

The house is too big. Too perfect. Victoria seems nice enough. Mike doesn't have a lot to say. Neither does my niece, Brittney. My father's wife, Lillian, is here. I'm not sure what I think of her. There's no reason to dislike her, really.

Tomorrow Mike and Victoria are driving Lillian home. They fully expect me to go with them, back to the apartment where I grew up. Where my mother died. I just can't! L

I closed the laptop and set it on the floor. Everything in the room was color coordinated. The sage green paint on the walls matched the pink and green Amish quilt on the bed. A pink and green cross-stitched WELCOME GUESTS hung above the dresser in a wooden frame.

The guestroom had its own bath, painted the same green. I brushed my teeth, washed my face, and dried my hands and face on a fluffy pink towel. The whirlpool tub was big enough to hold several people. Maybe I'd try it tomorrow.

I undressed and sat on the queen size bed in my underwear. I'd forgotten to bring pajamas. I slid under the quilt. The room was completely underground and had no windows. When I turned off the bedside lamp, it was absolutely dark.

Images of the funeral filled my head. The small gathering of black-clad mourners, their backs turned to the chilling wind. The simple coffin sitting beside a gaping hole in the ground. The bearded men swaying, caught up in the fervor of their prayer for the dead, their voices rising above Lillian's quiet sobs.

I saw my father's body inside the pine box, wrapped in a white burial shroud, his shoulders, in death, draped in the *tallit* he hadn't worn since his bar mitzvah. I shot up and turned the light on. I stacked the pillows behind me, picked up the book I'd bought in San Francisco, and stared at the pages.

Chapter 16

"Louise?" Someone was tapping on the door. "Louise?"

I opened my eyes. I'd slept with the bedside lamp on. What time was it? "Huh?"

The door opened a crack. "Louise? Are you awake?" Victoria peeked in. "Breakfast will be ready in a few minutes, Honey."

"Oh …"

"Come on upstairs when you're ready. We'll be leaving in an hour to take Lillian home."

"Thanks."

I felt a chill and looked down. I was undressed. I yanked the quilt up to hide my bra. Victoria closed the door and her footsteps went up the wooden stairs.

The temperature in the basement had dropped overnight. I shivered as I dug a clean pair of jeans and a sweatshirt out of the suitcase and put them on. Next, socks and Reeboks on my ice-cold feet. In the bathroom, I let the water run in the sink while I examined my face in the mirror. My skin looked as dry and tight as it felt. I tested the water temperature, washed my face, and brushed my teeth.

I did what I could to make my hair presentable and put on a pair of small gold hoop earrings. Without the humidity to plump my skin, new wrinkles had appeared at the corners of my eyes and the sides of my mouth. I never use lotion. In Hawai'i, it's unnecessary. I got my Chapstick out of my purse, applied it to my chapped lips, then to my entire face. I rubbed it in with my fingers. That was better.

The smell of coffee and bacon reminded me of happier mornings, when I still believed my mother could make everything right. The kitchen table had been expanded to seat six. Victoria, Brittney, and Lillian sat at the table, while Mike worked at the stove. Nigel waited at Mike's feet, ready to catch any spills. Gabrielle must have Saturdays off.

"Good morning," I said.

"Come sit with us." Victoria went to the cupboard and got out a mug. "Coffee?"

"I'd love some." I took an empty chair.

"Did you sleep well?" Victoria asked.

She set the mug of coffee in front of me. I wrapped my hands around it and inhaled the steam.

"I don't think I slept very long."

"Jet lag will do that to you," Lillian said.

She appeared more rested than she had yesterday. She wore jeans, a blue and white striped sweater, the same black boots, and had taken the time to put on makeup and pearl earrings.

Mike set plates in front of Lillian and me. Each held a large omelet and a generous serving of hash brown potatoes. "There's no meat in these."

"Thank you, Mike," Lillian said.

Victoria's and Brittney's omelets were ham and cheese, with hash browns and four slices of bacon on the side. Mike set a basket of buttered toast in the middle of the table, and joined us with his ham and cheese omelet.

Nigel hopped onto Lillian's lap and peered over the table. An awkward silence ensued as everyone concentrated on their food. I remembered reading somewhere that if, on a first date, an awkward silence goes on for more than four seconds, the game is over. This was sort of like a first date.

I glanced at Brittney. She was such a contrast to Emmeline, who never stopped talking. They were the same age. If they knew each other, would they be friends? Probably not.

Finally, Victoria said, "I thought it was a lovely funeral,"

Mike and Lillian agreed.

"It was good of your friend to come, Louise," Victoria said.

"He wanted to say *kaddish*."

"Please, thank him for me," Lillian said. "It's a *mitzvah*,"

Victoria asked, "Does he live in New York?"

"For now. He travels all over for his work."

"What does he do?"

"He's the stand-in and stunt double for Trent Nellis."

That got Brittney's attention. "Really?"

"Really," I said. "Did you see the movie, *Mountains on Fire*?"

Brittney glanced at Mike, then Victoria. "I'm not allowed to see anything rated R."

"I saw it with your father," Lillian said. "We enjoyed it."

"The movie was shot in Hawai'i," I said. "I met Ilan when he was working on the set and he invited me to watch them film part of it."

"Did you meet Trent Nellis?" Brittney asked.

"No, I didn't. I went to the wrap party, but I passed out before I had a chance to meet him."

Eyebrows went up around the table.

"That's a story for another day."

Brittney said, "I wish I knew last night that he was a celebrity. I would've asked him a million questions. And I would've gotten his autograph."

"I can ask him to send you his autograph, if you want."

"Sweet!"

We rode in the Audi. Lillian sat in front with Mike, Nigel on her lap. Victoria, Brittney and I sat in the back. I was too warm in my coat, but there wasn't room to take it off. We made a left on Brigadoon Circle and a right on the two-lane highway we'd taken from the airport on Friday.

Brittney had her iPod ear buds in, effectively cutting herself off from the rest of us. Every now and then, her phone vibrated, and her thumbs flew over the keys as fast as Emmeline's did. The two girls had something in common, after all.

The rest of us sat in silence. I turned to the window. Tires had left black ribbons on the slush-coated streets. Last night's snow clung to skeletal trees like cotton balls and lay in pathetic gray heaps along the roadside.

Thirty minutes into our trip, traffic slowed to a stop. We were approaching a tollbooth. I'd almost forgotten about toll booths.

Another half hour and three or four tollbooths later, the steel beams and cables of the George Washington Bridge reached skyward in front of us like a reversed arch. We inched our way to a toll booth at the foot of the bridge. Mike paid eight dollars, and we started across what had to be the busiest bridge in the world. With five people in the car, I supposed it was a bargain.

Gusts of wind caught the car and made it sway. Mike negotiated the agonizing traffic jam without breaking a sweat. At the top of the bridge, we crossed from New Jersey into New York. I stared at the city on the other side of the river. The brick and concrete towers appeared rose-colored, softened by distance and a thin fog that swept in from the Atlantic.

After twenty minutes on the bridge, we exited onto Harlem River Drive. From the six-lane highway we had an unobstructed view of the Harlem River that separates Manhattan from The Bronx. The road turned south and became Franklin D. Roosevelt East River Drive. On FDR we passed through a series of three-sided tunnels, with only the river visible on our left. Between the tunnels, Manhattan loomed to our right. Everywhere, gaudy Christmas decorations brightened drab buildings.

Lillian turned to me and said, "Do you see the Pepsi Cola sign?"

I looked across the river, to Queens, where the landmark sign stood. "It's moved."

"The bottling company closed in 1999. People were so upset when the sign was dismantled, it was erected again a short distance upriver. Now, they're building an apartment complex that will have a view of the sign."

We came around a bend and I caught my first glimpse of the angular red brick buildings of Stuyvesant Town, my childhood home. My heart beat faster. Until now, I'd managed to stay calm by distracting myself with the scenery. I rubbed my clammy hands together, then touched the drops of sweat on my upper lip.

Mike turned on Fourteenth Street, made a right on First Avenue, and pulled to the curb. A blast of cold air filled the car as Mike, Lillian, Victoria, and Brittney got out. They slammed the doors shut.

Nigel scampered under a chain to a patch of grass and peed.

Lillian groaned. "Oh, God. My knee is so stiff." She walked in a circle, testing her legs.

Brittney texted with her eyes on her phone. Mike opened the trunk and set Lillian's small suitcase on the sidewalk.

Victoria said, "Brittney, please take Grandma's bag."

Brittney put her phone in her pocket, grabbed the handle of the rolling suitcase, and started down the walkway.

Mike got back in the car and put his seatbelt on before he noticed me in the rear view mirror. "You can get out here," he said. "I'm going to park in the garage."

I opened the door and got out. My legs had been in the same position for an hour and a half and didn't want to unfold. I limped to the sidewalk, forced myself upright, and looked at the fourteen-story building.

"Does it still look the same?" Lillian asked.

"Everything is so much smaller than I remembered. I feel like Alice in Wonderland"

"Time will do that."

"I think there used to be more trees."

"Don't even get me started on that."

Nigel trotted over to us and we walked together to the entryway. Lillian opened the door with a key card. In the lobby, six-packs of empty beer bottles sat against the wall beside a shrink-wrapped pallet of new plungers.

"Plumbing problems?" I asked Lillian.

"To say the least."

Rough plywood had been nailed across one wall and painted beige. "Where did the mail boxes go?"

"What you see here is our management's answer to three or four broken mailboxes.Now, everyone in the building has to pick up their mail at the post office, Monday through Saturday, between the hours of eleven and two."

The elevator door slid open and stuck. A high-pitched alarm went off. Lillian put her fingers to her ears and winced. We stepped into the elevator and Lillian jabbed at the black dime-sized buttons until the door closed and the alarm stopped.

The elevator panels were grimy white. I distinctly remembered them as bright red. The elevators had all been red, blue or green, and I always thought we'd really lucked out to get a red one. My girlfriends would come over, and we'd put on my mother's old clothes and well-worn high heels. We spent hours riding up and down the elevator dressed this way. What a kick that was! In those days, it was perfectly safe for us to do so. Today, parents would never allow children to roam the elevators unattended.

As we passed each floor, there was a shrill beep. The sound effects had been added since I was last here.

We stopped with a lurch on ten, which is actually the twelfth story. The street level is called Terrace. The second level, Main, opens to an extensive area of playgrounds, lawns, walkways, the large Oval with its fountain, and still more playgrounds. Above Main, the floors are numbered one through twelve, thus avoiding an unlucky thirteenth floor.

The door rattled open and stuck. The alarm screeched behind us as we stepped out onto a dizzying brown-and-gray-patterned carpet. Food smells mixed with a faint odor of vomit and excrement given off by the stained carpet. Sounds of televisions and conversations carried into the H-shaped hallway, and I recalled knowing some of our neighbors by their voices alone.

Lillian unlocked the door to 10D and went in. Brittney followed, leaned the suitcase against a wall, and sat beside Victoria on a black leather sofa. With her ear buds still in, she pulled her phone out and started texting. Lillian took one of two identical chairs across from the couch. Nigel went around a corner to the kitchen and lapped water from a dish.

I closed the door behind me and looked around. It was as if an alien energy had manifested itself here. Our traditional furniture, oriental rugs, paintings, and lace curtains were gone. The temporary pressure wall that created a third bedroom—Mike's room—had been removed. Now, the living area was twice the size and a dining area had been opened up next to the kitchen. I glanced down the hallway and couldn't bear to think what must've become of my bedroom.

The walls of the living room were painted blood red. A splayed zebra skin stretched across the parquet floor. African masks hung behind the sofa. Statues carved in ebony—unclothed women with sagging breasts, scrawny old men, mothers with children—stood in corners and on shelves.

All that remained of my mother was her baby grand piano. Although many families owned pianos in Stuyvesant Town, our baby grand was considered something of a status symbol. When my parents moved in, the piano was too large for the elevator. I often heard the story of how it had been hoisted by straps attached to the roof of the building and brought in through the living room window. Even the window frame had to be removed, then re-welded on.

Now, the piano sat in the corner, closed and seemingly forgotten, hidden beneath a brightly colored tapestry. It would never leave the apartment—at least not in one piece.

Lillian put a hand on the chair next to her. "Come, Louise."

I didn't move. The chair was upholstered in what appeared to be wildebeest hide. Was that even legal? I looked from the chair to the zebra skin.

"It's okay to step on it," Lillian said.

I walked across the butchered zebra and sat on the edge of the wildebeest chair before I could talk myself out of it.

"You have some interesting things," I said.

"Thank you. I collected them during my years in Africa."

"Africa?"

"Yes. My first husband was Ghanaian."

"I didn't know that. How did you meet him?"

"When I was twenty-five, I spent a summer traveling through Europe. On a train from Belgium to Switzerland, I noticed a tall man with ebony skin. I think I must have been staring at him. He nodded to me, and I said hello. He started a conversation, though I can't recall what we talked about. I'd never spoken to a black person before. George was his name. We kept in touch—back then it was all by letter, of course. A year later, I sailed to Africa on a cargo ship, which was an adventure in itself. George and I were married, and I stayed in Ghana for thirty years."

This had to be in the late fifties, when it was still illegal in most states for a white woman to marry a black man. "Were your parents okay with it? I mean, you marrying a black man? And living in Africa?"

"My father was gone by then. My mother had fits over it, of course. But after our daughter was born, my mother came to visit us in Ghana."

"You have a daughter?" That meant I had a step-sister. I'd always wished for a sister.

"Her name's Kamili."

"That's pretty."

"It means 'perfection'. But she was a chatterbox, and her nanny called her Chiku. The name stuck. She still goes by Chiku. She's a bit older than you, forty-seven, now. She lives in England. She's married and has a son in college."

I not only had a stepsister, I had a step nephew.

Nigel hopped onto the sofa between Brittney and Victoria and curled up on a cushion. I noticed a pair of lamps on either side of the sofa. The white oval shades depicted intricate scenes with elephants, birds, and vegetation. They sat in carved wood bases.

"Those lamps are amazing," I said. "I've never seen anything like them."

"They're made from ostrich eggs. When I turn them on at night, shadows of the scenes are cast on the walls."

The intercom sounded. Lillian stood, and I watched her walk to the door. I was looking at a courageous woman. My mother had been courageous, in her own way. But she was also very conventional. Lillian had lived her life outside the box. How had my father ended up with someone so different from my mother? How had his marriage to Lillian changed him?

Lillian pressed a button on the wall.

"It's me. Mike."

She buzzed him in.

"Should I make some tea?" Victoria asked.

"That would be lovely," Lillian said.

Victoria went to the kitchen. I heard water running and metal clanking against metal. Brittney fidgeted on the couch. The room was too hot. Sweat prickled inside my shirt. The blood-red walls were closing in on me.

My head began to spin. I needed air. I got to my feet and put my purse over my shoulder. "I'm going for a walk."

I hurried past Lillian and out the door.

In the hallway I pressed the elevator button. It was taking too long. I pressed it again and again. Finally, it rumbled to a stop with an ear-piercing beep. The alarm screeched as the door slid open.

I was face to face with Mike.

Before he could speak, I said, "I'm going outside for a bit." I pushed past him and punched the buttons until the door closed between us.

Outside, a glacial wind stung my nose and cheeks. My eyes watered.

In the 1940's, developers razed eighteen square blocks of Manhattan. Five hundred buildings were demolished and three thousand families relocated. All to create the utopia for the middle class that they called Stuyvesant Town. Some said it failed to deliver on those promises. But for my family, it was an affordable haven in the middle of Manhattan that embodied all the best qualities of the modernists' thinking.

Just across the street, tenements, brownstones, and storefronts still date back to the turn of the century. As a child, the textures of the older buildings dazzled me. They seemed a colorful bazaar in contrast to the orderly, symmetrical world I lived in. I put on my gloves, pulled my scarf tighter, shoved my hands in my pockets, and crossed First Avenue. Evidence of Christmas was everywhere.

The Lower East Side always had an intensity all its own. The unexpected mix of immigrants—Ukrainians, Poles, Puerto Ricans, Jews, Italians, Asians—all brought their cultures, flavors, and music into one boisterous community. But the neighborhood had become chic in my absence. Markets now advertised organic produce. Art galleries had sprouted on almost every block. Boutiques sold goods I'd never seen offered on these streets.

The frigid weather hadn't kept people indoors. I was jostled by the crowd as I walked over uneven, cracked sidewalks, past basement windows sealed against the winter. The foreign accents that reached my ears didn't belong to immigrants, but to well-dressed European tourists. Pricey cars cruised the avenue and parked against curbs strewn with unidentifiable trash. Cold seeped through my Reeboks and numbed my toes. I scanned both sides of the street for something familiar.

Twenty minutes later, I stopped at the corner of First and Delancey. Ratner's Deli had been doing business on Delancey since the 1920's. I'd loved to stop there on my way home from school for their hot onion rolls and vegetarian pâté. It was once as familiar to me as my mother's kitchen. Sometimes, the guy who worked there would slip me a loaf of *challah* to take home.

I turned left, walked two blocks toward the bridge, and stopped. A mattress shop called Sleepy's occupied the space where Ratner's used to be. The bodega next door, where I bought *plátanos*, was gone, too. Puerto Rican men sitting outside the bodega used to whistle and call out *Chica!* or *Mamacita!* as I passed by. Once, I came with a girlfriend. When the men made their kissing noises and called out to us, she said *moricon* under her breath. I had no idea what it meant. One of the men jumped up, and my friend took off running. I followed without a backward glance, and didn't return to the bodega for several weeks. It was an education, and good preparation for the years I would later spend in Mexico. Pedestrians hurried past me in both directions without breaking their stride. I stood for a moment in front of the mattress shop, then headed back the way I came.

At Allen Street, I ducked into a Starbucks to get out of the cold.

Christmas music played on unseen speakers and a decorated tree stood in one corner between tables.

I picked up a gingerbread man from a display next to the cash register and studied his puzzled expression. "This, and a venti coffee of the day," I said to the barista.

"You want milk wich yo coffee?"

"No!" It came out harsher than I intended.

The barista put her hands up. "I gotcha, Girlfriend. You don' like no*body* messin' wich yo coffee."

"I'm sorry." I gave her an apologetic smile. "No, I don't. I like mine hot, strong, and black. And I could make a joke here ..."

The barista waved a hand. "No need, Honey. I just had me a *vision*."

We laughed.

At a table by the window, I sipped my coffee and watched the New Yorkers go by. A very long time ago, I'd been one of them.

I checked my phone. No calls. I was anxious to hear what Freddy had found at Lago Bar and Grill. It was only five-thirty in the morning in Hawai'i. I'd have to wait. I scrolled through my phonebook and pressed Ilan's number.

Chapter 17

"... a skinned zebra, black masks on the wall with empty eyes and gaping mouths on a sea of blood. I swear, I heard drumbeats. Maybe it was my own heart. I couldn't stay a minute longer."

"They'll be wondering where you are," Ilan said.

We walked side by side on the crowded sidewalks, our hands in our pockets. He was dressed for the New York winter in jeans, a down jacket, hiking boots, and a knit cap.

"I called Mike and told him not to wait for me."

"How will you get back?"

I shrugged. We were a good sixty miles from Mike's house. I'd figure it out when the time came.

We turned down Eldridge Street. Hebrew chanting drifted from an open doorway, and I stopped to look up at the ornate old building. Its Moorish architecture and stained glass windows clashed with the Chinese businesses on either side of it. This kind of jarring cultural collision is one thing I love about the Lower East Side.

Ilan said, "This is one of the oldest synagogues in the country."

I pondered, for the first time, how New York's Jewish history is also part of my own history. "It's beautiful."

"The City spent twenty million renovating it. Now it's a National Historic Landmark."

Ilan led me down East Broadway. "Chinatown has spread out to absorb this whole neighborhood. It's taken over Little Italy, too."

"You're kidding."

"All but one street, where there are still some Italian restaurants."

From Chatham Square we could see Chinese, Vietnamese, and Indonesian restaurants, as well as a Subway.

"Are you hungry?" Ilan asked.

"Not really. You?"

"I can wait. Should we catch a bus?"

"I'm enjoying the walk."

We came to a wrought iron gate. Beyond it, eerie rock formations, worn smooth by time, protruded from the earth. A brass plaque set into a slab of marble read:

The First Cemetery
of the Spanish and Portuguese Synagogue
Shearith Israel
in the City of New York
1656-1833

"Ever been here?" Ilan asked.

"Never."

He shook the gate. "Sometimes it's unlocked. Not today. Very few people know about this place. The oldest headstones date back to the sixteen hundreds and are engraved in Ladino. Twenty-two Jews who fought and died in the Revolutionary War are buried here."

"I didn't know Jews fought in the Revolutionary War."

"At the time of the Revolution, about two thousand Jews lived in the New World. They were some of the biggest financiers of the war."

He started walking and I followed. "When did your family come to the US?" he asked.

"My father's family arrived here in the early thirties. He was born in the Bronx, in 1934. My mother was born in Ireland. Her family came later, in the forties."

Strings of tiny golden lights covered the bare trees. We passed a Burger King that was filled to capacity. Across the street, people crowded into the Century 21 department store, where a sign advertised tee-shirts eighty-five percent off.

As we neared Ground Zero, the crowd on the sidewalks grew more dense. We walked around tourists who craned their necks to see over the barriers that walled off the Ground Zero construction site. All that was visible were a few red cranes reaching skyward.

At the gate to St. Paul's Chapel, a Hispanic man in a construction hat called out, "Ground Zero photos!" He held up images of smoky desolation, taken immediately after nine-eleven.

"Did you take these?" I asked.

"Yes. I helped clear the ground, and I took these photos myself."

A block away, a sign on the ground floor of an apartment building read, Amish Fine Food Market.

Ilan reached for the door. "Let's go in here. I think I'm ready to eat something."

As we went in I was hit with the fragrances of coffee, spices, garlic, and baking bread. We stood in line by a glass deli case. The blackboard menu offered salads, wraps, Panini sandwiches, brick oven sandwiches, pizza, sushi, desserts, and more.

"If they opened a place like this in Hawai'i, the line would stretch for miles," I said.

"While you're here, you should have a real New York pizza."

"That sounds perfect."

"What do you like on your pizza? You're a vegetarian, aren't you?"

"And a purist."

"Just cheese, then?"

"Yes."

When we reached the front of the line, he said, "Give me a large Bianca," to the guy behind the counter.

A sweaty man in a stained chef's coat spread marinara and sprinkled three kinds of cheese over a circle of dough and shoved our pizza in the oven.

When it was ready, Ilan carried it up a narrow staircase and we sat at a small table. The dining area was nearly empty. Christmas music drifted from the ceiling. I took a slice of pizza from the box and bit into it. The paper-thin crust was crispy and the cheese melted in my mouth.

I grabbed my napkin and wiped my chin. "Oh my God. I haven't tasted anything this good since…never."

Ilan bit into his slice. When he pulled it away, strings of cheese stretched between his teeth and the pizza. He nodded with his mouth full. While he worked on his pizza, I studied him. He hadn't taken time to shave this morning. In the three years since I'd seen him, his face had filled out. Faint lines crinkled at the corners of his eyes when he smiled. The man sitting across from me now was a mature adult. The eight year difference in our ages didn't seem to matter as much as it once had.

He caught me looking at him.

"Can I ask you something?" I said, to cover myself.

"Of course."

"When you lived in Kāne'ohe, do you remember a restaurant called Lago Bar and Grill?"

"Sure. We used to go there for drinks. It was more bar than grill, really. The only bar in the area."

"Did you ever see the owner?"

He thought for a moment. "I think it was owned by several brothers. One of them was the boss, though. He dressed better than the others and ordered them around."

"Did he ever have a woman with him?"

Ilan raised an eyebrow. "Are you interested in him?"

"Yes. I mean, no. Not like that."

I told him about Enid.

When I finished my story, Ilan said, "The boss sometimes came in with a woman. I remember her because she looked … odd."

"Odd how?"

"The way she dressed, for one thing. Skirts so short they barely covered the essentials, and the highest heels you ever saw. I mean, she could barely walk in them. But no makeup. She made me think of a kid playing dress up. The boss acted protective of her. Territorial might be a better word. He'd sit her at a table in the back, sometimes with a couple of other women. She'd nurse the same drink all evening. I thought she looked too young to drink."

"What did she look like?"

"Small. Skinny. Long, black hair. Dark skin."

"Dark skin?"

"Yeah. Very dark."

That sounded like Enid, except for the skin. Could she have had a predecessor? If so, what had happened to her?

Chapter 18

At the ferry terminal, we pressed through the crowd.

"It's much worse on weekdays," Ilan said. "And when the weather's warmer."

I spotted the ladies' room. "Do I have time to go to the restroom?"

Ilan looked at his watch. "Sure. We have twenty minutes until the next ferry."

I found an empty stall, shut the door, sat, and dug my phone out of my purse. There were two new voicemails.

The first was from Mike. "Louise, we want to head back home. Are you sure you won't come with us?"

I called him back and his voicemail picked up. "Go on home. I'll get a ride back later."

The second call was from Brian. "Hey. Just wanted to hear your voice. I miss you."

It was nine in the morning, Hawai'i time. I called my home phone. Brian picked up on the third ring.

"Hey," I said.

"How's it going?"

At the sound of his voice, tears stung my eyes. God, I was homesick. "All right." My voice caught in my throat.

"Are you okay?"

"It's just weird being here ..." I sniffed. "... after so many years." I grabbed some toilet paper with my free hand and wiped my eyes and nose.

"Did you go back to your old apartment?"

"This morning."

"How was that?"

"For a few minutes, I was okay. Then I freaked out. I ran outside and started walking. I kept going until I reached the Staten Island Ferry Terminal."

"Man, you walked halfway across Manhattan."

"I know." A tear trickled down my cheek. I wiped it away and blew my nose. "Is everything okay at home?"

"Everything's fine. Emmeline's been by to play with Sage and take her for a walk. Her little brother's been over here, too. He's a great kid."

"Have you seen Dan?"

"Not at all." A pause. "I miss you."

"I miss you too. I'm about to get on the ferry. I'll call you later."

I disconnected, grabbed more toilet paper, and blew my nose again before calling Freddy. His voicemail picked up.

"Freddy, it's Louise. I'm going to be away from my computer all day. Call me on my cell if you get a chance."

When I came out of the restroom, Ilan was waiting on a bench. He stood and looked into my eyes. "Are you okay?"

I must look a mess. "Sure."

"Let's get in line."

Ten minutes later, the crowd began to inch toward the ferry. As we boarded, Ilan rested his hand on the small of my back and let it linger there. Heat from his body penetrated my layers of clothing and spread up my spine to my neck. My face burned.

We followed the hardiest folks to the top deck, found a spot at the railing, and leaned against it. The big engines kicked in and the great orange concrete vessel eased out of the terminal.

Time, which moves at breakneck speed in the city, slowed to a crawl. The wind cut through my coat and jeans, stung my face, and made my nose run. I didn't care. It was a great feeling of freedom, no one breathing down my neck, no one expecting things I wasn't prepared to give.

Barges, tugboats, and ferries chugged through the harbor. Pleasure boats wouldn't venture out in this weather. The Statue of Liberty reached her arm skyward against a backdrop of dismal clouds. She's so much smaller than she should be, I thought. My mother was twelve when she came to this country. Had she felt the same when she saw the statue for the first time?

"Let me take a picture," Ilan said.

He put an arm around me, held his phone at arm's length, and snapped. He touched the screen a couple times. "It's on Facebook."

"That fast?"

"That fast."

We exited the ferry on Staten Island, followed the signs, and got in line for the return trip. On the way back, we found a bench on the second level, out of the wind, and watched the Manhattan skyline through the plastic window.

Our waiter introduced himself as Savas. He set the plates in the center of the table and said, "Here we have crostini with artichoke tapenade, olive tapenade, and fig and almond spread. And on this plate, five kinds of cheese. *Fromage de Chevre*, made from the goat. *Gorgonzola Dolce*, made from the cow. *Caccio de Roma*, made from the sheep. *Manchego*, also from the sheep. And *Rocchetta*, made from the cow, the sheep and the goat." He pulled a pad and pen from his apron. "Are you ready to order your dinner?"

Ilan ordered for both of us. "The lady will start with the fig and olive salad, followed by the carrot and thyme soup. I'll have the *pollo de Ibiza* salad, and the grilled chicken and lamb."

"Very good." Savas pocketed his pen and pad and refilled our glasses from the bottle of *Castillo di Monjardin* Chardonnay.

We'd arrived early enough to be seated on a Saturday night without a reservation. By the time the waiter returned with our salads and a basket of freshly baked bread, every table was filled, with standing room only at the bar. Most of the diners had dressed up for their evening out, and I regretted my sweatshirt and sneakers.

Ilan dug into his meal while I sipped my soup and nibbled at my salad. "How's the soup?" he asked.

My mother taught me never to say I'm full, because of the unpleasant image it evokes. "It's wonderful. Everything's great."

Ilan refilled our glasses and held up the empty bottle. "Should I order another?"

"Oh no. This is fine. Thanks."

I took another drink of wine. I should have stopped at two glasses, but I was feeling reckless.

I dipped a piece of bread in olive oil and balsamic vinegar and said, "You love New York."

"I do. It's different from any other place in the world. I mean, it's the people here that are different. In public, there can be a ... detached ... feeling. People have to maintain some kind of personal space among the hordes of human beings moving around the streets. But when you get to know them, New Yorkers are more intimate and accessible than people in—say—Los Angeles."

"Why do you think that is?"

"I really believe the absence of natural beauty in the geography has a positive effect on people here. With no nature to relate to, they focus more on each other. Humans are the dominant life form. We *are* nature in New York City. Besides concrete and steel, we're all there is. So people are more willing to connect. I think this is why there are so many creative types here—singers, dancers, actors."

"I never thought of it that way."

He cleaned up the last bit of meat from his plate and leaned back. "Dessert? Marzipan cake, or the *chocolat pot de crème*?"

I laid a hand on my stomach. "As good as it sounds, I couldn't eat another bite."

Ilan signaled the waiter for the check. I reached for my purse, but before I could open it Ilan handed him a credit card.

"Please, let me," I said.

"Absolutely not. You traveled all the way to New York. Buying you dinner is the least I can do."

He was being so nice. But I wondered, was this just a meeting of old friends for him? Or was it something more?

He pushed the door open and the cold hit me like a slap in the face. Even so, it wasn't enough to sober me. I rarely drink. When I do, I limit myself to a single beer or glass of wine. Tonight I'd polished off half a bottle of Chardonnay.

Cars filled the streets, but we had the sidewalk to ourselves. I concentrated on putting one foot in front of the other without staggering, but wasn't doing a very good job of it.

I swayed.

Ilan caught my arm. "Are you okay?"

I nodded, embarrassed. He put his arm behind my back and we continued walking. The wind whipped a light snow past the streetlights. Here and there, snow stuck to the ground.

I stumbled again. This time, I leaned into Ilan and let him steady me. His body blocked the wind. I felt his warmth and smelled his cologne. We walked a few blocks past gaily lit buildings and trees.

Ilan stopped in front of an older brick building and stood at the bottom of the steps. I looked up at him. He met my gaze, held it for what seemed like a very long time, then tilted his head toward the doors.

I followed him up the steps, through the lobby, and into the elevator. He pressed the button for the top floor and the door slid closed.

I leaned against the wall and felt the elevator rumble. What was I doing? I needed to get back to Mike's house, but I couldn't bring myself to say goodbye to Ilan. My heart pounded. Why did he bring me here? What was happening? What did I *want* to happen?

Since the day we met, I'd allowed myself to indulge in fantasies about him. It seemed harmless, because he was so inaccessible. Now, that fantasy was becoming a reality. I wasn't ready to say the words that would end it.

We got out of the elevator. Ilan led me down the hallway. He unlocked a door, opened it, and turned on the lights. The apartment was a single room, thirty feet long and not more than eight feet wide. Smaller than my living room.

"Have a seat." He gestured to a leather sofa. "I'll be right back." He threw his coat across a chrome barstool and went into what must be the bathroom.

I laid my purse and coat on the sofa and sat down. My phone vibrated. I ignored it. I closed my eyes, but it only made my head spin faster. I opened them and took in Ilan's home.

Just inside the door was tiny but modern kitchen with stainless steel appliances. The dark wood floor reflected recessed lighting in the ceiling and two skylights. Opposite me, a wall of exposed red brick ran the length of the apartment. A dresser held a flat screen TV. A queen size bed, neatly made in solid black, filled the far end of the room. Only ten or twelve inches of space remained between the foot of the bed and the wall. Everything was immaculate. A laptop, a few pens, and a stack of mail on a fold-down table were the only evidence that someone lived here.

Ilan joined me on the sofa.

"This is a great apartment," I said.

"I really lucked out. I found it on VRBO. It came furnished, and I rent it month to month. There's no view, but the location is perfect. There's a lot to do in the area, and I'm close to work."

I leaned my head back.

"Should I make coffee?"

"It might not be a bad idea."

"Do you like Israeli music?" he asked as he filled the coffee maker.

"I love it. Do you have any Idan Raichel?"

"He's my favorite."

He sat on a barstool at the fold-down table, opened his laptop, and put on the music. The coffee maker gurgled and the smell of coffee filled the room.

He got out two mugs. "Black, right?'

I nodded. He added cream and sugar to his coffee and sat beside me. We listened to Idan Raichel's traditional Hebrew, Aramaic, Arabic, Zulu, and Hindi, songs written to a unique blend of Middle Eastern, Indian, and African rhythms. The strong coffee tasted good, and helped sober me. Conversation was easy, with none of those awkward silences I'd felt at Mike's house. This was the perfect first date. Or maybe it wasn't a date at all.

"Have you ever been married?" Ilan asked.

"Never."

"Ever wanted to?"

I wasn't sure how to answer. "There was someone a few years back. We were together fifteen years."

"That's a long time. What happened?"

"He died."

"I'm sorry."

I looked past him to the room's only window, on the far side of the bed. It was impossible to see out through the frosted glass. "His name was Amos Moses," I said.

"That's a great name."

"I thought so. I fell in love with his name first, then I fell in love with him. We met at folk dancing in Seattle. I was twenty years old, Amos was thirty-two. He was a singer and musician, and his job took us all over. The summer after we met, someone offered him a gig in a hotel in Portugal. When that ended, we backpacked across Europe and ended up in Greece. Amos worked in Mykonos for a few months. When everything closed up for the winter, we caught a boat to Israel and stayed there for a year. You know that part of the story."

"That's when you lived on the kibbutz."

I nodded.

"And after Israel?"

"In Jerusalem we met a musician who played with a band in London. He needed a guitarist, and invited Amos to join him there."

"I love London."

"I might have loved it, too, under different circumstances. For a year, I spent my nights following the band from one pub to another. I slept all day, in an old house that had no heat. We shared the house with lots of other people who came and went at random. I didn't even know most of their names."

"Did you do any sightseeing?"

"I never got out during the day. The train trip into town cost six dollars each way, and I couldn't afford it."

"That's really a shame. It's such an amazing city, with so much history. I wish I could take you there and show you around."

"Really? You'd do that?"

"If there was any way, of course I would. How'd you finally get out of London?"

"Amos was offered a job in L.A. By then, we were more than ready for warm weather and sunshine. We lived in California for a while, then moved on to Acapulco. We got to know an Israeli who wanted to start a commune on the Big Island. He owned land there and was filling a big lava tube with supplies, getting ready for Armageddon. We weren't concerned about the end of the world, but we liked the idea of Hawai'i.

"There were always eight or ten people living in the commune, all of them artists or musicians. A few had young children. Eventually, Amos and I moved out of the commune and rented a house in Hawi. He got a night job singing in a bar and I worked in a little store down the road from our house. After all the years of moving from place to place, we thought we'd found Heaven on Earth. We were sure we'd stay forever."

"It sounds like a dream."

"It was the happiest time of my life. Back then, Hawi was a hippy town. Lots of drugs, and they were easy to get. Amos liked to get high, and he loved to surf while he was high. Made him feel closer to God, that's what he said. One winter day, he went out in search of the perfect wave. I told him not to go. The waves were too big, it was too dangerous. He laughed at me."

I sipped my coffee, closed my eyes, and listened to Idan Raichel sing a love song from the Song of Solomon.

"He never came back," I finally said. "They didn't find his body until the next day. He'd been dashed into the rocks. His skull was fractured and he drowned."

"I'm sorry," Ilan said for the second time.

I didn't want his pity. "How about you? Ever wanted to get married?"

"Yes."

"And she didn't?"

He looked away, then let out a long breath. "No."

"Echo?"

He nodded. "We met at Cal State and lived together for eight years. Our first goal was to finish school. We put everything else aside and concentrated on our studies. We graduated, and both got good jobs. She as a professional diver, me with the film industry. We were making money. Things were good. I figured the next step was to get married, buy a house, and start having kids."

"That wasn't what she wanted?"

"No. At least she said it wasn't."

This came as a surprise. When he'd e-mailed me about their breakup, he hadn't told me the specifics. I'd assumed Echo was the one who wanted to settle down and raise a family, and Ilan couldn't work it into his lifestyle.

"She's married now, right?"

"Married and expecting her first child."

"How did that happen?"

The corners of his mouth lifted in a half-smile.

"That's not what I meant. If she didn't want marriage and children …"

"I ask myself that question a hundred times a day."

The music had stopped. Ilan got up and put on some soft jazz. Our tastes in music had to be a generation apart, but he did a good job of picking what I like.

He held out his hand for my empty mug. "Refill?"

"Sure."

He filled our mugs and sat again. "So, what are you going to do?"

"I don't know what to do. I need to get to the airport Monday morning, and all my things are at Mike's house."

"You're welcome to stay here tonight."

Chapter 19

Ilan didn't have a hair dryer. I did the best I could with a towel. My clothes rattled in the dryer on the other side of the wall. This was one of a very few New York apartments that had its own washer and dryer, tucked into a space that had once been a closet.

The hot shower had eased the pain in my neck, but I still had a killer headache. What had I been thinking, drinking that much wine? Maybe Ilan had some aspirin. I opened the medicine cabinet. On one shelf, a razor, shaving cream, a tube of Polo Blue aftershave, toothbrush, toothpaste. On the bottom shelf, a green bottle of Excedrin and a yellow prescription bottle of little white capsules. What were they? I turned the bottle around. No label. I swallowed two Excedrin with water from the tap and slipped into the pajama bottoms and oversized sweatshirt he'd loaned me.

I guess I was more relieved than disappointed last night when Ilan made it clear I'd be sleeping on the couch. I needed a friend, not the kind of complications another lover would bring. Especially one who lived thousands of miles from me.

I sat on the disarray of sheets and pulled on a pair of Ilan's sport socks. They came up past my knees. I crossed my legs and pulled the quilt over my shoulders. My mouth tasted like a dead thing. Gray light filtered in through the skylights. No sound penetrated from outside. I missed open windows, the colors of sunrise, the sound of the wind rustling the palm branches, the chorus of birds announcing morning in Hawai'i.

I checked my phone. The battery was low and I'd left the charger at Mike's house. I had four missed calls. I was about to listen to my messages when a key scraped in the doorknob. I turned the phone off to save the battery and shoved it back in my purse.

Ilan came in with two large Starbucks cups in one hand, a couple of plastic grocery bags in the other, and a newspaper tucked under his arm. He set everything on the kitchen counter and opened the bags.

"I got coffee, croissants, and yogurt. And these are for you." He held out a toothbrush and toothpaste.

I went straight to the bathroom to brush my teeth. When I came out, Ilan had put away my bedding and folded my bed back into a couch. He'd made his own bed before he went out this morning.

He brought the coffee, yogurts, and bag of croissants to the couch and handed one of the cups to me. "Black."

I held the hot cup in both hands and took a careful sip. "This is exactly what I need right now. Thank you so much."

"Do you like Greek yogurt?"

"Greek yogurt? I've never tried it. I don't think we have it in Hawai'i."

"Here." He handed me a yogurt and a plastic spoon. "I got blueberry. I think you'll love it."

The yogurt was thick and sour, perfect with the tart blueberries. "This stuff is good."

Ilan bit into a croissant and took a sip of his coffee. "So, what do you want to do today?"

"I'd like to go back and visit Lillian. I want to see the apartment again, without Mike and Victoria and Brittney. Maybe take a walk around outside, too. It'll be my last chance before I head back to Hawai'i."

"Your flight is tomorrow?"

I nodded and scooped some yogurt into my mouth. "Ten in the morning. I'm supposed to check in at eight."

"I can drive you to the airport."

"It's a long way. Are you sure?"

"No problem at all. We'll be going against the traffic. If we leave here at seven it should give us enough time. We can swing by Mike's house on the way."

We ate in silence for a few minutes. Then he asked, "Would you like me to come with you to see Lillian?"

"Would you?"

"Sure. She'll be sitting shiva. We can pick up something at a bakery or a deli on the way."

Stuyvesant Town's Oval and surrounding playgrounds were deserted. The fountain wasn't in use. Ice sparkled from the same monkey bars I'd climbed on more than thirty years ago. Snow had been cleared from the sidewalks, but covered the grass and lay in piles ten inches deep around the garbage bins and on the bench seats. It was much too cold for anyone to sit outside, anyway.

"Why is all the grass chained off?" Ilan asked.

"No one is allowed on the grass. Security always saw to it that the rule was followed."

"What's the use of having so much grass if the kids aren't allowed to play on it?"

"It's funny, but I grew up believing grass was not to be stepped on."

We continued through the deserted grounds. A few joggers trudged past us, huffing out breath in white clouds. An Asian couple walked a small dog. Even the dog was bundled in a winter coat and boots.

"Look at this." Ilan pointed to a yellow sign that read, NO MUGGING ZONE $200 FINE.

He used his phone to take a photo of it.

"Is that going on Facebook?"

He touched the screen. "Already there."

I shivered and hunched my shoulders. "I can't stay out here much longer. Let's go see if Lillian is in."

We walked to the door and I pressed the intercom.

"Who is it?"

"Lillian? It's Louise."

"Louise?"

"Yes. My friend Ilan is with me. Can we come up?"

"Of course."

The door buzzed. Ilan opened it and held it for me.

We stood outside 10D. I lifted my hand, hesitated, then rapped on the door with one knuckle.

A moment later, Lillian opened it. "Louise, Ilan, please come in."

Nigel sniffed our legs and twirled his tail. Ilan reached down to give him a pat.

"These are for you," I said to Lillian. "Whole wheat bagels and a spinach quiche."

"Thank you so much. Would you like to have some now?"

"That's okay. We just ate."

"You can just leave them in the kitchen, then."

Yesterday, I hadn't seen the kitchen. It was just as I remembered it, shaped like an open-ended triangle that fit back-to-back with the kitchen next door, like pieces of a puzzle. The cabinets and countertops were the same ones I grew up with. Even with Lillian's peculiar decorative touches, it looked much as it always had. I pushed memories of my mother from my thoughts, put the bagels on the counter, and opened the fridge. It was filled with glass casserole dishes that must have been brought over by friends who came to sit shiva with Lillian. She wouldn't have to cook for a long while. I set the quiche on top of one of the casseroles.

When I came into the living room, Lillian was telling Ilan about the ostrich egg lamps. I took a seat beside him on the sofa, and Nigel jumped up and settled between us. Lillian was in one of the wildebeest chairs.

"The kitchen still looks the same," I said, for something to say.

"They only renovate the apartments when someone moves out. Then, everything is updated and they can charge market value for the rent. This apartment has been in the family since the sixties, and all the original fixtures are still here. The rent is still affordable, too. I imagine when I'm gone Mike will try to find a way to hold onto the apartment."

"The building doesn't seem to be maintained as well as it used to be," I said.

"When the new management took over, they had grand plans for improving everything. Unfortunately, it all fell through. They started with a landscaping beautification project. Block by block, the old landscaping was ripped out. Seventy-year-old trees were removed, with the promise they'd be replaced with new ones. A landscaper from California was hired to do the work. He brought in thousands of trees, and hired undocumented Mexicans to plant them. Instead, they threw half the trees into the Hudson River and tried to ride them home to Mexico."

"You're kidding me," I said.

"Absolutely not. I couldn't make up a story like that if I tried. Eventually, the rest of the trees were planted. But they'd been left lying on the ground so long, many of them died."

"We noticed the signs outside," Ilan said. "Good to know this is a no mugging zone."

"That would be the latest brilliant idea by the head of security, in response to a rash of assaults here."

"I thought it might be a joke," Ilan said.

"I don't know if I should laugh or cry." Lillian waved her hand. "I'm glad you came by today, Louise. I have some things I wanted to give you. Let me go get them."

"She seems really nice," Ilan said, when Lillian left the room.

"She is. I always resented her for taking my mother's place. Now that I'm getting to know her, I actually like her."

Lillian returned with a shoebox. "Mike took most of the family papers and photographs with him when he moved out. But Howard held onto a few things that belonged to your mother."

She handed me the box and I set it on my lap. She started to pull her chair closer to the couch.

Ilan jumped up. "Here, why don't you sit by Louise, and I'll take the chair."

Lillian sat beside me. "Go ahead. Open it."

I lifted the lid a crack and peeked under it.

"Go ahead."

I set the lid aside. The box held a stack of letters in envelopes, tied with a piece of white ribbon. The envelope on top was addressed to my mother, postmarked 1964, before she was married. I lifted the letters. Beneath them were loose photographs. Many were old black-and-whites, four inches square. The color photos of me and my brother as infants and children were more faded than the black-and-whites. My school pictures were here. I found my parents' wedding photo and studied it. Other photos I recognized as my mother when she was a young girl. I picked up a sepia portrait of a woman I didn't recognize, and turned it over. On the back, in my mother's precise handwriting, it said, Helen Louise Geraghty, 1938.

"This is my grandmother."

"Let's see," Ilan said.

I handed it to him.

"She was beautiful. Is she still alive?"

"Both of my mother's parents passed away when I was young. I barely remember them. They changed the spelling of their last name to G-A-R-R-I-T-Y when they came to New York."

There was a folded piece of paper tucked under the photos. I pulled it out and unfolded it. "It's a certificate of Baptism. Louise

Esther Golden. I was baptized? In the Catholic church?"

"Apparently so," Lillian said.

"That makes me Catholic, I guess. I had no idea." I stacked everything back in the box and put the lid on. "These are real treasures. Thank you so much, Lillian."

"You're very welcome. I have something else I want to give you." She got up, took a dark blue velvet case from a bookshelf, and handed it to me. "Your father's *tallis* case."

I ran my fingers over the Star of David embroidered in gold thread. Inside the star, Hebrew letters spelled out *tallit*. I wondered why I'd never seen it before.

"Your grandmother, your father's mother, embroidered it."

"It's beautiful."

"Do you want to take these things with you now, or should I mail them to you?"

"It would be great if you could mail them."

"While you're here, would you like to see the rest of the apartment?"

I glanced at Ilan. He gave me a little nod.

"Okay."

We stood and followed Lillian. She flipped the light on in the bathroom. A black cloth had been draped over the mirror.

When I was growing up, the bathroom had been pale pink: the shower curtain, bath mat, toilet tank and lid covers, and contour rug. As a child, I liked to play with the pink bobbles around the tank lid. We'd had pink towels, pink bars of soap, and even pink toilet paper. Lillian's taste leaned toward primary colors and bold patterns. A red towel hung on the bar, and the shower curtain had a geometric print in red, green, and black. The toilet was bare, and there were no rugs on the floor. The only decoration was a large African painting on the wall.

Lillian opened the door to the room that had once been mine and we were hit with the odor of oil paints and thinner. On one side of the room was a sewing machine and neat shelves of supplies. On the other side, two unfinished paintings sat on easels, and several more leaned against the wall. Her favorite subjects were sunny landscapes and seascapes in warm tones.

A foghorn sounded. I moved to the window and looked out. "I loved lying in my bed on winter mornings and hearing the foghorns." Most of the curtains in the next building were closed. "I used to stand here and look at the boy in the apartment down there. I watched him do his homework, practice his violin, and sometimes entertain friends." I turned away from the window and looked at Lillian's paintings. "These are very good."

"A little hobby I started when I retired," she said. "I still take classes."

Lillian led us to my parents' room. I froze at the door. Life had begun and ended in this room. My brother and I were conceived here, and this was where my mother died. Some of my happiest memories and worse nightmares took place right here. Could I bear to see it again?

Ilan gave my shoulders a squeeze and whispered in my ear, "It's okay."

I didn't know if he meant it was okay to go in, or okay if I chose not to. I stepped through the doorway.

My mother's vanity was gone. I used to sit at it for hours, trying on her makeup, perfume, and jewelry, while she lay on the bed and chatted on the phone. Now, the room held nothing familiar. Like the living room, it was decorated with African textiles, art and statues.

Lillian's eyes met mine. I nodded, said, "Thank you," and turned to leave.

Laurie Hanan

Chapter 20

We took the subway to the Museum of Natural History. The sixteen dollars admission bought us a whole day of entertainment. In the Rose Hall planetarium, on the first floor, we saw the world's largest meteorite. We went upstairs to the Hall of the Universe and played with the interactive astrophysics exhibits. A movie in the IMAX Theater educated us about the evolution of species. My favorite exhibits were in the Fossil Halls, which take up the entire fourth floor.

We stood in front of the Apatosaurus skeleton. I wished Emmeline and Jackie could see this place. "This would be so much more fun with kids," I said.

"I've come here with my sister's kids. They love it."

We went back down to the first floor and had a late lunch of soup and sandwiches in the café. Ilan took a small bottle from his pocket and emptied two white capsules into his hand. They looked like the pills I'd seen in his medicine cabinet.

He noticed me watching him. "Pain pills," he said, and washed them down with a gulp of coffee. "I hurt my back in a stunt last year and it's still bothering me."

A year seemed a long time to be on pain pills, but I didn't say anything.

We walked past storefront windows with elaborate Christmas displays, then crossed over to Central Park. Last night's snow had transformed the Park into a fairyland. All scale and detail was lost in the blanket of white. Icicles glinted on bare branches. Here and there, a spot of bright color stood out in the monochromatic landscape: red-ribboned wreaths hanging from lamp posts, a pink pom-pom atop a little girl's hat, a green umbrella floating above an old woman like a flying saucer, a delivery boy churning through the slush on his bicycle with a red pizza box.

"Do you like Israeli dancing?" Ilan asked.

"I love it."

"There's dancing tonight over on Broadway and 105th. We could hang around here, have dinner, then grab a cab over there."

"That would be great."

We wandered through the park. The black pathway showed through where pigeon footprints marked the snow.

"I wonder if I could make a snowman," I said.

"There isn't much snow."

I formed a snowball and rolled it over the ground, leaving a path of bare grass. When it was the size of a basketball, I set it on a bench. I made another the size of a grapefruit and set it on top of the first. Then a third, the size of a baseball, for the head. Ilan found two small branches and stuck them in the sides for arms. We collected pebbles to make the eyes, nose and mouth.

Ilan took his phone out. "Sit next to it."

I sat on the snowy bench and put my arm behind the snowman. Ilan snapped a photo.

"Facebook?" I asked.

"Of course."

There was no dramatic setting of the sun. The sky simply turned increasingly darker shades of gray until it was night.

"Hungry?" Ilan asked.

"Not really."

"Let's get a coffee and warm up."

We sat in a little café with bowl-sized mugs of frothy cappuccino and hot pretzels. Ilan popped another pain pill.

"Is your back still bothering you?" I asked.

"It's worse when I'm on my feet a lot. Which I am, most days."

We took a taxi a few blocks to the building where the Israeli dancing was held. Everywhere, holiday lights glinted off the snow, turning the landscape into a rainbow of color.

Ilan led me up a steep stairway. The music from upstairs was so loud, the steps vibrated under our feet. At the top of the steps, a woman sat behind a table with a metal cash box. A sign on the table said the entrance fee was ten dollars.

The woman came around the table, hugged Ilan, kissed him on the cheek, and said something into his ear. He laughed and said something back. While they greeted each other, I pulled a twenty from my wallet. When the woman sat again, I gave her the money.

"*Shneichem b'yachad?*" She asked if we were together.

"*Ken.*"

She stamped the backs of our hands with a Star of David, and we went in. The wooden floor shook under the weight of a hundred or more dancers. Colored lights swirled from the ceiling, disco style, and reflected off mirrored walls. A DJ at one end of the room oversaw the music.

Someone had probably paid several hundred dollars to rent the space for the evening. In Hawai'i, where folk dancing is not a major form of recreation, dance organizations can only survive as non-profits. Membership is encouraged, but not required. Members pay small yearly dues, and donations are collected at the dance sessions. I belong to several of the non-profit dance groups and sit on the board of the international dance organization.

It's different on the mainland, where Israeli dance is one of the fastest growing dance forms, with millions of followers. Dance leaders are incorporated, and folk dance is big business.

Men in the room outnumbered the women. A few women sat in chairs along the wall, but most danced with partners.

Young Israeli men gathered in the corners, watching, waiting for a turn to dance, maybe looking for a pickup. The mass of dancers moved in a clockwise direction, the more expert dancers in the center, those less confident forming an outer circle.

The song ended. Most couples changed partners as the music started again. Those who stayed with the same partner were probably married couples, or steady dance partners.

The dancers ranged in age from twenties to sixties, with a few in their seventies. The majority were in their forties and fifties, I guessed. The men were dressed in street clothes, the women wore leggings or tights with short skirts, like high school girls in a jazz dance class. Once again I felt out of place in my jeans, sweatshirt, and sneakers.

I laid my coat over a chair.

Ilan leaned over and shouted, "Would you like to dance?"

The song playing was unfamiliar, the choreography complicated. These people must spend hours every week learning the dances.

"I don't know this dance."

"Can you follow?"

"Can you lead?"

"Let's try."

He took my hand and we moved into the outer circle.

Dancing is an intimate act. It involves a surprising amount of physical contact. But it's more than that. Dancing with a partner reshapes the way two people interact. To dance well together, each must develop a heightened sense of the other's body. They have to be in sync mentally, too. The couple then becomes part of the flow of the roomful of dancers. I don't know if I should compare it to a religious experience, but that's how it feels when everything is just right. Until now, I'd connected on this level with only two men—Amos and Brian.

Our eyes locked. I resisted the temptation to look at the couples around us, and let him lead me. He anticipated the steps, gave me cues, and took me flawlessly through turns, dips and spins.

We caught a cab and arrived at the Chinese restaurant in Chelsea just before they closed at eleven. I stopped to read the handwritten sign that took up most of a front window:

We would like to extend our thanks to the Jewish people. We do not completely understand your dietary customs but we are proud and grateful that your GOD insist you eat our food on Christmas. Happy holidays.

We laughed and Ilan snapped a picture of the sign before we hurried inside.

Back at his apartment, Ilan said, "Let's have a picnic."

I spread the white carry-out boxes, chopsticks, and napkins on the floor in front of the couch. Ilan got a bottle of white wine from the fridge and opened it. He brought the bottle and two stemmed glasses and sat on the floor beside me, so close his knee touched mine.

He poured the wine and lifted his glass. "To friendship that spans the miles."

Friendship. Not love, or anything that resembled it.

He opened one of the boxes, used his chopsticks to take out a piece of broccoli, and tasted it. "This is really good. Try some."

I reached for the box. Instead of handing it to me, he took out another piece of broccoli and held it to my mouth.

What is *this*? I searched his eyes for an answer.

He smiled.

I opened my mouth. As I took the food from his chopsticks, a wave of heat started at my neck and flushed through my body. And it had nothing to do with the spicy food. A ringing started in my ears and for a moment my vision blurred.

I picked up my glass of wine, took too big a gulp, and choked. I put my hand over my mouth and coughed.

"Are you all right?"

I nodded and coughed again.

I finished my wine and Ilan held up the bottle.

"Just one more," I said. "And if I ask for a third glass, please say no."

He laughed and filled my glass.

When all the food had been eaten, Ilan picked up the empty containers and threw them in the trash under the sink.

He sat next to me on the floor again and handed me a fortune cookie. "Here. Open it."

My hands were trembling. I fought with the plastic wrapper, gave up, and tore it open with my teeth. Ilan already had his open. He broke his cookie and took the fortune out.

"Let me see," I said.

He held it out of my reach. "Open yours first."

I cracked my cookie and pulled out the slip of paper.

"What does it say?" he asked.

"It says, *Love is for the lucky and the brave.*"

"Are you lucky, or are you brave?"

"Not much of either."

"That's too bad."

"Now tell me what yours says."

He grinned. "It says, *Decide what you want and go for it.*"

"You're making that up."

"I am not. Here, read it for yourself."

He'd been telling the truth. That was exactly what his fortune said. Our eyes met. I wanted to look away, but forced myself to hold his gaze. He leaned toward me, took my chin in his hand, and gave me the most perfect kiss.

"Stay," he whispered into my hair. "Don't go back to Hawai'i."

Laying in the dark with my head on his chest, it was easy to imagine staying. What did I have to go back to, really? A job that was more drudgery than fun, a rented house that was barely furnished, a ten-year-old car ... I had no family in Hawai'i, no close friends. Brian would have no problem finding another dance partner, and another woman willing to take him into her bed.

Then I thought of Sage and Moondance. And Bob. What would happen to them? Who would Emmeline sit with in the evening to talk over her day? Who would give Gene a reason to keep playing his music?

And what about Enid? If I didn't come home, would Freddy continue searching until he found her? Or would he drop her when the next big news story came along?

"I can't. And much as I want to say yes, I can't."

He pulled me tighter to him and drew the comforter around us. "You've been trying to outrun something your whole life. One of these days you're going to have to stop running from the beast. Stop running, and let it catch you."

Chapter 21

I sat cross-legged on the dirty carpet. My cell phone and laptop were plugged into a wall outlet. At two in the afternoon, San Francisco was forty degrees, windy, and overcast. Inside the terminal, it wasn't much warmer than outside. I pulled my coat closed and sipped my hot latte.

I opened the laptop, logged into Yahoo, and scrolled through more than three hundred e-mails that had come in over the weekend.

There was one message from Freddy:

> From: FFriedman
> To: GoldenGirl
> Subject: Re: Raymond & Enid
> Date: December 19 03:58
> I checked out Lago Bar & Grill tonight. Sat at the bar, had a couple drinks and some pupus. On the way to the restroom I looked around but didn't see anyone who fit Enid's description. Raymond came in around 11. I knew it was him by his clothing and manner. I introduced myself and told him I want to do a story on his restaurant. He hesitated, like he didn't want anyone poking into his business. Then he invited me to a back office. We talked, and he started to relax. Comes across as a real nice guy. I think I convinced him I'm legit, and a story about his restaurant would bring in customers. I'll do the story so he doesn't get suspicious. He told me a lot about himself and his family but nothing that would pinpoint where he's keeping Enid. I'll fill you in on the details when you get back. See you soon. Freddy

Freddy assumed he'd be seeing me soon. He had no idea how close I'd been to not coming back. In Ilan's arms it was easy to imagine a life with him in New York—or where ever he happened to be.

This morning, Ilan and I had arrived at Mike's house at a quarter to eight. No one answered my knock. I called the house phone and Mike answered after several rings. He'd been asleep. It hadn't occurred to me that the whole family was on Christmas break, and they'd be sleeping in.

Mike came to the door in pajamas and a bathrobe. Ilan stayed in the car while I went inside to pack my things. Victoria and Brittney didn't get up. I said an awkward good-bye to Mike and was out the door.

Well, Mike should know I'm lousy at good-byes.

Ilan pulled up to the curb at Stewart Airport. He took my suitcase from the trunk and set it on the sidewalk. We stood in a tight embrace. He gave me a long, tender kiss, in defiance of the security guard who told us to move it along.

I eased myself out of his arms. "Bye."

He hesitated. I thought he wanted to say more, but all he said was, "Bye."

I watched him over my shoulder as I dragged my suitcase down the walkway. He waited by his car. When the terminal's automatic door opened, he waved to me. I waved back and went in. The door slid shut behind me.

Now, it was almost ten o'clock, San Francisco time. Almost eight in Hawai'i. I dialed my home phone and the answering machine picked up.

"Brian, it's me. I'm in San Francisco. I'm boarding in an hour, and scheduled to land in Honolulu at seven-twenty this evening. If you can't pick me up, I'll take a taxi. No problem." What else should I say? Did I miss him? Was I looking forward to seeing him? "Okay … I guess I'll see you tonight. Bye."

I exited the Jetway and walked through the chilly waiting area. The automatic doors opened with a hiss and I was greeted with Honolulu's heavy, moist air that smelled of plumeria and pikake. I was home.

I passed up a ride on the Wikiwiki Bus and made the long trek to Baggage Claim on foot. I pushed through the three hundred and fifty passengers from my flight and waited for my bag to come around.

No one checked my claim tags when I left the terminal. I could've been leaving with anyone's suitcase. Tourists wearing sweet-smelling lei packed the sidewalk with their luggage. Some carried surfboards. Taxis lined up at the curb waiting for fares to Waikīkī.

Brian wasn't there. I opened my cell and found his voicemail saying he was on his way. I sat on the hard edge of a stone planter to wait. Sweat prickled at my skin inside my sweater. I should've brought along a tank top, but I hadn't been thinking past the funeral when I packed to leave Hawai'i.

The funeral. Had it been only three days ago? So much had changed for me in that short time.

The crowd thinned until only a few people were left. My Z-3 pulled up with the top down, Brian at the wheel, Sage leaning out the passenger window.

Brian ran around the car and wrapped me in a bear hug. "God, I missed you," he whispered in my ear.

"I missed you, too," I said, and realized it was true. I'd missed everything about being home, in familiar surroundings, with people I've learned to read and predict.

When Sage heard my voice she let out a shrill yip and struggled against her leash.

"Sage!" I lifted her out of the car. "Oh, Baby. I missed you so much."

She squirmed, grunted, and wagged her tail double-time.

"I guess you missed me, too."

Brian put my suitcase in the trunk, then opened the passenger door for me. We got on the H-1 eastbound and merged with the slow-moving evening traffic.

"Does it feel good to be home?" he asked.

"More than I can say."

We didn't speak for the rest of the drive. The sights, sounds and smells were comfortable and familiar, and at the same time strangely new. Maybe it's a good thing to leave home from time to time, if just for the joy of coming back.

We took the Pali off ramp, made a left on Wylie Street, and a right on Alewa Heights Drive. Brian found parking near my house He carried my suitcase up the steps and opened my door with the key. He hadn't set the alarm.

The living room was neat and clean, everything in place. It felt so good to be here, I wanted to spin around with my arms spread wide. Instead, I said, "I need to change my clothes,"

Sage followed me as I rolled the suitcase into the bedroom. I pulled off my sweater, jeans, boots and socks and left them in a pile on the floor. I took a pair of flannel pajama bottoms and a loose tee-shirt from my dresser, put them on, and walked barefoot back to the living room.

Moondance was asleep on top of the piano and hadn't stirred since we came in. I picked her up and hugged her to my face. She purred but didn't bother to open her eyes.

Brian came out of the kitchen, a beer in each hand and sat on the couch. I joined him and settled Moondance on my lap. Sage jumped up and lay between us. Brian took a couple of generous swigs of his beer. I sipped mine and laid my head against the back of the couch.

"So, how was New York?" he asked, staring straight ahead.

"Freezing."

"Has it changed a lot?"

"It was like visiting a place I'd never been."

He drank some more. "Did you have a good time?"

"I didn't really go there to have a good time. I went to bury my father."

Brian finished his beer and stood. "I'm getting another. You want one?"

My bottle was still three-fourths full. "No, thanks."

He went to the kitchen and came back with another beer. He sat beside me and drank. Minutes passed.

"Marta said she saw you on Facebook," he said.

Ah…that explained his surly attitude. He knew I'd seen Ilan. "Marta?" I said, to give myself time to think. Marta has a big mouth, apparently.

"She said it looked like you were having fun."

I tried to remember the photos Ilan had posted on Facebook. There was the one of us on the ferry, with the Statue of Liberty in the background. Another of me in Central Park, sitting beside my snowman. Nothing incriminating, but I'd been smiling in both.

"I wouldn't call it fun."

"What would you call it, then?"

"Remember Ilan, the stunt man I met here three years ago?"
"Not really."
"Well, he's living in New York now. He came to the funeral."
"He must be a pretty close friend."
"For a Jewish man, attending funerals is a commandment."
"Then you went out with him after the funeral?"
"It wasn't like that."
"Like what?"
"Like going out."
"Why don't you tell me what it *was* like, then."

It was Brian who had never wanted our relationship to be exclusive. He hardly had the right to grill me about Ilan. On the other hand, Brian and I had been dating for five years, and now we were living together. I owed him some sort of explanation.

"The day we took Lillian home, I freaked out and ran from the apartment. That was when I talked to you. After walking miles, I met up with Ilan."

"You just happened to run into him on the street?"

"I called him. I was upset. I didn't know what to do or where to go. There was no one else to call."

"And he came to your rescue."

"You could put it that way. He looked out for me, made sure I was safe. He took my mind off everything and gave me a chance to get my head sorted out."

Brian drank more beer. He still hadn't looked at me. "Is there something going on between you and Ilan? Something I should know about?"

From the start, I'd wanted commitment from Brian, but he made it clear commitment wasn't his thing. He needed to be free to come and go. Hard as it's been, I accepted his conditions and learned to live with them. Apparently, the same rules didn't apply to me.

I turned to face him and tucked my legs under me. "Ilan is eight years younger than me. More like a kid brother than anything else." And what does that make me? "We walked around for a while, then he drove me sixty miles back to Mike's house."

Brian searched my eyes for any hint of deception. He once told me I'm easy to read, like an open book. Could he see I wasn't being totally forthcoming? I've always considered myself an honest person. And, until now, there'd never been a reason to lie to Brian.

At that moment I hated myself, and hated Brian for forcing me into the position of needing to deceive him.

He put his empty bottle on the floor, took the half finished beer from my hand, and set it down. His arms wrapped around me and he pulled me close. I breathed in his Irish Spring scent.

His mouth crushed against mine and his tongue forced its way between my teeth. His teeth cut my lip and I tasted blood. I tried to pull back, but he only pressed harder, his eyes staring into mine, full of desperation.

He let me go, set Sage and Moondance aside, and knelt on the floor in front of me. He started to lift my shirt.

I grabbed his wrists. "Brian."

His breath came fast. "What's wrong?"

All my life, I'd been completely monogamous, even when my partners may not have been. I'd never slept with two men in the same year, much less the same day. I couldn't do it.

"Brian. I've been traveling for the past eighteen hours."

"So?"

"I'm sweaty and exhausted."

"Do you want to take a shower?"

I nodded. A shower would give me time to decide how to handle the situation.

Brian stood, took my hand, and pulled me to my feet. I didn't resist as he led me to the bathroom, turned the shower on, lifted my shirt over my head, and eased my pajama pants down my legs. I'd run out of excuses.

I woke from a restless sleep. The ceiling fan turned slowly, pushed by a gentle breeze that blew through the open window. Outside, nothing stirred. What time was it? Brian's leg rested across my thigh, weighing me down. I couldn't turn over to see the clock without disturbing him.

I closed my eyes and tried to go back to sleep. I took slow, deep breaths, counting them. Every time my thoughts strayed, I started over at one. When I got to one hundred, I started counting backwards.

What is Ilan doing right now? He must be at work. Is he thinking about me? I closed my eyes and imagined I was back in Ilan's bed, imagined it was his shoulder my head rested on, his leg across mine.

No. What am I doing? This is so *wrong*, laying in bed with one man and pretending he's someone else. I eased myself from under Brian's leg, swung my feet down, and flinched when they touched the cold floor.

"Where are you going?" He rolled over to face me.

"I'm sorry I woke you. I need to go to the bathroom. I'll be right back."

I walked to the bathroom and closed the door behind me.

Without turning on the light, I sat on the toilet, rested my elbows on my knees, and put my chin in my hands. Oh, God. What kind of person am I? I've become the very thing I've always despised. Is this how cheating happens? I hadn't planned on sleeping with anyone while I was in New York. It had been the furthest thing from my mind. One thing led so easily to the next, and before I knew it, I was being unfaithful to Brian. And enjoying every moment of it. Did I regret it? Not at all.

I stayed in the bathroom long enough that, hopefully, Brian would be back to sleep. I flushed the toilet and looked into the bedroom.

Brian lay on his side, propped on his elbow. He held the comforter up. "C'mon."

I crawled into bed.

He wrapped his body around me. "The bed is so cold without you."

Laurie Hanan

Chapter 22

Tuesday morning I was back at work. With Christmas three days away, the volume of mail was heavier than ever. The sky was overcast, the wind strong. It poured hard, then drizzled, then poured again. Typical Christmas weather on the windward side. The going was slow as I delivered my load of cards and parcels.

When I got home, Emmeline, Jackie, and Dazy were waiting on my front steps. I got out of the car with a groan and shut the door.

Dazy ran down the steps to greet me. Emmeline followed, shoving her phone into her pocket.

"It's so good to see you," I said.

She threw her arms around me. "You're wet."

"After spending three days in the snow, rain doesn't seem so bad."

"I saw snow once, in Las Vegas. I loved it. But Jackie cried because his feet got cold. Mom put him in the front seat of the car with his feet on the heater."

Jackie stood and waited for me to notice him.

"Hi, Jackie."

"Auntie Louise! I brought you sumpin."

"What have you got there?"

He held up a fifteen-inch Norfolk pine in a plastic pot. "It's a Christmas tree. So you can get presents."

"Let's see." I climbed the steps.

Cellophane-wrapped candy canes hung from the branches, a string of popcorn looped over them. The star at the top of the tree had been cut from yellow construction paper and glued to a Popsicle stick.

"It's beautiful."

"I made the decorations myself."

Sage whined and scratched inside the door.

"C'mon in. We'll find a place to put the tree."

Dazy and Sage greeted each other while I looked around the

living room. I had no coffee table or end tables. I got a plate from the kitchen, laid it on top of the piano, and put the tree on the plate. "There. I hope Moondance doesn't knock it down."

Emmeline came out of the kitchen with the leash. "Can I walk Sage?"

"Me, too!" Jackie said.

"No. You stay here," Emmeline said. "I'm tired of you following me everywhere I go."

"Emmeline," I said. "That's pretty mean."

"Yeah, well, he's pretty mean, too." She hooked the leash to Sage's collar and led the dogs out the door without a backward glance.

I was left alone with Jackie. "You want to watch the Disney Channel?" I asked.

"Nah. Forget it." He ran to the door and slammed the screen on his way out. His footsteps pounded down the stairs.

I headed for the shower. When I came out of the bedroom dressed in jeans and a sweatshirt, Brian was sitting on the couch watching the evening news with a beer in his hand.

"Hey, Babe," he said.

"Hi. Where's Emmeline?"

"Sitting on the front steps with Sage."

I made a cup of tea and took it outside. "Can I join you?"

"Of course. I was waiting for you."

I sat down.

"I missed you," she said.

"I missed you, too."

"Really?"

"Of course I did."

"Did you have a hard day at work?"

"It's rough going back to work after a few days off."

"You must be tired."

I nodded. "I flew back from New York less than twenty-four hours ago. Then I didn't sleep well last night. Today I had to work three hours overtime to get all the mail delivered."

Emmeline was silent for a while. For once, her phone was silent, too. I sipped my tea and gazed at city skyline.

"Is he your boyfriend?" she asked.

"Brian?"

"Yeah."

Brian was only a few feet away and could probably hear our conversation. I thought how best to answer her question.

"He's my dance partner."

"I thought he was your boyfriend. Because he lives with you."

"He's been a good friend ever since I moved here. He's done a lot for me. He just started a new job, and he needs a place to stay for a little while so he can save some money."

Emmeline was quiet again. Finally she said, "There's a boy I like."

I knew it had to happen sooner or later, but I'd hoped it would be a while longer before she started liking boys.

"Does he go to your school?"

"He's in high school."

"High school? How old is he?"

"Fifteen—almost sixteen. He's a sophomore."

Uh oh.

"I'm thirteen and a half, so there really isn't that much difference in our ages."

Enough difference to make it a scary situation. The boy would be driving soon, if he wasn't already.

"So how did you meet him?"

"At church. The youth group started a band. I play keyboard, he plays bass guitar." She turned to look at me. "Louise, how do I keep a boy interested in me?"

Like I knew the answer to that one.

I wanted to tell her she's much too young to be worrying about such things. But of course I had my first crush when I was thirteen, on the boy who lived below us in the next building over. The one I watched through my bedroom window.

I thought for a moment. "Your question should be, 'What does he have to do to keep *me* interested'."

"Sometimes it's hard to figure out what boys are thinking."

"Don't I know it."

The screen door opened. "Okay if I make dinner?" Brian asked.

"Sure."

"Spaghetti with mushroom sauce okay?"

"Sounds wonderful."

The street lights were blinking on. "I still have this stupid curfew," Emmeline said."My dad still thinks I'm like eleven years old."

"You know it isn't safe to be walking around after dark."

"I'm not a little kid. I can take care of myself. Sometimes my dad is so irritating."

With that she dragged herself up and trudged down the stairs.

"Bye," I said.

She lifted her hand in a wave, but didn't look back.

We ate dinner on the couch, our plates balanced on our laps. I lifted a forkful of angel hair pasta and took a bite. The mushroom sauce was rich with butter and garlic. I washed it down with white wine.

"Where'd you learn to cook?" I asked.

"You like it?"

"This is the best mushroom sauce I've ever had."

"The trick is adding a little wine to it. I've spent a lot of years by myself. I got tired of fast food, but I hate to sit in a restaurant alone. I started experimenting in the kitchen. I only know how to cook a few things, but I do them well."

"You sure do."

I bit into a piece of garlic bread. It was browned just right and had the perfect amount of crunch.

I took a sip of wine, then turned to Brian. "How's the job going?"

He shrugged. "It's okay. I can't say I enjoy it, but the money's decent. He pays me a hundred dollars for each car I detail, and more for body work."

"A hundred dollars to detail a car?"

"Some of them are really bad. Dave buys Febreeze by the case."

I didn't know how to say what was really on my mind.

"Is something wrong?" he asked.

"No." I hesitated. "I'm just wondering if you'll be looking for your own place soon."

A wounded look crossed his face. "Is that what you want?"

Was that what I wanted? I didn't reply.

"I thought we had a good thing going here," he said.

"We do. Of course we do. I just had the idea it was temporary, until you saved up some money and found a place to rent."

"If money's the problem, I'll pay half the rent. I've already been buying the groceries."

"Money isn't a problem. Don't worry about it."

"Then what is it? Are you seeing someone?"

"No."

"Are you sure?"

I met his eyes. "Of course I'm sure."

He finished his wine and stood. "More spaghetti?"

"No, thanks. It was wonderful."

He took his plate to the kitchen, and came back with the wine bottle. "More wine?"

"I'm good. I have to drive tonight."

He filled his glass and drank. "You're going out?"

"I'm meeting Freddy. The reporter. While I was in New York, he looked into locating Enid. He wants to tell me what he's found."

"Why can't he tell you on the phone?"

"He's paranoid about phones."

"How late do you plan to be with him?"

"I'm not sure."

We sat in Freddy's truck and watched a steady stream of people go in and out of Lago Bar and Grill.

Freddy said, "Raymond told me his family raises fighting cocks on Guam. They developed their own line of roosters by mixing several breeds they brought back from Texas. Lago roosters are known all over the world for their speed and intelligence, and fetch a price of a thousand dollars apiece. The Lago family has done well for themselves."

"Cock fighting is illegal. How do they get away with it?"

"Cock fighting has been outlawed in all fifty states. But breeding, selling, and even training fighting cocks is still allowed in any state."

"You're kidding me."

"A few years back, I did a story on cock fighting in the Pacific Islands. In some US territories, including Guam, it's not only legal, it's sanctioned by the government. On Guam the sport dates back to Spanish rule. Now they hold fights every day of the week, in a big arena with bleachers."

"I don't see how you can call it a sport. It's barbaric."

"I agree. But in a lot of places it's as much a part of the culture as bull fighting is in Spain. No village feast on Guam is complete without a cock fight."

"How did Raymond end up in Hawai'i, in the restaurant business?"

Besides raising chickens, the Lago family owns a store in their village. They sell groceries and cold drinks. In the back they have a pool table, and a television hooked up to cable. It's a hangout for everyone in the village who has nothing better to do.

"Raymond told me he took over the family store right out of high school, which doesn't quite mesh with the story Enid told you. He never mentioned being in the army. He claims that even at age eighteen, he had a better head for business than his parents or any of his twelve siblings."

"There are *thirteen* kids in his family?"

"That's not at all unusual on Guam. Once he got the hang of running the store, he wanted more. He knew he could do better. His parents begged him to stay on Guam, but he talked two of his brothers into moving with him to Hawai'i. They started out leasing ag land from the State for a dollar a year, and growing chocolate and coconuts. They added a herd of pigs to the farm. When they'd saved some money, they opened Lago Bar and Grill. It's been successful, in part, because it's the only bar in the area."

Raindrops spattered the windshield. We closed our windows. Soon, heavy drops began pelting the truck.

Headlights turned onto the street.

"Don't let them see us!" Freddy shoved my head against the seat back and pressed his lips against mine as the headlights washed over us.

What's this?

I struggled. My scream of protest was stifled by his mouth. He pulled back just enough to speak. "*Shhhh.* Pretend we're kissing. We don't want them to see our faces."

Huh?

I stared into his eyes, an inch from my own. How does one *pretend* to kiss without actually doing so?

He closed his eyes, leaned forward, and touched his nose to mine. His lips found mine again and he ran his hands through my hair. His lips were gentle, his mouth tasted salty.

Just as I gave in to the kiss, the headlights moved away. Freddy sat back in his seat and looked out the window. A black pickup was pulling into the parking lot in front of Lago.

My breath came in gasps and I tried to calm it so Freddy wouldn't hear. While his head was turned, I ran my fingers across my lips. What had just happened?

"Is that them?" Freddy asked.

It took a moment to find my voice. "That looks like Raymond's truck." I spoke in a whisper, as if Raymond might hear me from sixty feet away.

The doors of the black pickup opened. Raymond got out.

"There he is," Freddy said.

Raymond walked casually toward the restaurant through the rain.

Two women got out of the passenger side. They grabbed each other by the arms and dashed through the downpour without an umbrella. Their squeals reached us through the closed windows.

"Those must be his sisters," I said. "The fat one looks like Tatum."

"Enid isn't with them."

"They must've left her at home—if she's still alive. What do we do now?"

"We'd better wait for them to come back out, then follow them."

"It could be hours. I have to work in the morning."

"Need a cup of coffee?"

"Sure."

Laurie Hanan

Chapter 23

"My father is a retired marine," Freddy said.

My body still tingled from the kiss, but Freddy seemed to have taken it in stride. "You must have moved around a lot as a child," I said, for something to say.

"I was born in Hawai'i, and lived here until I was two. Then we moved to Okinawa. I spent ten years there"

I sipped my hot venti latte. In spite of the strong coffee, my eyelids felt heavy. I needed to keep the conversation going or I'd fall asleep. "What was Okinawa like?"

"It was home for most of my childhood."

"Both of your parents are Jewish?"

He nodded. "Conservative."

"Is there a synagogue in Okinawa?"

"There isn't. But there was always a Jewish chaplain stationed there. Services were held in people's homes. It was okay when I was young, but when they expected me to study for my bar mitzvah, I rebelled."

"So you didn't have a bar mitzvah?"

"We left Okinawa when I was twelve, and moved to San Diego. My mother enrolled me in Hebrew school there. I had my bar mitzvah a year later."

"You must be a fast learner."

"I aced the Hebrew, then forgot it the moment the bar mitzvah was over."

"How long were you in San Diego?"

"I went to middle school and high school there. I hated it at first, but in time I got used to it. The year I graduated, my father retired. We moved back here."

"What did you do after high school?"

"I studied journalism at UH."

"So you've always wanted to be a reporter."

"Yup."

"Not a Marine, like your dad?"

"He always assumed I'd follow in his footsteps. When I was very young, I thought so, too. I finally realized killing isn't my thing. I started writing and it became a passion."

"Was your dad disappointed?"

"If he was, he didn't show it. My parents have been supportive of me."

"You're lucky. Do you have brothers and sisters?"

"I'm the oldest of three. My brother is two years younger than me. He's a marine. My sister is four years younger, and she's married to a marine. I'm the only rebel."

But he hadn't let his hair grow out. Or maybe he had, before the baldness set in.

The rain slowed to a light mist. Runoff from the street gurgled in the gutters like small rivers. Our breath had fogged the windows. Freddy took a rag from under his seat and wiped them.

He checked his watch. "It's ten thirty. I think I'll go inside. Maybe the sisters will tell me something Raymond didn't."

"You're leaving me alone out here?"

"Keep the doors locked. Give me a call if you see anything."

He opened his door and it *ding-ding-dinged* as he got out. He shut it and trotted across the street.

I double checked that the doors were locked and looked up and down the deserted road. I turned the key and the radio came on. It was already set to my favorite station. I cracked my window and inch, and sang with the music: *We got a thing goin' on/we both know that it's wrong/but it's much too strong ...*

Fifteen or twenty minutes passed. My coffee had gone cold. I finished it and set the empty cup in the drink holder.

Nothing much was happening across the street. How much longer would Freddy be in there? What would I do if I needed to pee? I pondered the logistics of peeing in the narrow paper cup.

A sharp rap on my window startled me. I turned. A dark-skinned man leaned against the truck with one arm casually on the roof, his face nearly touching the glass.

My mouth fell open, but no sound came out.

My eyes drifted from his face, which was hidden in the shadow of his hoodie, to the hand he kept in his front pocket.

He eased his hand from the pocket. The black barrel of a gun stared at me. Light from the streetlight glinted off the top of the shiny revolver.

I froze.

"I suggest you get outa here," he said.

If you want to get a message across, pointing a gun in someone's face is an effective way to do it. I wasted no time jumping to the driver's seat and starting the engine. I slammed the transmission into drive and stomped the gas. The big tires gripped the wet road, and I was outa there.

I barely slowed at the stop sign, then hit the gas again as I made a right. I gripped the steering wheel in an effort to control my trembling hands. Two blocks down, I pulled over. My heart pounded and I fought for breath. I left the engine running and watched the rear view mirror while I dialed Freddy's number.

"Yes?"

"A guy with a gun ..."

"Say that again?"

"There's a guy with a *gun* ..."

"Where?"

"Outside."

"Okay. Yeah. I'll meet you there first thing in the morning." He hung up.

He must be with someone. Maybe he was talking to the sisters. Now what? I watched the street while I waited. A few cars went by, none of them suspicious. The gunman must have stayed near the restaurant. What would he do to Freddy when he came out?

My phone rang. "Freddy ..."

"It's Brian." He hesitated. "Where are you? Do you know what time it is?"

The dashboard clock said eleven-eighteen. "I'm staking out the place where Raymond works."

"By yourself?"

"Yes, I'm by myself."

"It's late. Why don't you give it up for tonight and come home?"

My phone beeped. "Yeah, I think I will. I'm on my way." I hung up on Brian and picked up the incoming call. "Freddy?"

"Yeah, it's me. What happened?"

"This guy came up and knocked on the window. He pulled a gun out of his jacket and pointed it in my face. He told me to leave, so I did."

"Where are you?"

"A couple blocks away."

"I'm walking to the corner. Swing by and pick me up."

"Be careful."

I spotted Freddy and pulled over. He got in on the passenger side and fastened his seat belt.

"Did you see the guy with the gun?" I asked.

"There was a big guy leaning against the building across the street with hands in his pockets. I didn't see a gun."

"I'm not going back there. I want to go home."

"You've had a lot of excitement for one night. Let's go to your car."

I got home just before midnight. Sage threw herself against the screen door as I climbed the steps. The front door was open, the screen unlocked. Brian was watching TV with a beer in one hand, the remote in the other.

"You really should keep the door locked at night," I said.

He glanced at me then turned back to the TV.

I picked Sage up, closed and locked the door, and set the alarm.

I sat beside Brian. "What are you watching?"

He drained his beer and set the empty bottle on the floor with five others. "I don't know. Some stupid science fiction movie."

A commercial came on and he started switching through the channels.

"I'm going to bed," I said. "I have to get up early."

He ignored me.

I stood with Sage in my arms and walked toward the bedroom. "Good night."

I lay in bed with Sage, closed my eyes, and tried to tune out the droning of the TV on the other side of the wall. I'd kissed three men in three days. How had I managed to become the very kind of woman I've always despised? Of course, the time with Ilan was three days out of time. It had nothing to do with my real life.

And my kiss with Freddy tonight—that was only a pretend kiss. He said so himself. Pretend kisses don't count.

What makes a kiss just pretend? What makes it real? Is it what we're thinking during the kiss? What had I been thinking while Freddy kissed me? I couldn't deny it. Once I'd gotten over my surprise I thought, *I like this. It feels just right.* But that's not what Freddy had been thinking.

Do *both* people have to enjoy the kiss to make it real? When Brian kissed me last night, was that real? Or was it pretend?

Laurie Hanan

CHAPTER 24

Every table in the little restaurant was taken. I looked around and saw Freddy seated next to the window. He was wearing a white button-down shirt with the sleeves rolled to his elbows. The white set off his dark skin.

He saw me, smiled, and waved.

"Good to see you, Louise. Thanks for coming."

He stood and I thought he was going to give me a peck on the cheek. Instead, he pulled out my chair.

When we were seated I said, "It's good to see you, too."

And it really was. It felt surprisingly good to be with him again. I opened my menu, started to look it over, and felt his eyes still on me. I looked up.

"You look tired," he said.

"So people keep telling me."

"Hard day?"

I nodded. "I guess the bags under my eyes and my Phyllis Diller hairdo give me away."

"You look fine."

He'd just told me I look tired, but I let it go. I wasn't fishing for compliments.

"Where did you park?" he asked.

"There was no street parking. I ended up in a lot a couple blocks from here, across the street."

"I could have picked you up. Then only one of us would have to pay for parking."

"That's okay. Thanks."

"Don't want me to see where you live?"

"It isn't that." I tried to think of an explanation for why I didn't want Freddy at my house.

A waitress set a glass of water in front of me. Her floor-length Thai dress was jade green with elaborate gold embroidery. The other waitresses wore similar costumes, each in a different color.

"Ready to order?" she asked.

"Let's start with vegetarian spring rolls," Freddy said to her. Then asked me, "What do you feel like eating?"

Brian had made dinner earlier, and I couldn't disappoint him by not eating it. I didn't feel like I could eat another bite. "I'm not sure." I looked again at the menu.

"Give us a green papaya salad," Freddy said.

"I'd like the coconut curry vegetables," I said.

"The coconut curry here is fantastic. Should we have a broccoli tofu dish, too?"

"I really can't eat a lot"

"That's okay. I'm starving. Sticky rice?"

I nodded.

The waitress repeated our order.

"Everything mild," Freddy said to her. "And everything vegetarian. No fish sauce." Then he looked at me. "Is that okay with you?"

"Sure."

The waitress left.

"How'd you know I'm a vegetarian?" I asked.

"You're a vegetarian?"

"Yes."

"Me too."

"So we do have something in common."

The waitress returned minutes later with a platter of spring rolls, lettuce leaves, mint sprigs, and slices of cucumber.

I reached for a spring roll, burned my fingers, and dropped it. "Ouch."

"Watch out. They're hot."

We each wrapped a spring roll in a lettuce leaf, added mint leaves and a slice of cucumber, and poured sauce over it.

I took a cautious bite. "Mmmmmm."

"Isn't it great?"

I nodded while I took a second bite.

"How long have you been a vegetarian?" Freddy asked.

"About twenty years. I lived on a kibbutz in Israel and had to work with the animals. I couldn't stand looking into their eyes, knowing they'd be served up for dinner. Israel has the second largest vegetarian population in the world, percentage-wise. They accept it as a matter of course."

"It's the easiest way to keep kosher."

"Is that why you're a vegetarian?" I asked.

"That's only part of it. When I was going to UH, I worked for a professor of psychology. He was from Sri Lanka, and was also a Buddhist monk. He wore an orange robe around campus. At first I thought he was pretty freaky. Then I got to know him, and was impressed with the way he lived his life and the values he held. He never spoke to me about his religious beliefs, until one day when I asked him. Long story short, I became a Buddhist."

"I thought you were Jewish."

"A Jew never stops being a Jew, no matter what religion we practice. Anyway, Judaism is compatible with my Buddhist beliefs."

The waitress came back with the rest of our meal and fit the platters between us on the small table. While Freddy loaded food onto his plate, I pondered what he'd just told me.

He looked up at me. "Sorry. I'm really hungry."

"Go right ahead." I put some green papaya salad on my plate and used my chopsticks to taste it.

"You like it?" he asked.

I nodded. "It's good." I took another bite, then asked, "How can you be two religions at the same time?"

"You never heard of a Jew-Bu?"

I shook my head and laughed. "A Jew-Bu? What's that?"

"A Jew who practices Buddhism. There are lots of us. If you see a white person meditating with Buddhists, odds are they're Jewish."

I thought I'd heard of everything, but this was a new one. I let out another laugh. "I'm sorry. I wasn't making fun. It's just that you live in a world I'd never imagined."

He smiled. "Here—you've gotta try this curry."

I put a little on my plate and tasted it with the sticky rice. It was great, but I wasn't hungry.

While Freddy dug into his food, I checked out the activity on the other side of the window. We were on a busy stretch of Waialae Avenue, not far from UH. The area is home to a variety of ethnic restaurants including Thai, Japanese, Greek, Indian, and Italian. A steady stream of traffic passed by. Each time a car pulled out of a curbside spot, another was there to take its place. Couples and groups of students walked past the window.

"Not hungry?" Freddy asked.

"Not very. The food is great, though."

"We can pack some up for you to take home."

"No. That's okay. Really. I don't eat at home much." I needed to change the subject. "When you called, you said you had information for me."

He nodded, wiped his mouth with his napkin, and set it back on his lap. "Last night, after you left, I went back to wait for Raymond."

"What about the guy with the gun?"

"I parked in a dark spot, out of sight, but where I'd see Raymond if he left."

"How long did you wait?"

"They didn't leave until three A.M. I followed them."

He'd stayed three and a half hours after I left. And he'd done it for me.

He paused. From the look on his face, I knew he was waiting for me to urge him on.

"And…?"

"And I know where they live."

"You do? Where?"

"As you guessed, it's one of those small farms past the Hygienic Store. When they turned into their driveway, I kept going. I pulled off the road, gave them time to get inside, then turned around and drove up to their gate. It wasn't locked but a bunch of pit bulls guard the property. I made a note of the street number on their mailbox and left before anyone came out to see what the dogs were barking at."

"Enid must be in there. We have to think of a way to get her out."

"With all those dogs, no one could get past the gate and live to tell about it. It would be easier to wait until Raymond brings her out. He may take her to the restaurant sometime."

"Tomorrow's Christmas Eve. Maybe they'll all go to the restaurant to celebrate."

"We need to be there."

I took a drink of water, then rested my hand on the white tablecloth beside the glass. I gazed at the window, envisioning Freddy and I snatching Enid from Raymond's grasp as they arrived at the restaurant. We'd need a plan, and we'd have to be quick.

Freddy rested his hand on mine. I started. His touch sent a wave of warmth through me.

"I'm really sorry about last night," he said.

"Sorry? For what?"

"For what I did." At least he had the grace to look embarrassed. "I mean …"

I said it for him. "Sorry you kissed me?"

He shrugged and gave me a sheepish smile. "I was thinking on the fly."

"It's okay. I understand. We were just pretending." I held his gaze, wanting him to deny it.

He looked away, but his fingers closed around my hand. "I'm sorry."

"It's alright. You did a great job of hiding our faces. What they saw instead was a bald guy kissing a blond. Raymond is no fool. How long do you think it'll take him to put two and two together?"

"It was …"

A sharp rap against the window interrupted him. I jumped, pulled my hand to my lap, and turned to the window.

Janet from folk dancing grinned at me through the glass, a smear of red lipstick across her upper teeth. She gave me a wave and was gone.

Laurie Hanan

How Far Is Heaven

CHAPTER 25

December 24—the longest day of the year for postal workers. Every inch of my truck was packed with parcels and cards. I needed to hit the road and start my deliveries early if I was ever going to finish. Instead, I abandoned my route and steered my mail truck toward Kahikili Highway.

The suburban landscape retreated as Kahikili merged into Kam Highway. I passed Mitsui's Saimin House on my left, surrounded by groves of coconut trees. The bright orange Hygienic Store stood alone, looking like an outpost in an old western. To the right, a huli huli stand, with rows of chickens on spits, billowed smoke. The two-lane highway narrowed where it spanned an inlet of grey-green water that rippled like silk. Mokoli'i Island, better known to tourists as Chinaman's Hat, rose out of the Pacific. Soon, small farms appeared on the mauka side of the road. On the makai side, vacation rentals fought for space along the beach. I slowed and watched the numbers on the mailboxes.

A half mile past the Hygienic Store, I saw it. The rusted green mailbox sat crookedly atop a wooden post. I waited for oncoming traffic to pass, made a U-turn, and pulled up to the mailbox.

A muddy driveway led into a thick growth of vegetation that hid the property from the street. A few yards down the driveway, a pack of pit bulls approached a gate. They fixed their eyes on me, barking and wagging their tails. Beyond the fence, chickens and geese roamed, unafraid of the dogs. Goats stood like statues, staring at me with yellow reptilian eyes.

In this job, I've learned to sense which dogs are simply barking to announce my arrival and which would take a piece out of me if given the chance. This bunch seemed good-natured. They were trusted with the livestock. But dogs can be unpredictable. Misjudging even one dog this size, much less a pack of them, could prove fatal.

A breeze brought a revolting whiff of animal feces through my window. I put my hand to my nose. Maybe two dozen black pigs wallowed in deep muck, halfway between the gate and a small red wooden house with a corrugated tin roof. The upstairs windows at the front of the house were open wide, the curtains pulled back. A dog stood in each of the windows and barked.

If Enid was here, she'd be at the back of the house. There'd be no easy way to get onto the property and get her out.

"Hi."

I jumped and took my hand from my nose.

Raymond's brother, Joseph, had appeared silently, out of nowhere. He leaned on his crutches and watched me with his good eye, while the cloudy eye strayed.

He gave no indication that he recognized me, but I couldn't be sure.

"Hi," I said. "Merry Christmas"

No response.

I put the truck in gear, waited for a car to pass, and pulled away.

That was awkward. If their carrier hadn't already been here, Joseph would wonder why I stopped but didn't put anything in their mailbox. Or maybe he wouldn't think twice about it.

My cell phone rang. The caller ID showed my home number.

"Brian?"

"Yeah. You still working?"

"I'm at the station, just finishing up."

"Don't forget we're supposed to be at Anita's house at six."

Anita's house? At six? I looked at the clock on the wall. It was a little after five-thirty.

When I didn't reply he said, "We're going caroling. Remember?"

It had totally slipped my mind. I'd arranged to meet Freddy at nine.

Brian and I caroled with the international folk dancers every Christmas Eve. Even if I'm not crazy about Christmas music, I love to sing. And Christmas Eve is a rare chance to and socialize with the other dancers. It's always a fun evening.

"I'll be home as soon as I can."

"What should we take for the pot luck?"

"We'll have to pick something up on the way. A few bottles of wine, maybe."

"I'll run over to Foodland now."

It was almost six when I got home. No time for a shower. We'd be late as it was. I ran to the bedroom and stripped off my uniform.

"You have something red to wear?" Brian asked from the doorway.

"Red?"

"To go with this." He held up two red velvet Santa hats. "I picked these up today." He tossed one to me.

I opened my drawer and looked through my shirts. "Nothing red." I took out a long sleeved white tee-shirt. "This will have to do."

He leaned against the doorpost and watched me dress in a pair of jeans, the white shirt, my Reeboks, and the Santa hat. He put on his Santa hat and joined me in front of the mirror.

"Cute," I said.

When we pulled up in front of Anita's house, the group of carolers was just heading out. Brian ran inside to put the wine in the fridge. With our Santa hats in place, we hurried down the sidewalk to catch up with the others.

Janet looked me up and down before letting her gaze rest on my hat. She wrinkled her nose as though something didn't smell right, before saying, "Hello, Louise."

I gave her a nod.

As we followed the group to the door of a tidy white house, she sidled up to me and said, "I see you're with Brian,"

Brian overheard and gave her a puzzled look.

The carolers broke out in song. *"O come all ye faithful/joyful and triumphant ..."*

Someone handed me a songbook and I joined the singing. The door was opened by a frail, elderly Japanese woman. She appeared confused, but was too polite to close the door in our faces.

"Come and behold Him, born the king of angels..."

A couple in their forties joined the old woman at the door, followed by two children of about eight and ten.

"O come let us adore Him, o come let us adore him..." The voices blended perfectly and created a lovely harmony. *"... Chri-i-st the Lo-o-o-o-rd."*

The song came to an end. The Japanese family bowed. We

bowed back. They didn't close their door until we turned and headed back down the walkway.

As the sunset colors faded to black, a chill filled the air. For the next hour and a half we made our way through the Nu'uanu neighborhood of big, old homes. Most of them were two-storied with peaked roofs, built in the days when lots were ten times the size of the houses that sat on them. Many had brick or lava rock chimneys. All were decorated with strings of colored lights. Some front lawns had bigger-than-life nativity scenes, snowmen, Santas, and reindeer.

Janet stayed beside me. Her singing was badly out of tune and I was tempted to sing louder to drown her out. "*O little town of Bethlehem/how still we see thee lie ...*"

By eight o'clock we'd been through the song book three times. Feet and backs ached, voices were growing hoarse. Everyone was ready to head back to Anita's house, take a load off, and fill ourselves with Christmas goodies.

While the women arranged the pot luck dishes on the oversized dining table, Anita went around the living and dining areas lighting candles of various sizes. Wine and champagne bottles were opened and toasts were made. Brian and I filled our plates and carried them with our glasses of wine to the living room. We sat on the floor and left the sofas and chairs for the older and less flexible.

With so many people in the house, it was too warm for a fire in the fireplace. Instead, dozens of candles and the lights on the tree lent a holiday glow. The seven-foot Christmas tree was real and gave off a wonderful piney smell. I flashed back to the day I sat beside Ilan in Mike's house, enjoying the smell of the oversized Christmas tree that seemed so out of place at a Jewish funeral.

Roger and Patty joined us on the floor, sat cross-legged, and balanced their plates on their laps. In their fifties, they've lived together over twenty years but never married or had children. At folk dancing, the music is too loud to carry on a conversation. Now, we caught up on what each of us had done over the past year, and talked about our various jobs.

The conversation moved to the inevitable stories of pieces of mail that went horribly astray or were damaged beyond recognition.

Brian stood with his plate and empty wineglass. "Refill?"

"No, thanks."

He headed to the dining room.

"Some people think writing *do not mutilate* on a package will prevent it from getting caught in the sorting machines," I said to Roger and Patty. "It isn't like we sit around mutilating the mail unless instructed not to do so."

Roger drank half his glass of wine and forked stew into his mouth. He cleaned his handlebar mustache with a napkin. "I hear the postal service is going to have layoffs after Christmas …"

I only half-listened as I watched Janet approach Brian from behind. He was filling his glass. She said something to him and he turned to look at her.

Roger had finished speaking and was waiting for my response.

I said, "They hire hundreds of temporary workers for Christmas. After the holiday rush is over, their contract will end. Most of them will collect unemployment, then get hired again for tax season."

Janet's back was to me. She gestured as she spoke to Brian. Whatever she said made him freeze. He recovered, downed a full glass of wine, and poured himself another.

Patty was asking me a question.

"Sorry. Excuse me," I said, and hurried to my feet.

"Hi. What's going on?" I asked Brian.

"Let's talk outside." I knew him well enough to recognize the too-calm tone.

He set his glass on the sideboard and walked out the door, leaving it open behind him. I had no choice but to follow. He had the keys to my car. Janet's expression said she'd finally bested me at something.

I closed the door and ran down the steps. The lock beeped on my car. Brian walked around to the driver's side, got in, and shut the door quietly. He threw his hat to the floor, sat with both hands on the steering wheel, and stared straight ahead.

I slid into the passenger seat, closed my door, and pulled the stupid Santa hat off.

Minutes passed.

"When were you going to tell me?" he asked.

"Tell you what?"

"Don't play games." His voice broke—just a little. He looked at me and in the light of the streetlamp his eyes were red-rimmed. I'd seen him angry before, but I'd never seen him near tears.

"What did Janet say?"

"I want to hear it from you. What's going on?"
"Nothing's going on."
"You're lying to me."
"I am not."

He turned the key. The engine started and the radio came on. He slammed the radio button with his fist and shoved the car into gear.

Chapter 26

There was no place to park on the street. Brian drove up Dan's driveway and turned onto the grass behind my house. He shut the car off, got out, closed the door, and headed up the steps to the back door.

Up the hill, rows of colored lights outlined Dan and Doug's house. Their friends mingled behind the picture windows with drinks in their hands. Their Christmas tree twinkled red, green and white. Conversation and muted music drifted across the lawn.

My house was dark and deserted, the only one on the street without Christmas lights. Brian unlocked the door and Sage hurried to the grass. I waited for her to finish her business, then carried her in.

In the semi-darkness, Brian leaned against the kitchen counter with one hand and held a beer in the other.

I left the light off, set Sage down, and waited.

"Who is he?" Brian asked, staring out the window.

I took a few deep breaths to calm myself while I considered my answer. I had nothing to offer Brian but the truth. And the truth was, there was nothing going on between Freddy and I. We'd kept our relationship strictly professional. Even the pretend kiss, to hide our faces from Raymond, was executed with the utmost propriety. No tongues.

"I met with Freddy—the reporter—last night. He's helping me look for Enid. I told you about that."

Brian straightened and turned toward me, his face moving into the shadow.

"Janet saw us," I continued. "You know how she likes to twist the truth and make it into something it's not."

"So then *you* tell me. What *is* the truth? She said she saw you and *Freddy* in a restaurant with white tablecloths and candles. Are you going to deny that?"

"No ... but ..."

"Sounds pretty cozy to me."

"It wasn't like that. Freddy hadn't had dinner, so he …"

"She said you were holding hands."

"We *weren't* holding hands. Freddy …"

"Freddy. What kind of name is *Freddy*? People name their *dogs* Freddy."

I could think of nothing to say.

"Janet said he's *bald*." His voice rose. "You were sitting in a restaurant, holding hands with a *bald* guy."

I started to speak but he cut me off.

"What do you see in a *bald* guy? Named *Freddy*?" He was shouting now. "It's like a bad joke."

"I'm not …"

"Do you find *bald* men sexy now? Is that it?"

"*No.*"

He stared at me for a long moment, then flung his half-full beer bottle at the window. The window shattered. The bottle bounced off the window, hit the countertop, fell to the floor unbroken, and rolled.

I froze.

Brian walked past me to the bedroom and slammed the door.

My only thought was to clean up the broken glass before somebody got hurt. I took a tentative step and my foot slid in beer. I inched toward the light switch on the wall by the back door. A stabbing pain shot through my right heel as a sliver of glass pierced it. Warm blood pooled under my foot. I reached for the light switch and flipped it on. First, I looked around for Sage. She'd wisely retreated from the kitchen.

I made a wide circle around the broken glass to get the mop from the laundry room. Blood leaked from my foot and mixed with the spilled beer, making it look like more than it really was.

"Louise? Are you okay?"

"Oh ... Dan."

He stood outside the back door. "I saw your car parked on the grass, and then I heard glass break," he said through the window.

He had to have heard Brian shouting, too.

He opened the back door and stepped in.

"Keep your slippers on," I said. "There's glass on the floor."

"Who did this?"

"It was an accident. I'm so sorry. I'll pay for it."

Dan's eyes moved from the beer bottle in the middle of the floor to the darkened living room. "Where's Brian?"

"He's sleeping."

Dan looked back to the splotches of blood on the floor. "You're hurt."

"It's nothing. Just a little cut."

Dan took the mop from me. "You go take care of your foot. I'll clean up in here."

"It's okay. Really. You should get back to your guests."

"Douglas is with them. Go. Wash your cut and get a bandage on it. Make sure there's no glass in it."

I walked to the bathroom, stepping on the ball of my right foot. I closed the toilet lid, sat on it, and rolled up the leg of my jeans. I stuck my injured foot in the tub and ran water over it. The cut was small and there didn't seem to be any glass left in it. I dried my foot and wrapped it in gauze.

My cell phone rang in my back pocket. I dug it out and looked at the time. It was nine-fifteen. I was late meeting Freddy.

"Freddy," I said, not caring at this point if Brian overheard.

"Louise. Where are you?"

"I'm still at home. Sorry. My window broke and my landlord's over here. I'll be there as soon as I can."

"I'm parked across from the restaurant now. Raymond went inside about fifteen minutes ago with two men and three women. I'm pretty sure one of them is Enid."

Enid was at the restaurant. This might be our one and only chance to get her away from Raymond. I had to get over there.

I went to my purse for my car keys. Not there. They must still be in Brian's pocket. I opened the bedroom door. Brian lay on the bed, fully dressed, with his back to me. His anger was a palpable presence in the room. I wasn't about to be the first to break the silence, and I sure wasn't going to reach into his pants to search for my keys. I grabbed a jacket from the closet and closed the door soundlessly.

"Dan?"

The kitchen floor was clean, the beer bottle disposed of. "I think I got all the glass, but you'd better not walk barefoot in here."

"Thanks so much." I hesitated. "Dan, I have a huge favor to ask."

"What's that?"

"I need to run over to Kāne'ohe and ..." I didn't want him to know I'd been fighting with Brian. What reason could I give for not driving my own car? "One of my tires is shaky and I worry about driving it over the Pali. Would be okay if I take your car? I'll be gone a couple hours or so."

He reached into his pocket, pulled out a keychain, and removed a key. "No problem. Make sure you get that tire looked at as soon as possible."

"I will." I took the key from him. "Thanks."

"You know, anyone could come in through this window."

"Brian's here. We'll be fine."

He took one more look at the broken window. "Merry Christmas," he said, and went out the door.

Where was Sage? I'd better take her with me. In the mood Brian was in, I didn't trust him. He wouldn't harm her intentionally, but he might be careless and leave a door open. I switched the living room light on.

"Oh, *no*."

The little Norfolk pine that Jackie gave me lay on its side, half out of its pot. The candy canes and popcorn string were strewn around it. The top of the piano and the fallboard were covered in dirt. How could Brian do something so ... *childish*?

I strode to the closed bedroom door and yelled, "Thank you very much, Brian, for ruining my one little bit of Christmas!"

I went back to the piano. That's when I saw the neat pile of cat poop half buried in the dirt. Brian wasn't the culprit. Moondance had left her own little gift under the tree.

Chapter 27

I slid a pair of slippers on my feet, careful not to push the bandage out of place, and snapped Sage's leash onto her collar. As I walked past my car, I remembered the Santa hats. They'd be perfect to hide my hair, and Freddy's lack of it. From a distance, no one would recognize us. Good thing I'd forgotten to lock the car. I grabbed the hats from the floor and walked up the grassy slope.

Dan's black Crown Vic Police Interceptor is his pride and joy. He bought it last year at an auction, pimped out with as much equipment as is street legal for a civilian vehicle. I turned the key and the big engine rumbled to life. I drove down the driveway and headed toward the Pali on deserted roads.

What a fool Brian must think I am, yelling at him for ruining my Christmas. Like that was the only comeback I could think of after he broke my window. Since when had I ever cared about Christmas?

Jackie's gift had touched me. Having a Christmas tree made me feel connected to the rest of the world in a way I hadn't since my mother died. Like I was part of something bigger than myself. When I saw it lying on its side, destroyed, I immediately jumped to the conclusion that Brian had done it. I really believed he'd been that petty, and I had to say something petty in return.

Idiot.

On the other hand, Brian had been completely unfair in accusing me of cheating. Well, with Freddy, at least. Brian and I were both guilty of jumping to wrong conclusions.

But there are some lines that should never be crossed, no matter what. Brian crossed one of those lines when he threw the beer bottle. He had a lot of pent up rage, and it scared me. I knew I'd have to ask him to move out of my house.

Brian's outburst had frightened Sage, too. Now, she leaned out the passenger side window as far as her leash would allow and rested her chin on the side view mirror.

The big car purred up the hill and over the Pali. The air held a chill and stars glinted in the night sky. In Kāneʻohe, the 7-Elevens were doing good business. Everything else was dark and deserted. Two blocks from Lago Bar and Grill, I pulled over and dialed Freddy's number.

"I'm outside Napa Auto Parts, in a black Crown Vic. Why don't you leave your truck over here and get in my car. They won't recognize it."

"I'll be right there."

Freddy parked behind me and leaned in my window. "How about I drive?"

"Sure." I moved to the passenger side and lifted Sage onto my lap. She pulled away from me and was all over Freddy.

"Who is this little guy?" He scratched her behind the ears with both hands.

"This is Sage. And she's a girl."

Sage wagged her tail and sniffed Freddy's mouth. He laughed.

"She just wants to know what you've been eating."

"She's a doll."

I took Sage back and Freddy pulled away from the curb. "Man, I love this car," he said. "Whose is it?"

"My landlord's. I asked him if I could borrow it."

"Good thinking."

"Dan—my landlord—says it helps him get through traffic. People think he's a cop and want to get out of his way."

We drove two blocks and parked across the street from Lago. It was close to ten o'clock and the parking lot was full.

"Looks like they're doing good business tonight," I said.

"See that guy standing outside?"

An oversized thug leaned against the wall near the restaurant's door, smoking a cigarette. He eyed our car but didn't move. "Yeah."

"He's been there the whole time. Security, I guess."

"I bet he has a gun on him."

"No doubt."

"What kind of restaurant needs a security guard with a gun?"

"I don't know, but I'd swear there's more going on here than bar and grill."

I handed him a Santa hat. "Here. Put this on."

"What's this?"

"A disguise." I put the other hat on and stuffed my hair into it.

"No one will recognize us in these."

Freddy hesitated.

"Go ahead. Put it on."

"Okay. Why not." He pulled the hat onto his head and down over his ears. "Merry Christmas."

Now it was easy to imagine him with a full head of hair. Not bad at all.

"How long have you had Sage?" he asked.

"Two and a half years. Emmeline—remember Emmeline? You met her at the funeral."

"Sure. Cute little kid."

"Back then. Now she's a teenager. She found Sage wandering in the middle of traffic. The poor thing was a mess of dirty, tangled hair, covered in ticks. Emmeline cleaned her up, then tried to find her owner. Sage wasn't microchipped, and no one ever claimed her. Emmeline already has a dog—Dazy—and her parents wouldn't let her have another one. By then, I'd fallen in love with Sage. I'm not supposed to have pets in my house, but my landlords had already let me keep a kitten I found. I talked them into letting me keep Sage, too. The vet says Sage is completely blind, and has been from birth."

"She's blind? I'd swear she's looking right at me."

"It took me a while to realize something was wrong. It's amazing how she senses her way through the world. She'll even fetch a ball."

A car pulled into the parking lot and we watched two men go into the restaurant. Another man came out the door. He said a few words to the security guy before disappearing around the far side of the building.

Without taking his eyes off the restaurant, Freddy said, "That happens every half hour or so. Someone comes out the front door and goes around the building."

"I wonder what's back there."

"There's definitely something." A minute later, he said, "A friend of mine, a reporter, moved to Guam a couple years ago. He's working for the *Pacific Daily News*. I asked him to see what he could find out about the Lago family, Raymond in particular. The family is still in the chicken business, and still owns the village mini mart. Word has it they have their fingers in a number of other lucrative enterprises."

"Such as?"

"Illegal gambling. Prostitution. Looks like Raymond isn't the only entrepreneur in the family."

"Prostitution?"

"They specialize in blonds." Freddy looked amused when I reached up, felt around the edges of my hat, and tucked a stray lock of hair into it. He continued. "They cater to Asian construction workers. These men leave their wives and children behind and send money home each month. They live in crowded camps under poor conditions. The pay is better than anything they'd get back in their countries. Of course the men get lonely. There aren't a lot of blonds in Asia, and they're willing to give up a good part of their paycheck for the novelty."

"I don't imagine there are a lot of blonds on Guam, either."

"Not outside the military bases. The Lago family sends recruiters to the mainland. They hire the blonds and bring them to Guam to work."

"Hire, or kidnap?"

"Kidnapping isn't necessary, apparently. There are enough women willing to do the work. They're paid well, rent their own apartments, and have their own cars. They're free to come and go as they please."

"I don't suppose prostitution is legal on Guam, the way cock fighting is?"

"No. But the law looks the other way where the Lago family is concerned. One of Raymond's uncles—Ben Lago is his name—is a police officer. Uncle Ben is a partner in the family business. My guess is members of the police force are some of their best customers."

"Makes sense, if blonds are so rare over there."

"The Lago family controls that corner of the market." He hesitated. "There's more."

"What?"

"Ben Lago had a wife—Millie—who owned a beauty salon. A few years back, Aunt Millie was found dead in her salon."

"*Dead?* How?"

"She was duct taped to one of her salon chairs. Her tongue was cut out."

My hand flew to my mouth. White noise filled my head and the car around me started to spin. "My God."

"Her mouth was taped shut. Her lungs filled with blood and she drowned."

I focused on a streetlamp and the spinning slowed. The white noise continued.

"Raymond's car was seen parked against the door of the salon around the time of her death."

"He killed his aunt?"

"He admitted to stopping by to see her that morning. But he swore she was alive when he left her. As the wife of a police officer, her murder was investigated thoroughly. In the end, detectives said there wasn't enough evidence to charge anyone with the crime. It's still unsolved. Shortly after her murder, Raymond joined the army."

Freddy turned to watch the activity in the parking lot. Every now and then a car went in or out.

I couldn't get the picture of Aunt Millie, duct taped to the salon chair and drowning in her own blood, out of my head. To distract myself, I asked, "What are we going to do when Enid comes out? Do you have a plan?"

"I'm thinking we drive up to her, open the car door, and tell her to jump in."

"What if she refuses? She's terrified of them."

"Then you'll have to pull her in."

"Me?"

"I'm the driver. I'll get us in and out of there before they have time to react. I know the back roads around here. If they try to follow us, I can lose them. All you have to do is get her in the car."

"Sounds like a shaky plan to me."

"You have a better idea?"

"No."

"Climb into the back seat now. When we see her, I'm gonna go—fast. I'll stop next to her. You jump out and get her into the car. Don't take the time to talk it over with her. Just get behind her, give her a good shove, and jump in with her."

"What about the guy with the gun?"

"Keep Enid on the floor until I tell you it's safe."

I climbed into the back seat and called Sage to join me. She moved onto Freddy's lap and he rubber her ears.

We watched the parking lot and waited.

I checked the time on my cell phone. Twelve-ten.

A few minutes later, the restaurant's door opened. Three women walked out arm in arm.

"That's Enid in the middle," I said.

"Here we go."

Freddy turned the key, flipped the headlights on, and hit the gas. He tore into the parking lot and cut the women off from Raymond's truck. The car skidded and came to a halt.

"Now!" he shouted.

There was no time to think. I threw the door open and jumped out. Enid, Tatum, and the other women stood frozen in dumb shock. I grabbed Enid's arm and yanked her away from the other two. She screamed and tried to pull free of my grip, but she wasn't very strong. She lost her balance and one of her high-heeled shoes came off. I pulled her toward the car and she stumbled. I got behind her and gave her a shove. She shrieked as she landed face down on the back seat. The other women were screaming now, too.

I dove in on top of Enid. "Go!"

Chapter 28

Freddy spun the car around. I held onto the edge of the seat for all I was worth, my feet still out the open door.

Boom! A hole opened in the side window. The glass spider-webbed and round-edged pieces rained on me. Thank God for shatterproof glass.

"He's shooting at us!" Freddy shouted.

No kidding.

"Stay down!"

I tried to pull my feet in, but couldn't.

Sage must be terrified. Before I could say a word to her, the car jolted over the curb.

Boom! Boom!

The tires screeched as we made a sharp right. I bent my knees and pulled my feet into the car a split second before the door slammed shut.

I was on top of Enid, my face pressed into her hair. I lifted my head. "Are they following us?"

"They're right behind us. In the black pickup."

All my weight rested on Enid. I was twisted in an awkward position, but managed to maneuver onto the floor. Enid was sobbing, no doubt in shock at being kidnapped on Christmas Eve by two people posing as Santa Claus.

"Enid. It's me, Louise."

She rolled to her side, closed her mouth, and stared at me.

"Do you remember me?" I pulled my hat off. "From the hospital?"

"Louise?" She sniffed and wiped her nose with the heel of her hand.

Street lamps flew by. The car careened left around one corner, then right around another.

Boom!

We hadn't lost them.

Boom!
A bullet pinged against the trunk.
Boom!
I ducked my head and covered my eyes as the rear window shattered.

If we continued west, we'd soon be on a dark, winding two-lane highway with no way out. If we headed back toward town, we'd have to go through one of the three tunnels. Either way, we could easily be trapped.

I looked between the seats at Freddy. He drove like a hellion, his Santa hat flapping in the wind.

"Where are we?" I asked.

"Still in Kāneʻohe." He made a hard left. "A lot of these roads go a mile or two, then dead end. I'd better not pick the wrong one."

"I thought you said you knew all the roads."

"I do. Don't worry."

Enid was crying again.

"Enid." I waited until I was sure I had her attention. "We want to help you get away from Raymond."

We tore down residential streets, barely slowing at each turn.

"I don't see them." Freddy said. "I think it's safe to get up now."

"Enid. Sit up so I can get off the floor."

She struggled to maneuver so her feet were down and her head up, and tugged on her mini skirt to cover her underpants. I climbed up and sat beside her.

"Where's Sage?" I asked.

"On the floor," Freddy said. "She's fine."

I doubted very much she was fine. She had to be scared out of her wits.

"Sage. Come to Mommy." She cowered on the floor and didn't budge. "It's okay, Baby Girl. Mommy's here and you're safe."

We headed down Kam Highway. Freddy moved into the right lane and got on the H-3 South. Once on the freeway, it would be fifteen miles before the next off ramp. Ours was the only car on the road. We'd be an easy target, but it would also be easy to see if we were being followed.

I looked through the hole in the shattered rear window. "So far so good."

We entered the tunnel. Enid still hadn't spoken, but she'd calmed down. In fact, she seemed drowsy. How much had she had to drink tonight, on top of whatever they kept her doped up with?

We merged onto the H-1 West and took the first exit we came to. We were on Moanalua Road in Aiea. The black Crown Vic blended with the rest of the cars on the road, except for its blown-out windows. We turned toward Kam Highway and followed it through Pearl City and into Waipahu.

Freddy made a right and slowed to a crawl as he negotiated the narrow roads of a residential neighborhood. Cars lined both sides of the street, leaving room for only one car to pass. In this neighborhood the bullet holes in our car would draw little attention.

In spite of its high crime, Waipahu has become a tourist attraction during the Christmas season. Gaudy Christmas lights covered every house and lit up the night, making me think of Whoville in the Grinch movie.

A few more turns, and we were in a neighborhood of newer homes. Freddy pulled into a driveway and pressed a remote. The garage door opened.

"Where are we?" I asked.

"Waikele. My parents' house. We're going to switch cars, just in case."

We left the Crown Vic in the garage and got into a green Prius..

"Whose car is this?"

"My mom's. I'll call her in the morning and explain."

And I would have to explain to Dan why his car is riddled with bullet holes and the windows shot out. Would his insurance cover that?

We got on the H-1 and continued west.

"Where are we going?" I asked.

"My boat."

We wrestled Enid out of the car, got her into a standing position, and draped her arms over our shoulders. Freddy held Sage in his free arm and we half-carried Enid down the steps, then along the pier.

Freddy climbed onto the boat while I steadied Enid. He took her by the arms and pulled while I pushed. "At least the girl you decided to kidnap is a lightweight."

We lowered her to the cabin below, put her to bed with her clothes on, and covered her with a quilt.

Freddy took two more quilts from a cabinet. "Can you take these up to the deck?"

"Sure."

I settled on a bench with Sage on my lap. She still panted with fear, but rested her chin on my leg when I wrapped a quilt around us.

Freddy came up with a bottle of Chardonnay and two Lucite wine glasses. "I think we could use a drink." He sat beside me and handed me the glasses.

"I thought Buddhists abstain from alcohol."

"But Jews don't. I'm always a Jew first." He touched his glass to mine. "To a job well done."

It had been well done. We worked together with precision and pulled off the snatch, right under the noses of an armed guard and Raymond's sisters. And Freddy had done all this for me. He'd risked his life to help me. I couldn't think of any other person in the world who had literally put their life on the line for me. "Thank you."

He smiled and gave a little shrug.

I laughed.

"What's so funny?"

I tapped my head.

"What?"

"You're still wearing it."

He reached up and felt the hat. "I forgot." But he left on.

"What now?" I asked.

"Now we both could use some sleep."

I nodded. "I mean what will we do with Enid?"

"I have some friends here in the marina, a family with three young kids. They're sailing down to Tahiti in a couple days, then eventually to Washington State. I thought I'd ask them if Enid could ride along."

"How can she go to Tahiti without a passport?"

"Anyone on a private vessel is supposed to report their arrival to the authorities, but it's on the honor system. No one checks. Enid could live on their boat in Tahiti pretty much forever, and no one would know."

"You're kidding me."

"Not just in Tahiti. Boats come and go here at the marina all the time, from every part of the world. I know for a fact some of the people on them are illegals."

"With all the talk about border security, I can't believe it's that easy to enter the U.S."

"Believe it."

A minute later he said, "I'm going to sleep up here tonight and keep an eye on Enid. After all we just went through, I don't want to risk losing her again. If you like, you can sleep here too. She'd never get past the two of us."

I wasn't anxious to go home to Brian and the confrontation that surely awaited me. "That sounds like a good idea. I have to work in the morning, but not until nine. I'll need time to pick up Dan's car and drive it home so I can change for work."

"You have to work on Christmas?"

"Only eight hours. No overtime.

"What do you do at the post office on Christmas? It's closed, isn't it?"

"We still deliver the Overnight Express Mail. You wouldn't believe how many people wait until the day before Christmas to mail gifts, and expect them to be delivered on time."

Freddy moved to the port side of the boat and lay on the bench under his quilt. I folded mine double, stretched out, and covered myself. The thick plastic cushions crackled as I hugged Sage to me.

There was a rustling while Freddy got comfortable. "Good night," he said.

"Merry Christmas."

Laurie Hanan

CHAPTER 29

Rain fell in a light mist on my face. I opened my eyes to a dense black sky and pulled the quilt over my head. The rain came down harder.

"Louise?" Freddy said.

"Mmmm."

"Let's get down in the cabin.

Enid slept on her side with the quilt pulled to her nose. She didn't move when the light came on. I checked the time on my phone. Six-fifteen.

Freddy started a pot of coffee and turned a radio on. *Walking in a Winter Wonderland* was playing. "You don't want to hear this, do you." It wasn't a question.

He switched the radio off and we drank our coffee in silence. I could've closed my eyes and gone right back to sleep, but I needed to be on my way.

I watched Enid. Her face looked peaceful in sleep, but maybe it was the drugs. I felt no triumph at rescuing her, no horror in remembering the bullets ripping through the car. Those emotions would no doubt hit me later, after a decent sleep and time to process what had happened.

The rain let up. "Do you want to go to the restroom first?" Freddy asked. He held out the key.

"That's okay. You go."

When Freddy returned, I climbed off the boat and he handed Sage down to me. I carried her to the restrooms and set her in a patch of grass. When I got back, Freddy was talking to a man on the next boat over. I climbed onboard with Sage.

"Louise, this is Mack. He's going to keep an eye on Enid while I take you to pick up the Crown Vic."

We left Enid a note in case she woke up while we were away, and locked her securely in the cabin. Neither of us had much to say on the drive to his parents' house.

Freddy opened the garage and I got my first good look at the damage to Dan's car. Bullet holes riddled the trunk and the right side. The rear window and a side window would need to be replaced. How would I ever explain this to Dan?

"I'm sorry about the damage to the car," Freddy said.

"It wasn't your fault. This whole thing was my idea. If it weren't for your driving skills, we might not have made it at all."

He shrugged one shoulder as if it were nothing and handed me the key.

I parked in Dan's driveway and looked up at his house. After partying last night, they wouldn't be up this early. I closed the car door quietly and went home. Brian had my keys. I'd have to wake him to get into the house.

The smell of coffee reached me as I went up my back steps. He was already up. Or maybe he hadn't slept at all.

"Brian?"

He opened the back door.

I brushed past him, into the kitchen.

"Where were you all night?" There was no anger in his voice.

"I was with Enid."

"You mean you found her?"

"I found her, and I got her away from Raymond."

"How'd you manage that?"

"It's a really long story."

"Where is she now?"

"I took her to a friend's boat."

"I didn't know you had a friend with a boat."

"Well, I do." I headed to the bedroom to change.

"You want a cup of coffee?"

"That's okay. I already had one. I have to get ready for work."

"It's Christmas."

"I work every Christmas. Express Mail deliveries."

He followed me to the bedroom and sat on the edge of the bed. I turned my back to him and changed into my uniform.

"I'm really sorry about last night," he said.

I faced him. In all the years I'd known him, he'd never apologized for anything. I could never tell if he realized when he'd been unfair, or understood how much he hurt me sometimes. Now, I didn't know what to say.

"I'll get some wood to board up the window today," he said. "Tomorrow, I'll replace the glass."

I resumed buttoning my shirt.

"I know how wrong I was to talk to you like that. I've been under a lot of stress lately. Not having work, and now doing a job I hate. I have no right to take my frustrations out on you."

He waited for my reply.

"Louise, you mean a lot to me."

Since when? I tucked my shirt in and put on my belt.

He stood and took two steps toward me, but stopped when I held up my hand.

"Brian, I ..."

"What?"

"I don't know."

Since we met, I'd dreamed of a real, committed relationship with Brian. The kind where I wouldn't be afraid to say I love you, and he would say it back and mean it with all his heart. As sincere as he might be this moment, I knew he wasn't capable of the kind of commitment I need. The kind that means forever.

He took me in his arms. I tried to push him away, but he held tight. He spoke into my hair. "What don't you know, Babe?"

He pulled back and looked into my eyes. His face was a mask of raw pain.

I shook my head. "I don't know."

I couldn't bring myself to kick him out of my house on Christmas morning. I needed to put some distance between us. I needed time to think.

"I'm leaving for work now. Can I have my keys?"

On my way back through the living room I saw that he'd cleaned the piano, repotted the little tree, and put the decorations back in place.

Christmas Day has to be the easiest workday of the year. Everything is closed and traffic is almost nonexistent. All my customers are home, and they're overjoyed when I show up at their door with a package from Grandma or Auntie. The double-and-a-half paycheck helps to further lighten my load.

The day went by quickly and I got back to the station with time to spare. In the break room, a plastic tablecloth with a poinsettia print covered the utilitarian table. The skeleton crew of carriers sat on broken and mismatched chairs and enjoyed a small feast. I had some eggnog and pumpkin pie before heading home.

Everyone on my street was home for the day, and there wasn't an empty spot along the curb. I did what Brian had done last night, and parked on the grass behind my house.

A piece of plywood covered my broken kitchen window. I tried the back door. It was unlocked. Sage greeted me at the door and followed me to the living room.

Emmeline and Jackie were sitting on the floor. They jumped up, ran to me, and threw their arms around me.

"Auntie! Auntie!" "Louise!"

I hugged them. "Merry Christmas, you guys. Did you get lots of good presents?"

"Santa Claus didn't bring me a phone," Jackie said with a pout.

"You don't get a phone till you're twelve," Emmeline said. "Dad already told you that."

Jackie brightened. "But he brought me and Emmie new Boogie Boards and snorkels and fins and beach towels. And money."

"Mom and Dad gave us the money," Emmeline said. "They think we'll learn money management skills if we have to buy our own presents."

"Hey, Louise," Marta said from the couch. She and Brian each held a coffee mug, a plate of cookies sat between them.

Sage and Marta's dog, Ele'ele, stood over another plate of cookies that Emmeline and Jackie had abandoned on the floor. Moondance was probably behind the couch.

Speaking of Moondance ... I glanced at the piano. The little tree was undisturbed. No one would guess it'd been used as a litter box just last night.

What's this? A small silver box wrapped in red ribbon sat under the tree.

Brian got up and gave me a peck on the lips. "Hi, Babe. How was work?"

"Good." I set my purse on the piano bench.

"Would you like some coffee?"

"That would be great."

"Sit here with Marta. I'll bring the coffee."

"I made cookies today and brought some over," Marta said.

Jackie and Emmeline shooed the dogs away and took their places on the floor. Emmeline picked up her phone and started texting. Ele'ele watched Jackie select a cookie and cram it into his mouth. A string of drool escaped her mouth and fell to my Persian rug. Sage licked her lips.

Brian brought me a mug of coffee, then moved my purse to the floor and sat on the piano bench.

"Have a cookie," Marta said.

I picked up a sugar cookie with white icing and colored sprinkles and bit into it.

"Auntie!"

"What, Jackie?"

"Santa Claus left a present under your tree. Just like I told you he would."

I glanced at the silver box on the piano.

He jumped up, grabbed it, and put it in my hand. "Open it!"

The box was six inches long and two inches wide. I looked from Marta to Emmeline to Brian. I hadn't gotten presents for any of them. Which one had bought me something?

"Go ahead," Brian said. "See what Santa Claus left you."

Now Jackie and Emmeline were right in front of me. Behind them, Ele'ele and Sage scarfed cookies.

I pulled one end of the ribbon. The bow came undone and the ribbon fell away from the box. I lifted the lid. Inside, on a bed of cotton, was a diamond tennis bracelet.

I looked to Brian.

"Do you like it?" he asked.

I lifted the bracelet out of the box. "It's beautiful."

"Try it on!" Emmeline said.

I laid it across my left wrist and fastened the latch.

"That's gorgeous," Marta said. "Brian is one very special guy. If you ever decide you don't want him …"

I was looking at Brian's hesitant smile when there was a sharp knock at the back door.

Brian stood. "I'll get it."

The door opened and Dan's voice said, "I need to talk to Louise."

Oh, no. I'd forgotten to call him today about his car.

"Come on in," Brian said.

Dan rounded the corner into the living room, followed by Brian.

"I don't suppose you'd like to explain the bullet holes in my car?"

Chapter 30

"Bullet holes?" Brian, Marta, and Emmeline all said.

"Bullet holes! Oh, *cool!*" Jackie shouted. He took off for the back door, his feet pounding on the wooden floor.

Marta and Emmeline were right behind. Brian followed.

"Well?" Dan said to me.

"Uh…someone shot at me?"

Brian stopped in his tracks. "Someone *what*? What were you doing…?"

I hurried past Brian, out the door.

Jackie ran in circles around the car, shooting it with an invisible rifle. *"Peeeewww! Peeeeew! Peeeeew!"*

Dan caught up with me. I started to shake. Tears welled in my eyes and I covered my face. For the first time since the shooting, the reality of it hit me.

Dan wrapped me in a hug. "Hey. It's okay."

I leaned into him, and my knees buckled. He eased me to the ground. He sat beside me, put an arm over my shoulder, and pulled me close. I let go and allowed the tears to come.

Brian sat on my other side. Marta and Emmeline watched the drama from a few feet away.

"It'll be alright," Dan said. "I think my insurance will cover it."

I couldn't speak.

Jackie continued to shoot the car. *"Peeeeew! Peeeeew!"*

The dogs had joined us outside. Ele'ele lay in the grass, enjoying the sunshine, while Sage sniffed the plumeria tree. Moisture from the damp grass seeped through my jeans. We'd all have wet bottoms when we got up.

Dan said, "Before I tell the insurance company, I'll need to report the shooting to the police. What should I tell them? Who shot at you?"

I wiped my face with the neck of my tee-shirt, and took a deep breath. I told him the story, reliving the horror of bullets smashing into the car. I didn't mention Freddy. It was bad enough I'd gotten Dan's car shot up. He didn't need to know I'd let someone else do the driving.

Looking at the car, I knew the outcome could easily have been so much worse. "Enid is in a safe place now. Tomorrow morning, someone will help her get off the island. I don't want anyone to find out where she is. Not even the police."

"Don't worry. I'll edit the story so no one knows Enid was involved. I'll just tell the police I went for a drive, and someone shot at me."

I sniffed and wiped my nose again. "I am so sorry about your car, Dan."

"The car can be fixed. I'm just glad you're okay."

After a few minutes, Brian stood. He touched my shoulder, then joined Jackie.

Dan took my left hand in his and examined the bracelet. "Brian?"

I nodded.

Now Brian and Jackie chased each other around the yard in an imaginary shootout. Jackie shouted, "You're dead!" Brian clutched his chest and fell to the ground.

"So he smashes your kitchen window in a fit of rage, then tries to make up for it by buying you a diamond bracelet?" Dan spoke quietly so no one else would hear.

"I'm not sure that's how it was." But I wasn't sure that *wasn't* how it was, either.

"Next time, it might not be the window."

"Brian would never hit me."

"Don't wait to find out."

Brian ordered me to relax while he made dinner. I turned the TV on and switched channels. Good smells drifted from the kitchen. I settled on an old western.

Twenty minutes later, Brian carried our plates to the living room. "I thought you could use some comfort food."

He'd made mashed potatoes, soy 'chicken' patties, and fresh asparagus. No one had cooked a meal like this for me since my mother died. My throat tightened and I blinked away tears, hoping Brian didn't notice.

He said, "I used what I found in the kitchen. I'll do some shopping tomorrow when the stores open." He headed back to the kitchen. "Beer?"

"Sure." I quickly wiped my eyes.

He came back and sat beside me on the floor. "Burt Lancaster?"

"Yeah. I love his movies."

"Me too."

Sage waited patiently while we ate. Moondance slept on top of the piano beside the tree.

When the next commercial came on, I said, "Maybe we should plant the tree outside. Before Moondance decides to use it again."

"Tomorrow, I'll plant it in front of the house. Next Christmas we can string lights on it. It'll always be a reminder of our first Christmas living together."

The movie can back on.

When it was over, Brian said, "That was pretty amazing, what you did."

"What was amazing?"

"Pulling Enid away from Raymond's sisters like that. And you must've done some mean driving to outrun the guys who were shooting at you."

I nodded.

He leaned over and gave me a long, deep kiss. "I don't know what I'd do if something happened to you."

"Nothing's going to happen to me."

"I wish you had let me know what was going on. I could have helped. In the future, at the very least, I'd like to know where you are. In case something ... you know ... happens."

"It's over. Enid will be gone by tomorrow."

"Raymond is still here. He's got to be upset. He'll be out looking for her."

"He'll never find her. And he has no idea it was me who took her."

"Are you sure?"

"The one sister had never seen me before. The other one, Tatum, saw me only once at the hospital, and only for a few minutes. If you ask me, Tatum's not quite all there. She wouldn't remember my face. And, besides, I wore a disguise last night."

"Okay. But promise me you'll be careful. You have a way of

attracting gunfire like no one else I know."

"It's been three years since anyone shot at me."

"Until last night. Getting shot at twice in three years is pretty unlikely, at least in Hawai'i."

Sage licked the plates clean and Brian took them to the kitchen.

I followed. "I'll do the dishes."

"You go back and sit down. I'll take care of the dishes."

I touched the diamond bracelet. It glinted in the lamplight. Brian was trying so hard. Except for the one incident, our relationship was finally moving in the direction I'd always wanted it to go. So why did it make me so uncomfortable to have him in my house? Do I only want what I can't have?

Water ran and dishes clanked in the kitchen. A few minutes later, Brian came back with two bowls of ice cream.

"Mint Chocolate Chip? My favorite. You remembered?" It'd been years since we had ice cream together.

"Babe, I remember everything about you. Every word, every touch. And I'll never forget."

Chapter 31

I woke before dawn to a heavy rain beating on the roof. The wind howled and wet ginger plants slapped against the window. I left Sage in bed with Brian, brushed my teeth, and went to the kitchen to make coffee.

I sat at my desk and checked my e-mail. There was a message from Ilan. It said, simply, "I miss you."

I missed him, too. He was not only the sexiest man I'd ever met, he was probably the sweetest. Sexy and sweet are a rare combination in a man. But I could never keep up with his lifestyle. His career took him all over the world. Any woman in his life would either get left behind, or have to pick up and follow him around the globe at the drop of a hat. I needed a place to call home, a place I never had to leave. This island, with all its good and bad, was home now, and always would be.

"It's cold this morning." Brian said.

I jumped, and closed the e-mail. Had he seen it?

"Sorry. I didn't mean to startle you."

"I didn't hear you get up."

"Are you hungry?"

"Not really. Thanks."

He turned on the stove and dropped a pat of butter into a pan. I watched him crack three eggs into the pan and put two pieces of bread in the toaster. "You sure you don't want something? Eggs? Toast?"

I had no appetite. "I'm sure."

When his breakfast was ready, he took it to the living room, sat on the couch, and switched the TV to *CNN*.

I had to tell him today. While he ate, I rehearsed the words in my mind, over and over.

Sage walked through the kitchen and stuck her nose against the back door.

"Do you need to go out?" I opened the door.

Sheets of water cascaded from the roof. She turned around and headed back to the living room.

"What's the matter? You don't want to go potty in the rain?"

She sat at Brian's feet and sniffed in the direction of his plate. He took a last bite of his eggs, shoved the rest of the toast in his mouth, and set the plate down for Sage to lick. He took his dishes to the sink, refilled his coffee, and went back to the couch.

I sat beside him. "Brian."

He knew by my tone what was coming. He tensed and looked away.

I let out a long breath. This wasn't going to be easy. "It isn't working." I waited, but he didn't reply. "I'm sorry, but … you're going to have to move out."

He didn't ask why. He didn't want to hear me say it—that I didn't love him, that I was afraid of his temper. He didn't protest or beg me to change my mind.

I went to the bedroom, picked up the silver box with the bracelet in it, and held it out to him. "I know you're short of money. Maybe you can return it."

He shook his head. "It's yours. I want you to have it. For all the good times we had together."

He stood and went to the bedroom. Five minutes later, he came out with his guitar case in one hand, his duffle bag in the other. He set them by the front door and went to the kitchen to use the phone.

"Sorry to call so early … it's Brian … yeah … how are you? I was wondering, do you still have a room to rent?"

I unzipped the end of his duffle and stuck the bracelet inside.

"… is it okay if I come over now? … yeah … see you in a few minutes."

He opened the front door and picked up his things. "I'll be at Marta's house if you need anything," he said with his back to me. He went out and let the screen door close with a soft click. I locked it behind him and watched him head down the sidewalk in the rain.

Now what? I sat on the couch and stared at the window. The house across the street was invisible through the downpour.

My cell phone rang and I ran to get it from my purse. It was Freddy.

"How's Enid?"

"She's still a little groggy, but doing fine. My friend Becky—the one who's going to Tahiti—went to Walmart this morning to pick up some clothes and things for Enid. We got her settled on their boat. She seems to adore the kids. Becky and her husband will make sure someone is always watching her until they're out to sea. They'll set sail for Tahiti later today, weather permitting."

"I know I'll breathe a sigh of relief when Enid's away from here."

"Me, too. How are you doing?"

"Yesterday it hit me how close we came to not making it. I had a mini breakdown."

"I have to admit I was a bit worried when the bullets started flying. Are you feeling better today?"

I was miserable thinking about Brian. "Yes. I'm fine."

"Good girl. You can't spend too much time thinking about what might have been."

I nodded, even though he couldn't see me. "That's right."

Eventually, the rain let up. I took the decorations off my Christmas tree. "Come on, Sage. Let's go outside."

The Korean lady next door was working in her garden and I borrowed her spade. Sage watched me dig a hole in the front yard, far enough to the side so the tree wouldn't block the window if it ever grew big.

"What are you doing, Louise?"

"Hi, Emmeline. I'm planting the tree Jackie gave me."

"Can I help?"

"Sure. It's at the bottom of the steps. Bring it over here."

Dazy and Sage took off in a game of chase. Emmeline knelt with the tree, worked it out of its pot, and set it in the hole.

"Louise."

"Yeah?"

She hesitated. "When did you have your first kiss?"

So that's what's on her mind. She's way too young to be thinking of such things.

"Not until I was seventeen."

Which wasn't entirely true. When I was her age I experimented with kissing, with an older boy of fifteen. But nothing came of it, and a year later he was going steady with a girl he knew at school.

She pondered this. "When did you start dating?"

"I didn't have a boyfriend until I was seventeen. And even then, he wasn't exactly a boyfriend. We ran away from home together. I told you about that."

"My dad says I can't date until I'm thirty."

"That's probably good advice."

"Remember the boy I told you I like? From church?"

I nodded.

"He asked me to meet him at the movies. My dad says no, but I asked my mom to drop me off at the theater."

"Does your mom know you're meeting this boy?"

"I'm not sure."

She filled the hole with dirt and patted it around the tree, then stood and tried to brush the mud off her hands. "The tree looks good here."

"You did a good job." The tiny tree would barely be visible from the sidewalk, but with a little luck it would take root and start to grow. "By next Christmas it should be double its size. Let's go inside and clean up." I looked around for the dogs. "Sage? Dazy? Where are you?"

They came around the side of the house and stopped. They both had grins on their faces. Sage's entire bottom half was black with mud, and her face and head were coated in it.

"Oh, no. What have you done?" I laughed and they knew I wasn't really angry with them.

"I think we need to give them a bath," Emmeline said.

"Let's carry them in so they don't ruin my rug."

When the dogs were clean and dried with towels, we left them to play.

Emmeline opened the piano. "There's dirt on the piano. What happened?"

"Moondance knocked the tree over. Brian tried to clean it up but I guess he missed some."

She started to play *Toccata and Fugue in d Minor*. "There's dirt between the keys, and it's still out of tune." She closed the piano. "Can I have a cup of tea?"

"Sure. I'll make some for both of us."

She followed me to the kitchen. I filled two mugs with water, added tea bags, and put them in the microwave.

"How'd your window get broken?"

I'm never sure how much to tell her. "Brian got mad and threw a beer bottle at it."

"What was he so mad about?"

"He heard that I went out to dinner with someone. Another man."

"Did you?"

"I did, but he's just a friend."

"Do you even have a boyfriend? You said Brian isn't your boyfriend."

"Brian was getting close to being a boyfriend, but we weren't quite there yet."

"And there's nobody else?"

"Nobody."

The microwave dinged. We took our tea to the living room and sat on the couch.

A loud wail reached us from outside, and grew nearer.

"That sounds like Jackie," Emmeline said.

I went to the window and looked out. Jackie ran to my house and pounded up the stairs. I opened the screen and he stumbled inside. His lower lip was split and swollen twice its size. Blood and spittle ran down his chin.

My heart lurched. "Jackie, what happened to you?"

"Where's Brian?" he howled, tears streaming down his cheeks.

I leaned close and spoke gently. "Brian isn't here. Come on. Let's get you some ice."

I took his hand and led him to the kitchen. I wet a paper towel and carefully cleaned tears, dirt, and blood from his face.

"What happened? Did you fall?"

He shook his head.

I filled a Ziploc with ice. "What, then?"

"I want Brian," he sobbed.

"Here. Hold this on your lip."

"Dominic punched my mouf."

Dominic is oversized boy of about ten who lives a few blocks away.

"*Brian!*"

"Brian is at Auntie Marta's house. Do you know where she lives?"

He shook his head, on the edge of hysteria.

"Okay. I'll take you there and you can talk to Brian."

I hooked Sage's leash to her collar and grabbed my keys. "C'mon, Emmeline. We're going to Marta's house."

Jackie held my hand with one of his and pressed the bag of ice to his lip with the other, still sobbing. Emmeline led Sage on the leash and Dazy trotted behind.

"What's Brian doing at Marta's house?" Emmeline asked.

"I asked him to move out. He's renting a room from Marta now."

Brian's old white van was parked in the open carport beside Marta's shiny red one. Food smells drifted from the house, along with voices and an occasional laugh. Brian and Marta must be cooking together.

"Here we are," I said quietly to Jackie. "Brian's in there."

"Come wif me."

"Sorry, no. I can't. Emmeline, would you walk him to the door?"

She had her phone out and was texting. "C'mon on, Jackie."

I took Sage's leash from Emmeline and moved behind a dense red hibiscus bush. I didn't want Marta and Brian to see me and think I'd come over to spy.

Dazy looked at me and whined, then trotted after Emmeline and Jackie.

Marta answered the door. When I heard them go inside, I continued down the sidewalk. Gene lives a few houses away and I hadn't even wished him a merry Christmas yet.

We went up his front steps. "Knock, knock."

Pipsqueak rushed to the door. From his recliner, Gene said, "Oh, hi there, Louise. Come on in."

He struggled out of the chair and grabbed his cane.

I went in and greeted him with a hug. He was no taller than me and felt frail in my arms. "Merry Christmas. I know I'm a day late."

"That's okay. Did you have a nice Christmas?"

"I had to work."

"That's right. You always work on Christmas, don't you?"

"I do. But I'm off today.

"Then how about a little music?"

Pipsqueak and Sage chased each other around the crowded room while Gene and I looked through his boxes of sheet music.

He pulled out a yellowed sheet. "This one?"

"Perfect."

He made his way, slowly and painfully, to the piano. The way his gnarled fingers glided over the keys looked effortless, but I knew his arthritis made it painful for him to play. I stood beside the piano and sang, *Take my hand, I'm a stranger in Paradise/All lost in a wonderland, a stranger in Paradise...*

Laurie Hanan

Chapter 32

The parking lot at the Ala Wai Golf Course was nearly empty. I glanced around as I locked my car and climbed the stairs. I probably didn't need to worry about running into Brian tonight. He'd be getting settled in at Marta's house. But sooner or later he'd show up at folk dancing. When I asked him to move out, the decision included giving up my dance partner to the next woman waiting in line to grab him.

Frankie wasn't in her usual spot outside the door. I went in and saw her sitting in the DJ's seat, working the CD player. Her ever-present blue backpack lay at her feet. I ignored Linda's stare, picked up a folding chair, and set it next to Frankie. The dance circle was smaller than usual. A lot of the regulars were out of town for the holidays. The music was too loud for conversation, so I sat back and watched.

At eight o'clock, Patty stood at the front of the room and rang her dinner bell. "Announcements!"

Almost everyone headed to the lanai for a cup of water and cookies. I stayed inside with Frankie.

"Why aren't you dancing tonight?" she asked.

"I'm not in the mood. I just wanted to get out of the house and be around people."

"I know what you mean."

"What's going on with you?"

"I moved out of the place where I was living. Everyone in that house was insane."

"Where are you staying now?"

"I'm back on the street."

"That isn't safe."

"I sleep with my gun in my hand." She gave a nod toward her backpack. "And I always have my cell phone with me. Just call if you ever need anything."

Frankie changed the CD and pressed a button on the player. At the sound of the Balkan music, the dancers drifted back into the room. When the lanai was empty, Frankie stood and motioned me to follow her outside.

"This CD has eight good songs in a row," she said when we were out the door. "I have time for a smoke break."

I poured water into a paper cup and joined her on the concrete bench. She lit a cigarette, took a deep drag, and let out a stream of smoke. Out here, through the glass wall, the music was muted. I watched the dancers, middle-aged women and men holding hands and prancing in a circle like children, many of them wearing elf-like shoes with curled up toes. Suddenly, it all seemed ridiculous. Even so, it was such a way of life. I'd probably never give it up.

The music ended. The circle broke up and a new one formed as the next song came on. Janet pushed the door open and stepped onto the lanai.

"Where's Brian tonight?" she asked, a look of innocence on her face.

I held her gaze and it was she who ended the stare-off, for once.
"He's at home."

"He didn't want to come with you tonight?"

"He's exhausted. We had a busy weekend." I hoped to imply heavy romance going on.

Janet would learn the truth soon enough. Everyone would. But I wanted to put it off as long as possible. Once they all knew Brian and I had split up, I'd be fair game for gossip. And he'd be fair game for all the single women.

Janet looked as though she wanted to say more, but thought better of it. Frankie blew a cloud of smoke in her direction. Janet wrinkled her nose, waved a hand in front of her face, and backed away. She popped a cookie in her mouth and went inside.

It had been precisely two weeks since Brian moved in with me. I should have been happy to have my own space again, but I wasn't. The loneliness was a heavy weight in my gut, like undigested food. I crawled into the empty bed and pulled the comforter to my chin. The bed smelled like Brian. Tomorrow I'd change the sheets. Sage settled in next to me with a groan. Moondance lay on the window sill, where she could keep an eye on activity outside.

At the post office, two days after Christmas looked about the same as two days before Christmas. Even with a year to prepare for it, the holiday sneaks up on many folks. They mail their cards and presents well after the deadline for Christmas delivery. The volume of mail would remain heavy through the end of the year.

I was on the road when Freddy called, just before noon.

"I left you a message yesterday," he said.

The spark of pleasure I felt at hearing his voice took me by surprise. "Sorry. I guess I forgot to check my messages." Mental note: check phone messages more regularly.

"Enid is on her way to Tahiti."

"Thank God. I can barely believe we got her away from Raymond and off the island."

"It was pretty insane, wasn't it? This whole thing with Enid has probably been the most fun I've had in my life."

"I didn't think being shot at was fun at all."

"The biggest rush, then. It was wild."

"Wild, yes. But I hope I never repeat the experience. I've had all the excitement I can take for this lifetime."

"How did your landlord react when he saw his car?"

"Better than I expected. He's getting the windows fixed, but he wants to leave the bullet holes in the body. Knowing him, he'll have some fun with it. He'll make up a new story to tell each person who asks."

"We need to celebrate. Can you meet me after work?"

"I'll have to go home and change first."

"Will you let me pick you up at your house this time? Six o'clock?"

"I'd like that." I gave him my address.

"Wear a dress."

Minutes felt like hours. Each time I stopped on another street, I calculated the time left until seven o'clock. Which dress should I wear? The black one? I hadn't worn it in three years. Do I still have the shoes I bought to go with it? I should wear the pearl necklace and earrings. They'd look nice with the black dress. The evenings get chilly—I'll need a jacket. Will my hair be okay?

Haiku Gardens was my final stop before heading back to the

station at the end of the day. With one cluster of mailboxes for every twenty townhomes, delivery would be quick and easy.

I pulled to the side of the road and checked the time. Two hours and nine minutes until Freddy.

I grabbed the stack of letters and magazines from the tray, got out of the truck, and used my master key to open the backs of the mailboxes.

I heard footsteps and started to turn, ready to smile and say hello. Strong hands grabbed my arms and jerked them behind me. At the same time, a cloth sack was thrown over my head, pulled tight, and strapped around my neck. The world went dark.

A scream escaped my throat, and a hand clamped over my face. The rough burlap was crushed against my nose and mouth and I couldn't breathe. The envelopes in my hands dropped to the ground.

Something hard pressed into my temple and it didn't take much to imagine it was the muzzle of a gun. "Shut up or you're dead," a male voice hissed.

The hand eased off of my face and I gasped for air. The sack stank of mildew. A zip-tie tightened around my wrists, binding them together behind my back and cutting into my skin.

While one person grasped my arms from behind and held me in place, another worked at my belt buckle. I almost screamed again, but remembered the gun and thought better of it. My belt was slipped off, and with it the only weapon I carry—my can of pepper spray.

I had to get out of this alive. The best way was to cooperate, until I saw an opportunity to get away. And even that thought, I knew, was optimistic.

Rough hands groped in my pockets and took my phone and keychain. Someone locked the open mailboxes, then I was half-dragged down the sidewalk. A car door opened and I was shoved from behind. I lost my footing on the curb and landed face down on a car seat.

Someone got in from the other side.

"Get up." It was the same man who had spoken earlier. There were at least three of them, though I couldn't be sure how many. I was wrestled to a sitting position, then my head was pushed against my knees. The pistol pressed hard into the base of my skull. "Keep your head down."

The car started. We were moving.

Laurie Hanan

Chapter 33

Haiku Gardens was, for the most part, deserted this time of the day. But surely someone must have been home and glanced out their window when they heard the mail truck. Had anyone seen me being kidnapped? If not, how long would it be before my truck was noticed, abandoned at the side of the road? Would passersby help themselves to the parcels and envelopes in the open truck?

Sooner or later someone would notice something was amiss. Would they call the post office? The police? How long before anyone realized I was missing? How would they know where to find me? My hope of a quick rescue began to wane.

The other occupants of the car were silent. My face itched from the burlap sack, but there was no way to scratch. The sharp edge of the zip-tie cut into my skin. My hands tingled, then burned, and finally went numb. Would I lose my fingers? Would I even live long enough for it to matter?

After about fifteen minutes, we left the highway and turned onto a dirt road. The car came to a stop and someone got out of the front seat. I heard the creak of a gate, then the car was moving again, up a slight hill. The ground was bumpy and the tires kicked up rocks against the bottom of the car.

We stopped. The others got out, then the door next to me opened.

Nearby, several dogs panted. *Big* dogs.

A strong hand gripped my right arm. "Get out."

I stuck one leg out the door and the dogs started barking. They came closer and I pulled my leg back in.

"*Basta pachot-mu!*" a man shouted. The language was unfamiliar.

I heard a dull *whump* and a *yip*, as a shoe made contact with a dog.

The other dogs fell silent.

The man holding my arm said, "No worry. Dey no bite."

I didn't believe it.

He pulled me again. "Get out."

I stuck my leg out to keep from falling, then found the ground with both feet. I tried to stand, but my knees threatened to buckle. My heart pounded. There wasn't enough air inside the musty sack. He steadied me, and another pair of hands gripped my other arm. The two men held me upright and led me over a patch of rough grass.

"Steps here. Watch out."

The dogs panted at my heels as I was guided up three wooden steps and across a flat surface. I sensed a change in light and temperature. We'd entered a building.

A man's voice: *"Konne' gui' hulo'."*

A woman's voice: "What do you think you…"

"Fino' Chamorru! Maleffa yo'!"

"Dispensa-yo, Chelu."

They must be speaking Chamorro.

The man holding my right arm said, "Come." Our footsteps echoed as he led me across a wooden floor.

"Now, stairs."

I lifted my foot and found the first step. We took the stairs slowly, one at a time. I counted them as we climbed. On number seven, I stumbled. His hands tightened on my arm and stopped my fall. "Watch out," he said.

Someone followed close behind us. Sixteen stairs in all. We turned right, walked eight steps, then turned left. My shoe hit something soft.

He turned me around. "Sit."

The other person in the room walked over and two pairs of hands lowered me to a mattress on the floor. I waited.

The man who led me up the stairs kneeled on the mattress beside me, then shoved me onto my back. He leaned into me with his knee on my chest. I started to struggle, then felt the muzzle of the gun against my forehead. "Don't move."

I froze. My heart pounded, my body trembled. White noise filled my ears. I gasped for breath. Is this it? Are they going to kill me here and now? No. They wouldn't have brought me into their house just to shoot me. That could be done more efficiently in a cane field.

He took his weight off my chest but kept the gun on me. Slowly, one by one, he used his free hand to open the buttons on my shirt.

When he'd undone them all, he opened my shirt wide.

I knew the other man was still standing close by.

A cold knife blade slipped into one sleeve and cut it open. Then the other sleeve.

"Take it off," the other man instructed.

My shirt was yanked away.

Silence.

The gun left my head. My shoes and socks were removed. He slid the zipper of my pants down slowly, in no hurry. I lay still as he drew my pants down over my legs and pulled them off. All I had left was my undies.

He stood. What now? I felt their stare and wanted to press my legs together, but was too scared to move. I fought to control my trembling.

Finally, their footsteps retreated. The door closed. Metal slid on metal. A bolt lock?

They went down the wooden stairs.

How long until they returned?

I lay on my arms and struggled to draw air inside the smelly, oxygen-deprived sack. My head was spinning. As much as I longed for pure, fresh air, I was glad they'd left it on my head. As long as I didn't see their faces, I might have a chance of making it out alive.

It had to be Raymond's goons who kidnapped me. This could only be in retaliation for taking Enid. Was he here too?

Where had they taken me? What were they going to do to me?

A breeze drifted into the room from behind me. Through the musty sack I picked up the unmistakable stench of pig excrement. It mixed with the nauseating odor of mildew and urine that rose from the mattress. I dry-retched, then tried to calm my breathing. It wouldn't do to vomit inside the sack.

I listened. Outside, birds called to each other. Palm branches rustled. Chickens clucked. Geese honked. A dog barked half-heartedly. A rooster crowed. Then another. I was on a farm. Raymond's farm, or somewhere else?

I worked myself to a sitting position and inched backwards on the mattress, the zip-tie biting into my raw wrists. I came to a wall, leaned against it and drew my knees to my chest. My head touched what felt like a window sill.

Dogs scrambled up the stairs and through the room next door. A moment later, right behind me, toenails clawed against metal. The dogs whined and paced at the window. I flinched and ducked my head. How many were there? Could they get in here?

Downstairs, men and women discussed something, but I couldn't make out the words. A man shouted, *"Cho'gue hafa ilek-hu"!* and they lowered their voices.

Time passed. The room grew darker. The breeze turned cold and I shivered. Outside, the birds in the trees grew raucous for a while, then quieted. The dogs stopped pacing, but I could still hear their breathing right outside the window.

What time is it? Freddy would be at my house at six. Would he leave again, thinking I'd stood him up? How long before Darren realized I hadn't returned to the station with the mail? Had anyone found my truck?

Someone was coming up the stairs. The bolt lock slid.

I stiffened.

The door creaked as it opened.

I pressed my back into the wall. My breath came in gasps.

"I brought your food." A woman's voice. She set the plate on the floor and crawled onto the mattress. "I'm gonna take this off."

She undid the strap around my neck and slipped the sack off my head. Enough light came through the window so I could make out the mattress under me, but nothing more. Even so, I looked away from the woman's face.

"Now I'm gonna untie your hands so you can eat."

If they were feeding me, they must plan to keep me alive. At least for a while. Maybe the food was drugged. I scooted away from the wall and turned my back to her. She cut the zip-tie with a knife. I brought my arms around and tried to rub my numb hands together, but they wouldn't move.

She didn't seem worried that I might try to overpower her. I considered it for a moment, but dismissed the idea. From the corner of my eye she appeared strong—and she had the knife.

My hands were useless. Even if I managed to get past her, there would be the dogs to contend with. Not to mention the guys downstairs with at least one gun, probably more.

"Eat," she said. "If you gotta go batroom, use da bucket."

"I'm cold."

Without replying, she stood, went out the door, and locked it behind her.

I shook my arms. My hands burned as the blood started to flow through them. When I could move my fingers a bit, I opened and closed them until the feeling started to return.

Where had they put my clothes and shoes? I crawled around the room, feeling along the walls. In one corner, I found a plastic bucket with no handle and a roll of toilet paper. Nothing more.

I picked up the plate and held it under the window to get a better look. Dinner was chicken and a mound of dark-colored rice. Only a spoon to eat it with. The chicken had been hacked into bite-size pieces, bones and all, and boiled in a spicy, vinegary sauce. The taste would mask any drug added to it. Bile rose in my throat.

Outside the window, in the moonlight, three dogs lay on a four-foot width of corrugated tin roof. Beyond that, there was only darkness. It was impossible to see how far the property extended, what type of fence there was, or what was beyond the fence.

The dogs stood, stretched, and stuck their noses through the two-inch opening. I lifted one end of the mattress, scraped the chicken and rice to the floor, and let the mattress fall on it. The dogs whimpered and clawed at the window.

"Patience, fellas."

I remembered what Enid had told me about loosening the screws that held the window. I felt along the top edge of the window. A large screw was embedded in the wood on each side to keep it from being opened. I'd need a tool to get them out.

I examined the spoon. The end of the handle was squared. Would it fit into the slot in the screw? It did. It slipped a few times, but I finally worked one screw out of the wood. I placed it back into the hole and started on the other one. My captors didn't seem really bright. Hopefully they would think to check the window.

I set the spoon and the empty plate on the floor and leaned back against the wall. There were muffled sounds of eating and talking from downstairs. A TV came on, the volume high. Should I try to get out now, or wait until everyone was asleep? I hugged myself for warmth and tried to control my shivering.

Above the canned laughter of a sitcom, I heard slow, measured footsteps on the stairs. My heart raced.

The bolt slid back.

The door opened.

A light in the hallway silhouetted a man as he entered the room. I couldn't make out his features, but I knew it was Raymond. He closed the door and stood in the shadows, watching me.

I folded my arms across my chest and pulled my knees up. My heart pounded so hard it hurt. My body trembled.

He crossed the room, sat on the edge of the mattress, and folded his hands casually over one knee. The dial of his watch glowed in the dark.

I made a point of looking away.

"Do you know who I am?"

"No," I whispered. My teeth chattered.

"I think you do." He waited a moment. "And I think you have something that belongs to me."

"No." My voice quavered. "I don't."

"I want it back."

He reached out and fingered my hair. It took everything in me not to pull away. His hand brushed my face, his fingers felt the contours of my cheek. "And I think before too much time passes, you'll want to return what's mine." His thumb caressed my lips with a feather-light touch. "I'm a very patient man. In the end, I always get what I want."

He got up and left the room, closing the door softly behind him and sliding the bolt back into place.

Chapter 34

My hands shook and my body trembled, both from cold and from fear, as I lifted the corner of the mattress. I grabbed a few greasy pieces of boiled chicken.

"P*sssst*. Doggies."

They raised their heads and sniffed the air. Their toenails clicked on the metal roof as they approached the window. I dropped the chicken through the small opening. The dogs jumped on it, swallowed without chewing, and looked for more.

I pulled the loosened screws out of the window frame and raised the window six inches. I scooped up the rest of the chicken and rice and threw the food out. The dogs scarfed it up. They whined, stuck their noses through the window, and clawed at the wall.

I tried to clean the pungent, greasy sauce off my hands by wiping them on the bare mattress. If the food was drugged it should have some effect on the dogs. I lowered the window to its original position, curled up on the mattress for warmth, and waited. When the dogs realized there was no more food coming their way, they settled down.

Downstairs, the TV blared. I waited about half an hour, then eased up on my knees and looked outside. The dogs were asleep just outside the window. Should I cross the roof and jump off? What would I land on? How far was it to the fence, and how hard would it be to climb over it? And how many more dogs were down there?

Raymond might come back at any time. I tried to put the picture of his Aunt Millie—with her tongue cut out, her lungs filling with her own blood—out of my mind. But how could I? My only options were to stay here and take my chances with Raymond or jump off the roof. The choice was pretty clear.

I eased the window up. The breeze that blew in was chilly, tainted with the odor of pigs. The window scraped in the frame. I froze. The dogs didn't stir.

Slowly, I pushed the window up until it would go no further. I stuck one leg out, sat on the sill, and balanced, one leg out, the other in.

One of the dogs raised his head and wagged his tail, but didn't get up. I put my foot between the sleeping dogs, stepped onto the roof, and lowered the window. I crouched and inched toward the edge of the roof. Every sound was amplified by the corrugated metal, but if anyone heard me over the noise of the TV they'd think it was the dogs. Beyond the roof, nothing was visible in the darkness.

A light came on in the next room and lit up half of the roof and the sleeping dogs. I scooted back against the window, held perfectly still, and listened. Nothing.

I crept around the corner of the house until I was in shadow.

A back door opened and light spilled into the yard. The area was littered with old furniture, animal crates, stacks of boards, tires, wheelbarrows, and buckets. Joseph came out, balancing on his forearm crutches. Four dogs circled him, wagging their tails. He ignored them, sat on a wooden table, rummaged in his pockets, and lit a cigarette.

A brown horse appeared from the side of the house. It hesitated, then approached Joseph. He patted its flank, then looked into the distance. The horse started nibbling the corner of the table.

After a few minutes, Joseph looked in my direction. I pulled my head back, even though he couldn't see me in the shadows.

God, it was cold out here in nothing but my bra and underpants. The roof was like ice against my feet. I crouched against the wall, hugged myself, and shivered. The next time I looked at Joseph, he was gazing into the night sky.

Voices. I peeked around the corner again. Raymond was sitting beside Joseph. They spoke in Chamorro. A few minutes later, another man brought three beers from the house and joined them. This one was shirtless and looked like he spent a lot of time at the gym. "Hey, man," Raymond said. He handed beers to Raymond and Joseph, then took one of Joseph's cigarettes. Raymond apparently didn't smoke.

Now the conversation was in English, but I only caught a few words. Every now and then Raymond glanced at my window, and the other two would follow his gaze. Raymond stood and took another long look at the window before going back into the house.

No way could I chance jumping off the roof with them so near. They'd be on top of me before I got to my feet. Raymond had to be planning another visit to my room tonight. He might be on his way upstairs right now. If I stayed here, it would only be a matter of time before he found me. From what Enid had said, my trying to outsmart him could send him into a rage.

By now I was shivering so hard I could barely move. Maybe I should go back inside, where I'd at least be out of the wind. If I returned the window to its original position, no one would suspect I'd been out. Raymond wasn't going to kill me—at least not tonight. This was a game for him. He'd toy with me and drag out the fun as long as he could, sure that in the end he'd get everything he wanted.

He'd expect me to fight back. If I pretended I was drugged—totally out of it—he'd eventually lose interest. He'd leave me be until I could put up more of a fight. Then, once everyone was in bed, I'd sneak away.

No. I couldn't do it. The thought of Raymond touching me made me want to scream. I couldn't go back inside. My only other choice was to jump down. And that wasn't a good option until these guys went back in the house.

The roof above me was about nine feet up at its lowest point. Was there any way to climb up there? On this side of the house there was a darkened window, about two feet square. Probably a bathroom. Above it, a row of round vents just below the roof. Maybe enough to get a finger hold. I'd have to be sure of myself. A fall from here would be disastrous.

I stretched my leg up and got one foot on the window frame. My fingers gripped the top of the frame, and I eased myself up. The screen covering the vents was old, and ripped in some places. I tore one screen away, got my fingers into the vent, and held on. My other hand found the top of the roof. I wedged my toes against the top of the window frame and pulled my torso onto the roof. The sharp edge of the metal scraped my belly. I lay there with my arms stretched in front of me, my legs dangling. I got one knee onto the roof and slowly, quietly, brought the other up. I listened for a moment, then crawled up to the peak.

From this vantage point both sides of the house were visible. Joseph and the shirtless guy were still talking and smoking in the back. The horse had eaten away a corner of the table and was still munching. In front of the house, light from the nearly full moon glinted off the wet muck in the pig enclosure. The pigs huddled together at the far end of the pen. An acre or so of coconut trees grew in neat rows to the right.

"*Sona ba bi tsi,*" Raymond bellowed. He was below me, in the room I'd just left.

Shirtless hopped off the table and yelled, "What happened?" as he ran inside.

The dogs followed him into the house, and Joseph struggled on his crutches. Footsteps pounded up the stairs.

"She's gone!" Raymond shouted. "You stupid *idiots*! Find her!"

More footsteps on the stairs. Shirtless burst out the back door. The horse startled, tossed its head, and trotted to the side of the house. Shirtless walked through the debris that littered the yard, shining a flashlight over every possible hiding spot. A large pistol stuck out of the waistband of his jeans.

The front door slammed open and someone pounded down the front steps. It was Raymond. He must have a gun too, though I didn't see one. He walked calmly and deliberately through the property with a flashlight, as if he were in no hurry at all. Below me, inside the house, two women talked excitedly in Chamorro as they went from room to room.

The scrapes on my belly stung. I stretched out along the peak of the roof, shivering so hard I was afraid I'd shake myself right off.

A large vehicle—a truck or SUV—turned off the highway. Its high beams lit up the property. The dogs ran to the gate, barking. Raymond must have called for backup.

Instead of stopping to open the gate, the driver gunned the engine. There was a tremendous crash as wood splintered and metal ripped. The dogs scattered. The truck raced up the driveway with the mangled gate across its windshield.

For a split second, Raymond froze. Then he drew a pistol from his waistband, steadied it in a two-arm stance, and fired at the oncoming truck. It swerved into the pig enclosure, ripping the fence out before coming to a stop. The herd of pigs squealed and pressed against the far fence.

Someone in the truck fired several shots back at Raymond. The dogs barked from their hiding spots. Raymond got off two more shots as he dove behind the pig trough.

Silence.

It was impossible to make out anything of the truck or its occupants behind the glare of the headlights. Who was in the truck? Had they been hit?

Shirtless took cover behind an old Civic and fired several shots at the truck. Return fire blew out the Civic's windows. The pigs stampeded through the torn fence and scattered. The dogs barked.

Joseph hobbled out of the house on his crutches, a large pistol in his right hand.

"Joseph! Get down!" Shirtless yelled.

Joseph balanced on his crutches, took aim with both hands, and fired at the truck. Shirtless fired several more rounds as Joseph moved to join Raymond behind the trough.

All three of them opened fire on the truck. Someone in truck shot back. That meant at least one person in the truck was still alive, but they were outnumbered. They didn't have a chance.

Glass shattered in front of the house and the women inside started screaming.

The horse neighed and I turned to see if it was hurt. It stomped in circles, terrified, but appeared unharmed. The dogs on the roof still hadn't awakened.

Shirtless fired again from behind the car. Joseph hunched against the pig trough, reloading.

Where was Raymond?

The women stopped screaming. Footsteps pounded up the stairs. A window creaked open. Someone was coming out onto the first floor.

I froze. Had someone seen me?

Something scraped against the side of the house. I waited. A hand reached up and gripped the edge of the roof. Then another. A head rose, and Raymond's eyes locked with mine. He grinned. Then he reached down with one hand. He was going for his gun.

There was no time to formulate a plan. I stood and ran straight at him. He barely had time to register surprise before I dropped to my butt and kicked out with both feet. He let out a groan as my feet connected with his face. He lost his grip, landed with a loud thud on the roof below, bounced, and somersaulted. He got off one shot at me as he rolled off the roof and tumbled to the ground.

W*hump.*

I tried to grab the slippery metal, but the roof was too steep, my momentum too great. I went over the edge and slammed, belly first, onto the roof below. I lay there, stunned, unable to draw breath.

The gunfire had stopped.

Finally, the tightness in my chest started to ease. When I could breathe again, I stood and looked over the edge. There was no sign of Raymond. I made my way around to the front of the house.

A motorcycle roared off the highway and through the gate at high speed. Joseph stood, aimed at the motorcycle, and fired. It veered off the dirt drive and into the pigpen, spraying an arc of mud and pig excrement over everything. The stench was nauseating.

Joseph stood his ground and fired again. The motorcycle skidded, fell to its side, and slid twenty feet, heading straight for Joseph. He turned to run, but it was too late. The bike bowled him over.

Shirtless ran toward Joseph. The bike's engine screamed as the rear wheel spun a fountain of muck into the air. Shirtless raised an arm to shield his eyes as the black goo splattered across his face.

The biker pulled himself to his feet. He tried to run toward the pickup, but the knee-deep filth sucked at his legs. The motorcycle sputtered and died. All was quiet. Joseph lifted his arm and fired. The biker staggered one step, then another, and went down in the muck.

Sirens wailed.

Two police cars careened through the broken gate with flashing blue lights. Shirtless took off into the coconut grove and disappeared in the darkness. Joseph struggled, but was pinned under the motorcycle.

The police slid to a stop behind the truck. Four officers got out with their guns drawn. "Police! Drop your weapons!"

Joseph tossed his gun aside and raised his hands. A pistol dropped from the pickup and a pair of hands stuck out of each side window.

I stood and waved my arms. "Hey! Up here!"

The truck's doors opened. Someone stepped out of each side, but behind the headlights' glare I couldn't see them clearly.

"Louise?" It was Brian!

"I'm here, too!" And Freddy!

But how ... ?

I didn't care how. All I could think of was running and throwing myself into their arms, the way they do in the movies. But it was a long drop to the ground. Did I dare go into the house through a window? No way. Raymond might be in there. He'd take me hostage and that would be the end of that.

The horse was standing just under the edge of the roof. Could I slide down and onto his back? Then it would be an easy drop to the ground. Burt Lancaster did it in the movie I watched the other day. If he could do it, no reason why I couldn't.

I positioned myself just above the horse, lay on my belly, and dangled my legs over the edge. I gripped the corrugated metal with all my strength, eased off the roof, and hung by my fingers. My feet were still a good twenty inches from the horse. He started to move away.

"Wait, horsey!"

I lost my grip and landed with one leg over the horse's neck. He shied to the side and stomped. I clung to his mane and pulled myself up so I was centered on his back, one leg on each side.

An engine roared to life nearby. The horse bolted.

"*Wait ... stop ...*" I screamed, but he didn't listen. There was nothing to do but wrap my arms around his neck, clench his sides with my legs, and hold on for all I was worth.

In the dark, just ahead, I made out an ATV. It sped through an opening in the fence. The horse followed at a full gallop, through the narrow opening, and down a dirt path.

The ATV disappeared over a hill. The horse barely slowed as it raced down the steep embankment, into a shallow stream. He stumbled, and I was nearly thrown off. The ATV raced downstream, tossing up an arc of water on each side. I was soaked in the icy spray as the horse galloped behind the ATV.

"*Oh, God, Horsey, Please don't fall down ... please don't fall ... please don't fall ... oh, God ...*"

The ATV roared ahead of us, following the stream under the bridge at the highway. The horse, crazed with fear, stayed right behind. My crotch was pounded by the horse's bony back. His muscles labored under my bare legs. I pressed my face into his mane and held on, helpless to do anything else.

On the other side of the bridge, the stream flowed through a stretch of sand and emptied into a small bay. The ATV turned left, onto the sand. So did the horse. Maybe this was a good time to let go and drop to the ground. But I couldn't make myself loosen my grip.

The ATV came to a stop at the edge of the water and the rider got off. In the moonlight his features were clear. It was Raymond. He kicked off his shoes, dove into the small waves, and started swimming. He was getting away.

When the horse reached the water's edge, he didn't stop.

"Hey, no! Wait a minute!"

The horse fought through the waves. Before I knew it, he was swimming in the cold, black water.

How deep is it here? Don't sharks feed at night? Finally, I eased my grip on the horse's neck and let myself float off.

Raymond had reached a small powerboat, moored just beyond the breakers. He climbed into it and pulled the cord several times, trying to start the engine. It finally caught. He brought the boat around and headed straight for me. I swam as hard as I could toward shore, but the choppy waves and strong current slowed my progress.

The boat made one wide pass, then turned around and headed for me again. I took a deep breath and dove down. From below the surface, I saw the boat pass over me in the moonlight. When I couldn't hold my breath a moment longer, I came up.

The mooring line trailed in the water behind the boat. I grabbed the line and let it pull along me. Raymond looked back to see what was slowing the boat. He made a sharp turn and came straight at me. He was trying to run me over!

I let go of the line and backpedalled. The rope wrapped around the boat and caught in the propeller. The engine sputtered and stalled.

Raymond tipped the motor into the boat so the prop was out of the water and worked to untangle the line. He restarted the engine and looked for me. I dove below the surface again, trying to come up with a plan. I needed to get the boat away from Raymond. Then I could take it back to shore and get help.

I came up next to the boat and gasped for air. I grabbed the side of the boat and rocked it as hard as I could. Raymond fought for balance. Before he could steady himself, he fell backwards into the water. The engine dropped, the prop hit the water, and the empty boat took off.

Raymond screamed as he was pulled behind the boat. His leg

was caught in the mooring line. He fought to free himself as he was dragged past me, his face inches from mine. Our eyes met. He reached out and grabbed hold of my arm. My shoulder felt like it was being wrenched from the socket as the boat towed us both toward the horizon.

I bit his hand as hard as I could. It slipped down to my wrist, then his fingers loosened.

I was free.

I struggled against the current, fighting to reach the shore. Waves washed over my face and salty water went down my throat. I coughed and spit, but kept going.

I wasn't going to make it. I was too tired. I floated on my back and gasped for air. Little by little, the current washed me further from the shore.

My arm bumped something big in the water. It moved.

A shark!

Don't panic. That would only attract the shark. They say sharks are delicate, and a good hard kick or punch will frighten them away. I positioned myself to kick it.

Then I saw his head. It wasn't a shark. It was the horse, swimming back to shore. I swam to him, grabbed hold of his mane, and pulled myself onto his back.

"Oh, good boy. I'm so glad to see you. I really thought you were a goner."

Within minutes, the horse's feet touched bottom. He walked onto the beach and stopped. His head drooped, his sides heaved. I lay against his neck and vomited up sea water. My teeth chattered, my muscles cramped, my thighs and crotch ached from being pounded by the horse's back.

After a few minutes, the horse raised his head. He took one slow step, then another. He made his way across the sand and headed for the highway. He knew his way home. He crossed the road, found the driveway, and carried me through the opening where the gate used to be.

Laurie Hanan

CHAPTER 35

**Kidnapped Mail Carrier Freed
Investigators Turn Up Gruesome Discovery
By Freddy Friedman**

(Kāne'ohe, December 27) Police investigators discovered decomposed human remains at a Kāne'ohe farm Wednesday morning after the dramatic rescue of a kidnapped mail carrier.

Crime scene investigators worked throughout the day Wednesday, searching through two feet of mud and animal excrement after human remains were found in a pig enclosure. Two bodies believed to be those of young women were taken to the medical examiner's office for identification.

Louise Golden told police she was putting mail into a cluster of mailboxes in Haiku Gardens around 4 P.M. Tuesday when a sack was thrown over her head, her hands were bound behind her back, and she was forced at gunpoint into a waiting car. She was taken to a small farm in Kahalu'u and held in an upstairs room. Haiku Gardens residents reported the unlocked mail truck to the Kāne'ohe post office. "Louise is one of our best carriers," mail carrier supervisor Darren Saddler said. "She would never abandon her truck or leave it unlocked. I knew right away something was wrong and alerted the authorities."

Friends of Golden learned of her disappearance and started a search. They had reason to believe she might be at the home of the Lago family, owners of Lago Bar and Grill in Kāne'ohe and casual acquaintances of Golden. Three of Golden's friends entered the Lago's property and were immediately pinned down by gunfire. Police were called by neighbors who heard the shots. By the time police arrived, Golden had escaped her alleged captors by climbing from an upstairs window to the roof.

Joseph Lago, 53, was arrested for kidnapping a federal employee, firing a gun during the commission of a crime, and possession of a gun by a convicted felon. The crimes carry a maximum penalty of life in prison. Two of Joseph's sisters, Lourdes Lago, 31, and Tatum Lago, 29, both residents of the farm, were arrested as accessories. Another brother, Raymond Lago, 33, was seen fleeing across Kamehameha Highway and escaping in a small powerboat. An unidentified suspect also fled on foot. Both men are still at large.

Brian Griffith, 50, a friend of Golden, suffered gunshot wounds to the arm and chest. He remains at Queen's Medical Center in stable condition. Another friend, Francine Weiner, 58, was taken to Queen's with a gunshot wound to the leg. She is in good condition. Golden was taken to Castle Medical Center and treated for exposure, shock, and contusions. She was released the following day.

The Humane Society was called to the scene to take possession of approximately one hundred animals that were running loose on the property, including pigs, goats, dogs, ducks, geese, chickens, and a horse.

The story and photos of the arrests were on the front page of the *Honolulu Advertiser*. It continued on page three with photos of the search for bodies, and the animals being loaded into crates and trailers. What would become of the horse? He was a good horse and I wished him well.

I set the newspaper aside and stared at nothing. Sage slept beside me, her body stretched against my thigh.

There were footsteps on my front steps. Sage jumped off the couch and ran to the door. Someone knocked. My heart hammered as I crept to the window and peered through the closed blinds.

It was Freddy, dressed in Hawaiian print board shorts and a tank top that showed off his muscles. He looked like he'd either just been to the beach, or was heading there. I flipped the deadbolt, let him in, and locked the door behind him.

"Keeping yourself locked in?" he asked.

"Raymond is still out there somewhere. Not to mention the other guy." I moved the newspaper to the floor and sat on the couch. "Your story made the front page."

Freddy took the other end of the couch. "This story's going to make my career." He pulled Sage to his lap and she snuggled into him.

"Nothing like being in the right place at the right time."

"No kidding. And there's more."

"What more could there be?"

"When today's paper hit the streets, I got a call. An anonymous tip. The guy told me about a little side business going on at the bar and grill."

"Prostitution?"

"Yup. According to my informant, there were codes. The customer would sit at the bar and order a drink. Specific drinks meant he wanted specific services. His credit card would be billed accordingly, and the charge would look like a bar tab.

He'd be sent to one of several rooms, through a door around the side of the building. I passed the tip along to a friend in the police department. This is going to be another big story."

After a pause, Freddy asked, "Have you been to see Brian?"

"I visited him yesterday and again today. He's in a lot of pain. I feel horrible that this happened to him."

"So what is he ... your boyfriend?"

I looked away and shook my head. "No."

"Well, I can tell you he really cares about you."

My throat tightened and tears burned my eyes. I knew Brian loved me. He had looked so pitiful in the hospital—so sad. He didn't deserve the way I'd treated him lately. When he got out, I wanted to give our relationship another go.

Freddy said, "I tried to interview him, but he didn't want to talk about what happened."

"He didn't really talk to me about it, either. He's a very private person. He was wounded in Vietnam and this probably brought it all back."

I was in danger of bursting into tears, and needed to change the subject. I said, "I went to see Frankie, too. She wasn't very coherent."

"I tried talking to her. All she did was babble about aliens and government conspiracies. Is she always like that?"

"Off and on. She has her problems. How did Frankie end up at the farm, anyway? I don't get it, at all."

"She must have followed us."

"But … I don't understand any of it. How did you and Brian end up together? And what were you doing with Frankie?"

"You know I was supposed to pick you up Tuesday night at six."

I nodded.

"When I knocked on your door, Brian answered. He looked as surprised to see me as I was to see him. We stared each other down for a minute, and I thought he was gonna take a swing at me. I have to admit I was pretty pissed at you, letting him answer the door for you. Then he turned and went into the house without a word. He left the door open, and I took that as an invitation to follow him in. He sat on the couch and covered his face. I swear, the dude was crying behind his hands. I stood there like an idiot, no idea what was going on or what to say to him.

"Finally, he rubbed his face. He said, 'It was on the five o'clock news. Louise disappeared today on her mail route. They found the truck …' He covered his face again.

"I said, 'Oh my God. Raymond.'

"Brian said, 'He has her, doesn't he?'

"'I think so.'

"'I'm going to find him—and kill him.'

"'I think I know where he took her. But those guys are dangerous. They've got guns. You have a gun we could take with us?'

"'I know where I can get one.'"

"Frankie," I said.

"Yeah. Brian called her. We got in my truck and met her downtown. She looked like some kind of street person, but she's got a nice bike so I figure she's getting money from somewhere. She wanted to get in the truck with us, but Brian wouldn't let her. He grabbed the gun and an extra cartridge from her and told her to stay put."

"Poor Frankie."

"When we got to the farm, Brian acted like he was on a suicide mission. All I did was hunker down on the floor of the truck like a coward. Even when he took one in the arm, he kept on shooting. It wasn't until he was hit in the chest ... I thought we were done for. If the cops hadn't shown up when they did ..."

We each spent a few minutes pondering the alternate scenario.

Freddy checked his watch. "I have to get going. I just wanted to check in on you, see how you're holding up. Are you going to be okay?"

My eyes teared up again. I shook my head, but couldn't speak.

"Look," he said. "I'm heading out to Mokulē'ia. You want to ride along?"

The last thing I wanted was to be left alone with my thoughts. "Sure."

"Go change. We're going to the beach."

Minutes later we were in my BMW with the top down, Freddy in the driver's seat.

"Where's your truck?" I asked.

"In the shop. It needs a radiator, new windows and a lot of body work. I don't think I want to leave the bullet holes in it the way your landlord did."

I kept an eye on the rear view mirror, watching for Raymond's black pickup as we got on the H-1. By the time we merged onto the H-2 North, I was pretty sure we weren't being followed. The freeway ended and we drove past Schofield Barracks. Minutes later, the thick forest opened to a spectacular vista of Hale'iwa, Waialua, Mokulē'ia, and the ocean beyond. I began to relax as we headed downhill on Kuakonahua Road—also known as Snake Road—through acres of pineapple fields. After a few miles, the steep road began to twist and turn. Makeshift memorials for motorists killed on this treacherous stretch of highway appeared along the scraped guardrail: wooden crosses, arrangements of faded plastic flowers, a teddy bear, a deflated Mylar balloon flapping at the end of a length of red ribbon. A black skid mark on the pavement led to another reminder of heartbreak.

We made a left toward Waialua, passed the old sugar mill, and followed Farrington Highway into Mokulē'ia past horse farms and plantation era homes. Freddy pulled off the road. He left the car running while he got out and opened a padlocked gate that was almost invisible in thick bushes. He drove through the gate, closed it, and locked it behind us. No one would find us in here.

We followed two sandy ruts with scrub grass growing between them. The drive wound through a thick grove of ironwood trees that broke the sunlight into shards. We came to a bright clearing and stopped next to a small building made of plywood. Beyond the building, the turquoise ocean could be seen through a barbed wire fence.

Three horses appeared out of the trees and stopped a few yards away, curious about the car they didn't recognize. Freddy got out and they trotted to him. He patted their muzzles and murmured to them. Two more horses came around the building, stood on my side of the car, and watched me.

"Come on, Louise. Meet my friends."

I opened the door and stood. The horses approached me, looking expectant. I moved back until I bumped the car.

Freddy said, "Those two are Pano and Magic."

"Uh … hi …"

"These guys over here are Milo and Koa."

He kissed one on the nose, then scratched its ears. "And this beauty here is my special lady, Ipo."

All five horses were the same dark shade of brown. Ipo had a small, heart-shaped patch of white between her eyes, but the others were so alike, I wondered how Freddy could tell them apart.

"I didn't know you had horses."

"Ipo is the only one that's mine. The rest I take care of for the guy who owns this place."

"Why are their manes shaved off?"

"They're all polo ponies. We braid their tails for the games, too, so the hair doesn't get in the way."

"You play polo?"

Freddy was full of surprises. I realized I knew very little about him, and how he spent his time. I wasn't even sure where he lived.

"It's an expensive passion. Most polo players are born into it, their families have money. Then there are a few like me who bust our butts for years grooming for the players, just to be close to the horses and the game. I was lucky enough to work my way into one of the player's good graces. He taught me to play. Working for him is the only way I can afford to keep Ipo here."

"You drive all the way out here every day?"

"I love this place, there's nothing like it. And it isn't really that far. Thirty-five miles from Ko Olina. I have a cot in the office here so I can spend the night if I don't have any reason to go back to town."

He went into the building and came out with a bridle over his shoulder and a bareback pad in his arms. He laid the pad over a hitching post made from a smoothed log. The other horses watched him put the bridle on Ipo and tie her to the post. He brushed her and cleaned her hooves with a pick before throwing the pad over her back and cinching it tight.

"Come on. We're going for a ride."

"Who—*me*?"

"Of course you." He kicked off his slippers, pulled his shirt over his head, and dropped it across the post. He led Ipo to a bench at the side of the building, stepped on it, and hopped easily onto her back. "You're next. Come over here."

"I don't think so. Thanks any way."

Freddy had no idea of the wild ride I'd taken just two nights ago. If I never got on another horse in my life, it would be too soon for me.

"We'll go slow. I promise."

"No …"

"If you don't like it, we'll get off. I want to show you the beach here. It's gorgeous."

He wasn't leaving me a lot of options. I walked to the bench. "Now what do I do?"

"You got your swimsuit on?"

"Under my clothes."

"Then drop the clothes."

I stepped out of my slippers, undid my shorts, and let them slide down my legs. I tossed my tank top on the ground beside them. The other night, Freddy had seen me all but naked and soaked to the skin. I felt no shyness now as his eyes took in my body.

He said, "Now step up on the bench."

I did.

"Okay, grab my arm. Throw your leg up behind me and slide on. I'll help you."

I managed to climb onto the horse without incident. My thigh muscles screamed and my bones felt bruised from my recent ride. I let out a groan.

"You okay?"

"I think so." At least the bareback pad cushioned my sore bottom from the horse's backbone.

Ipo took a step and I nearly toppled off. I screamed.

"Put your arms around me. You'll be fine."

I clamped my arms around his waist. His muscles were solid under his warm skin, his abdomen covered in thick, wiry hair, hard as a rock. The horse walked toward a gate that led to the beach. My belly and breasts pressed against Freddy's back, my thighs rubbed his legs in time with the movement of the horse. The physical contact was too intimate. I wanted to pull back, but I also wanted to stay on the horse.

"Can you ease up just a little?" he said. "I can't breathe."

"Oh ... sorry." I loosened my grip, but just a little.

The horse made her way to the hard packed sand where a gentle surf lapped the shore. Further out, six-foot waves crashed onto the reef with a roar, sending up plumes of white spray. I looked up and down the unbroken beach. It stretched for miles in both directions and appeared deserted. We rode without conversation. A stiff breeze came off the ocean and whipped my hair. The sun warmed us.

Maybe a mile down the beach, Freddy stopped the horse. "I'm going to get down, then I'll help you off." He swung his right leg over Ipo's neck and slid to the sand. He reached up and put his hands on my waist. "Jump."

I leaned forward, grabbed his shoulders, and let him lift me to the ground. He removed Ipo's bareback pad and gave her a pat on the rump. She trotted to the water's edge. We sat on the warm sand and watched the horse. After a few minutes, she bent her legs, rolled awkwardly onto her back, and kicked at the air.

"What's she doing?" I asked.

"She loves the feel of the sand and the water. About once a week I bring all the horses out here to swim. It's good exercise."

"This is only my second time on a horse. The first time was two nights ago."

"I never would have guessed."

"I grew up in Manhattan. The closest I ever came to riding a horse was when my brother and I would gallop around the apartment, playing cowboys and Indians. We'd pull out a kitchen chair and jump over it, pretending we were on horseback. The old lady downstairs finally came up to complain to my mom about our clumping on the wood floor. We were told to stop."

He grinned.

"Sorry. I don't know why I told you that. I just remembered it myself."

"Don't be sorry."

I looked over my shoulder at the ironwood forest. It was a perfect hiding place.

"Worried?" he asked.

"I guess Raymond wouldn't have followed us all the way here."

"I doubt it."

"I wonder about the other guy who got away. I don't think he was related to Raymond. They spoke English with him."

"Probably just one of Raymond's paid thugs. If he's smart, he'll stay as far away from the Lago family as he can."

Freddy's phone rang. He pulled it from his pocket and listened. "Get photos, send me the details. I'll get the story in today."

He ended the call and speed dialed another number. "Big story. Tourists found a body in the water off Chinaman's Hat. Police think it's the missing Lago brother ... yeah ... Raymond. Alyn's there now taking photos ... you'll get it by tonight."

When he ended the call I asked, "What ...?"

"Looks like Raymond's body has been found."

"He's dead."

"Yes." He touched my arm. "You okay?"

I nodded. "I never wished anyone dead before, but I can't say I'm sorry."

"I know. Me, too." He put his arm around my shoulders and I let him pull me close.

A flock of sandpipers landed nearby and picked at the line of debris left by the tide. A wave chased them up the sand, and they followed it as it receded again. Back and forth, back and forth.

Freddy pulled away and searched my eyes. He reached up, slowly, and touched my face. He leaned closer and closer, until his lips found mine. Our tongues met. I closed my eyes. He eased me down onto the sand. Our legs intertwined.

Finally, he ended the kiss.

I struggled to calm my breathing while my heart pounded in my throat.

When I could speak, I said, "I guess that one was more than just pretend."

Idiot. Why do I always have to go and say something stupid?

He smiled. "Kisses are like tears. The only real ones are the ones we can't hold back."

GLOSSARY

Challah.....Judaism, a loaf of bread, usually braided, traditionally eaten on the Sabbath and holidays

Chamorro.....a language of the Northern Mariana Islands

Chica.....Spanish for *young girl*

Hapa.....Hawaiian Pidgin, borrowed from the English word *half*, meaning half-caste or of mixed descent

Hasapiko.....a Greek folk dance, literally *the butcher's dance.*

Huli huli.....Hawaiian, to rotate, flip over, or turn

Kaddish.....Judaism, a prayer of praise that is part of the daily liturgy, also recited by mourners

Kam Highway..... used as an abbreviation for Kamehameha Highway

Kugel.....Yiddish, a sweet casserole made from egg noodles

Ladino..... a nearly extinct language, descended from medieval Spanish, spoken by Sephardic Jews

Makai.....Hawaiian, *toward the sea*

Mamacita.....Spanish, literally *little lady*. Slang for a sexy girl.

Mauka.....Hawaiian, toward the mountains

Menorah.....Judaism, a nine-branched candelabrum used in celebration of *Hanukkah*

Minyan.....Hebrew, literally *count*. The quorum of ten men required for Jewish communal worship

Mitzvah.....Hebrew, a worthy deed, or the fulfillment of a commandment of God.

Moricon...Spanish, *faggot*

Mu'umu'u.....*Hawaiian,* a long loose dress that hangs free from the shoulders.

Plátanos .....Spanish, deep fried plantains

Shabbos.....Hebrew, also pronounced *Shabbat*. The Sabbath.

Shiva...Hebrew, the week-long mourning period for close relatives

Slippers.......Hawaiian Pidgin for thing sandals, also pronounced *slippahs*

Tallis.....Yiddish, a Jewish prayer shawl. Pronounced *tallit* in Hebrew

Laurie Hanan